Novels by Resa Nelson
Published by Mundania Press

.

The Dragonslayer's Sword

Our Lady of the
Absolute

Resa Nelson

A Mundania Press Production
Mundania Press LLC
6470A Glenway Avenue, #109
Cincinnati, Ohio 45211-5222

To order additional copies of this book, contact:
books@mundania.com
www.mundania.com

Cover Art © 2010 by Ana Winson
Arien Graphics (http://www.arien-graphics.info)
Edited by Judy Bagshaw

Trade Paperback ISBN: 978-1-60659-235-9
eBook ISBN: 978-1-60659-234-2

First Edition • June 2010

Production by Mundania Press LLC
Printed in the United States of America

10   9   8   7   6   5   4   3   2   1

CHAPTER ONE

Isis, help me, Meres thought. *My life has always been childless. Save me from living without hope.*

She stood waiting in the city's central park, preferring to stand in the direct sunlight and take comfort from its heat than seek shade. Today, like most days, the air felt dry and hot and smelled like lotus blossoms. The sun blazed high overhead in a cloudless sky, and red sandstone mountains jutted up at the edge of the White-Walled City. Rain and snow melt trickled down the mountain, supplying the city with six natural springs. Throughout the city, lawns were green and grassy, places like this park, a welcome sanctuary for the city's residents. Camels and donkeys grazed inside a corral by the park, and the heaviness of their scent in the air made her nose twitch.

She watched as a naked boy ran across the grass toward the hundred-foot-high granite statue of the Pharaoh. The boy's head was shaved, except for a side lock of hair, a symbol indicating his age lay between five and nine years old.

She frowned. The boy looked younger than five, making his haircut a lie. Clearly, he was not an orphan or he would have been beaten for such a lie. Despite the sun's warmth on her skin, Meres shivered. She had a dim memory of her parents and the day she'd been told they'd been killed by crocodiles. Mostly, she remembered the orphanage and the most important lesson she learned: follow the rules to the letter or face the consequences.

A slight breeze distracted her as it penetrated her lightweight linen dress. The narrow ankle length skirt billowed between her legs, cooling her skin. With her long blond hair dressed in tiny braids, she was grateful to feel the light air graze her scalp. She knew the black kohl she'd used to enlarge and extend her eyebrows and eyes should reduce the glare of the sun, but she squinted nonetheless. As much as she loved the desert sun, it could be hard on the eyes and especially on Meres' light golden brown skin.

Meres took a seat on one of the park benches and looked around at the lush greenery. It was hard to believe that the Black Land was a desert country. As her husband so often loved to tell her, its name came from the black silt deposited on the farmland when the Nile rose above its banks every year. Towns were few and far between, separated by miles of barren sand. Surrounded by a high white wall and guarded gates, the White-Walled City served as the royal hub of the Black Land.

In her late thirties, Meres thought of herself as a typical Black Lander. She lived in a simple house with her husband. She embraced the gods and goddesses of the Black Land's religion with open arms. She followed the Pharaoh's laws by the book.

Meres regretted only one thing: she and her husband Ramose had no children. The goddess Isis herself, known to Black Landers as Our Lady of the Absolute, had struggled against all odds and succeeded in having one child. Being a mother was what defined any Black Land woman as mistress of her own house.

Meres reflected that her husband Ramose was lucky. He loved his work and everyone respected him as a man who pulled his own weight. But without children, Meres felt as if she'd been locked out of the walls of the city on a cold desert night while everyone else celebrated at a festival: no matter how loud she cried out, no one could hear her. She felt invisible and lonely, the same way she'd felt growing up in the orphanage.

But Meres drew strength from her faith in the gods. Of all those deities, Meres most admired Isis, Our Lady of the Absolute, the goddess of all goddesses. Our Lady had suffered many hardships and conquered them all.

Lady Isis, she thought, *if I accomplish one thing in life, my wish is to become just like you.*

She looked longingly at families picnicking in the shade of oak and poplar trees. Donkeys and horses grazed on grassy fields while eyeing the park's fenced flower gardens. One donkey brayed mournfully, and as the wind shifted, Meres caught a whiff of its pungent, dusty scent.

Lotus blossoms floated in a long reflecting pool, flanked by spiky papyrus plants.

"Look at me!" The small boy shouted as he ran toward the Pharaoh's statue.

The gigantic stone image of the Pharaoh stood straight and tall, arms by his side, with one foot in front of the other as if frozen in mid-step. Bare-chested, the statue wore a white kilt and the official headdress of royalty.

The Pharaoh wasn't simply the king of the Black Land. He was its living god. He symbolized all gods that watched over the Black Land

and its people.

Most considered his image sacred, Meres included.

Her throat tightened with anxiety when the boy jumped up on the statue's bare foot.

Giggling, he peed on the statue.

Oh, no! Meres thought. *No one has taught him how to worship the gods! He's in violation. Someone has to stop him!* Meres gasped in horror and hurried toward him.

Breaking through a row of hedges behind the statue, a young woman raced to scoop the boy up in her arms. She looked like a teenager. Still urinating, a steady yellow stream arced away from the statue and soiled the young woman's dress.

The boy screamed and squirmed in the young woman's arms. "No!"

Meres remembered running away on the day her parents died. Someone had chased her down, and she'd tried to squirm away, just like this boy. *What if the same thing has happened to him?* Meres thought in a sudden panic. *What if that's why he's urinating on the Pharaoh, because he needs someone to blame for his parents' deaths?*

Meres looked up and scanned the park until she spotted the nearest Eye of Horus. She ran toward it, waving her arms and pointing at the statue, the young woman, and the boy.

The Eye was a small camera mounted on a tree limb. Dozens of Eyes peppered the White-Walled City. This one responded to Meres and pivoted to face the statue.

The young woman hurried away as the boy squirmed in her arms.

"Hey!" Meres shouted. Adrenaline rushed through her as she realized this woman might be a foreigner. Meres had learned at a young age that foreigners were dangerous and not to be trusted. Few were ever granted admittance into the Black Land.

The young woman ignored her, struggling to keep the boy in her arms. His wails pierced the still air.

Meres caught up and grabbed the other woman's elbow. "Stop!" Meres shouted. "Foreigner!"

The young woman's face flushed with shame and exertion. "Please," she whispered. "I'm a Black Lander. Let me go!"

"What's your name?"

Her eyes teared and her face sagged with fear. "Neferita."

"You can't just run away," Meres said. Although Meres' heart still raced, she knew the woman told the truth. "Neferita" was a Black Lander name, not a foreign one. Because Meres admired Isis, she treated every Black Lander like a sister or brother, especially when someone like Neferita so clearly needed help.

The boy let himself slide through Neferita's arms and plopped on the ground. When he tried to run back toward the statue, Neferita grabbed his arms and kneeled, spinning him around to face her. "Don't ever do that again!"

The boy tried to yank free of her grip. He failed, crying, "Let go!"

Neferita shook his shoulders. "Bad boy! If you ever touch that statue again, it will come to life. Then it will hunt you down in the middle of the night and kill you!"

The boy stared at Neferita wide-eyed for a few moments. He began screaming.

"Good god Osiris," Meres said, rolling her eyes. "That boy will have nightmares for the next ten years."

Neferita slapped the boy hard in the face. "Shut up!" she said, her face flushed with anger. "You're a big boy now. Act like one!"

Gazing in terror at Neferita, the boy choked back his screams.

Meres quickly stepped between them, shielding the boy. "He's been misbehaving, but he doesn't deserve to be treated like that," Meres said. "If he were mine, I'd never hit him. I'd never tell him to shut up."

Neferita's face flushed deeper, this time with anger. "He's not your son. He's mine."

A familiar sinking feeling numbed Meres. Neferita pointed out the truth: the boy did not belong to Meres.

It wasn't easy for Meres to live in the Black Land, a country dotted with fertile farmland that was a constant reminder to every childless woman of her own infertility. Every year the Nile flooded its banks and turned the fields into temporary swamps long enough for rich, black sediment from the river bottom to impregnate the farm land and prepare it for the year's crops.

Meres wished she could scoop the boy up in her arms, take him home to her husband Ramose, and have the family she'd always wanted.

But that would be no more acceptable to the gods than peeing on a statue of the Pharaoh.

A park guard with a shaved head hurried toward them. He wore only a white kilt and carried a large brass knife. His knowing glance toward Meres showed that he recognized her. "What's the problem?"

Neferita shrank, clutching her son. She froze when she finally spotted the Eye of Horus pointed at her. "There's no problem," she said.

Meres knew nearly everyone in the White-Walled City, but she'd never seen Neferita before. Meres felt sorry for the young woman, thinking how difficult it must be to bring a small child to a new place. Meres struggled between her compassion for the woman and her loyalty to the gods.

As usual, just the thought of shirking her duty to the gods sickened Meres. *Don't be afraid to tell the truth,* she reminded herself.

"I'm the one who waved down the Eye of Horus," Meres said. "The child urinated on the Pharaoh's statue."

Scowling with disgust, the park guard wrapped his beefy hand around Neferita's elbow.

"No!" Neferita slipped from his grip, hoisting her son up into her arms. "We're leaving now. Thank you, but there's no need. We're fine."

Meres' jaw slackened in amazement. First Neferita allowed her son to insult the gods and then she denied it? The woman's audacity made Meres glad she'd turned her in. No one with such a reckless attitude toward the gods should walk free. Clearly, Neferita was a troubled woman who could unwittingly cause trouble for herself, her son, and the people of the White-Walled City.

As the park guard vise-gripped Neferita, Meres shook off her earlier feelings of compassion, certain she'd done the right thing. Perhaps now, the young mother would get the help she so obviously needed. She watched in relief as the park guard dragged a protesting Neferita with her screaming son in tow from the park.

The Eye of Horus whirred as it pivoted to record their progress.

Remembering why she'd come to the park, Meres checked her watch. Worried, she scanned the grounds for someone who should have arrived ten minutes ago.

Meres grinned and waved when she recognized her sister-in-law Pu walking toward her.

Like her brother Ramose, Pu stood tall and slim, her long dark hair in dozens of braids. Her real name was Senetenpu, which translated from the old language to "She is our sister" but everyone called her "Pu." She never went anywhere without wearing her diamond stud earrings, a full broadcollar necklace comprised of several rows of gold and lapis beads, gold bangle bracelets, and a single gold anhk ring that identified her as a member of the Pharaoh's harem. Like her brother, she was strong-willed and made her own decisions.

Meres ran to kiss her cheek, stretching up on the balls of her feet. "Pu!"

Pu's brow furrowed, and she wrapped her arms around Meres' shoulders, clinging tight. "Thank you for coming."

"You're trembling," Meres said. "What's wrong?"

Pu stared into Meres' eyes. "Do you see any Eyes watching us?"

Meres shook her head. "There's one in the tree behind me. It should be looking the other way. Why?"

Pu glanced at it. "Most people want to believe what they want to believe. But then there are people who wake up one day and realize they need to hear the truth. People say, 'If you want to know what the truth is, ask Meres, because she's the one person who's not afraid to speak it.'"

With a start, Meres realized Pu was scared. "What's wrong?"

"Something has happened, and I can't tell anyone other than you because I know you can keep a secret."

"But what about Ramose? He's your brother. Why aren't you talking to him instead of me?"

"I can't. He's a man, and he'd side with other men, not with me." Pu took a deep breath as she squeezed Meres' hands. "I'm pregnant."

Meres felt as if she'd been slapped. Her own belly knotted with emptiness and envy. Why was it that every other woman in the White Walled City became pregnant so quickly and easily? Pu was already the envy of most women, and not just because she held the coveted position as a member of the royal harem. She was also one of Pharaoh's favorites. Pu wasn't simply beautiful and charming. She had already given four daughters to the Pharaoh.

Remember how much you love Pu, Meres reminded herself. *She's been kind to you for as long as you've known her.*

Meres gave Pu a genuine smile. "What good news! I'm so happy for you."

Pu shook her head. "You don't understand. Pharaoh isn't the father."

Meres' smile faded. Bound by law and honor to be faithful to the Pharaoh, Pu had never shown interest in any other man. After all, when you sleep with a god, how can you be tempted by a mere mortal?

"If Pharaoh finds out," Pu whispered, "he'll have me killed."

CHAPTER TWO

Meres and Pu sat at a small table tucked into a back corner in *Cleopatra's Cafe*. Pu stared glumly at a bowl of chicken soup. Meres picked at her salad.

"Are you sure the Pharaoh's not the father?" When Meres spoke, she kept her voice low, careful not to be overheard.

Pu did likewise. "I haven't been with the Pharaoh in months."

"You broke your promise to a god," Meres said. "That's unethical."

"The Pharaoh treats me like one of his gold statues," Pu said. "I met someone who loves me. Really loves me."

How could this be happening? How could Pu have broken not only the law of the land but a law that defied the Pharaoh himself? It was unthinkable. "But you've slept with another man," Meres said, trying to make sense of it. "You must have lied to Pharaoh. That's the same as lying to the gods!"

The women froze in silence as a man walked past their table, heading toward the restroom, just a few feet away. After he'd entered and the door swung shut, the women exhaled, neither realizing she'd been holding her breath.

Meres shut her eyes, feeling lightheaded. How could this be happening to her own sister-in-law? What Pu had done was far worse that peeing on a statue. If Meres had been quick to turn Neferita over to the authorities, shouldn't she do the same with Pu?

Taking a deep breath, Meres considered the situation carefully. Pu wasn't just Ramose's sister. She wasn't just Meres' sister-in-law. Pu had welcomed Meres with open arms from the beginning. Pu was a friend.

I should be true and loyal to the gods, Meres thought. *But how can I hurt someone I love?*

Meres stared out the window as if looking for an answer. All she saw were parents and their laughing children walking through the streets of the White Walled City.

Ramose and I could come up with a reason to hide her, Meres thought, suddenly seeing a way to benefit from Pu's misfortune. *We could make sure she's well nourished. And I could wear padding to make it look like I'm the one who's pregnant. And after she delivers, Pu would give her baby to me. Pu already has enough children. I'm the one in need, not her. Her life is already perfect. Why can't I be the one who's lucky for once?*

Whenever Meres had such thoughts, she didn't like the cold, hard edge she felt inside. It made her feel less than human.

Pu's face sagged. "I shouldn't have burdened you with my problem. How can I complain about one more child when you have none?"

"There's always a solution to any problem—we just have to figure out what that solution is," Meres said. She reached across the tabletop and held her sister-in-law's trembling hands. "We can figure this out." She brightened with a new idea. "We've been making this more difficult than it needs to be. Why not tell the Pharaoh the baby is his?"

"That's impossible," Pu said. "I haven't been with him for months—he'll know."

"Tell him it's magic. Tell him you prayed for his seed, and the gods delivered it to you."

Pu raised an eyebrow. "Isn't that unethical? Lying to Pharaoh?"

Meres nodded. Pu was right. It was quite unethical. It surprised Meres to realize she felt perfectly fine about suggesting an act she considered to be perfectly wrong. "There are worse sins."

"But lying to Pharaoh isn't one sin I'll be committing."

"Why not?"

"Because the father is a foreigner. The baby won't look like Pharaoh or any of us. It's more than just being unfaithful. Everyone will know I've conspired with the foreigner. That's why I'm sure Pharaoh will have me killed."

"That's impossible. The Pharaoh would never—"

"You don't know what I know," Pu whispered. "You don't know what every woman in Pharaoh's harem knows."

The emptiness in Meres' stomach twisted into fear. The more Pu talked, the more terrified she looked. "Then tell me."

A tear plunked from Pu's chin into her soup. Quickly, as if afraid of being caught, she brushed the tell-tale tracks off her face, smudging the kohl lining her lower eyelid. She leaned forward and whispered. "When you first join the harem, they tell you the rules, which are mostly about being faithful to Pharaoh and the gods and the Black Land. But they also tell you about Sekhmet."

"That doesn't make any sense." Meres frowned. Napkin in hand, she corrected the smudge on Pu's face. "Our Lady of the Absolute is Isis, not Sekhmet."

"Sekhmet is the name of a demon woman who lives under the city," Pu whispered. "She is the goddess's namesake. They say she has the power to turn herself into a powerful lioness. Anyone who commits a crime within the walls of the royal palace is given to Sekhmet."

Meres' eyes widened. For the first time, she questioned the sanity of her sister-in-law.

"I have to leave the White-Walled City and take my daughters with me," Pu said. "I can't leave them behind. Pharaoh's likely to make them pay for my sin."

This makes no sense, Meres thought. *Why would Pharaoh hurt his own children?*

Out loud, she said, "So what's stopping you?"

"You don't know what goes on. As long as I'm anywhere near the palace, Pharaoh's guards watch us all the time. They let me come alone today because I told them I was meeting you. Even so, if I'm not back at the palace in an hour, they'll come looking for me."

"They're protecting you. And him."

"Pharaoh doesn't want anyone touching what he thinks is rightfully his. No woman in the palace can leave without his permission. And even then, we can't be gone for long."

"How did you manage to have an affair with a foreigner?"

"It was a fluke. He's an advisor, and Pharaoh trusts him." Pu glanced at the clock on the wall. For the first time, her voice was calm and resolute. "I don't have much time left, and I need your help. You work at the temple. The Festival of Isis is next week. I need you to change the festival route."

"Change the route? Why?"

Pu withdrew a pen from her pocket. She took the paper napkin from her lap and spread it flat on the tabletop. She quickly sketched a simple map of the White-Walled City. "This is the path that The Festival of Isis parade takes every year." Pu drew a line that began at the Temple of Our Lady of the Absolute and ended at the royal palace.

Meres nodded. As the temple's scribe, she was in charge of the festival details, including the parade. More or less, Pu had drawn the correct route.

"I need the parade to take this route instead." Pu drew a new line from the royal palace that veered a few blocks toward the white wall surrounding the city and then headed back toward the normal route.

"That doesn't make any sense," Meres said, frowning. "The parade route follows the main streets. These are side streets."

"This is my only hope," Pu said. She added dots all over the map. "Here are all of the Eyes of Horus between the royal palace and the temple. Most of them swivel around in a circle, which means they see everything." She pointed to a dot by the altered route she'd drawn. "Except for this one. It's broken, but no one has gotten around to fixing it yet. If you re-route the parade so it goes by this Eye of Horus, then I can take my daughters through this city gate and no Eyes will see us leave."

"But all city gates are guarded. How will you get through?"

"You underestimate the appeal of the Pharaoh's women to his guards. Don't worry. I know most of the guards. I know which ones I can trust and which ones I can't. The men who guard this gate are men I can persuade."

Meres studied the map. "I don't have the power to change the route. Only the priests can do that."

"And you have influence over the priests. They like you."

Meres shrugged off the compliment. "We've been colleagues for many years. That's all."

"That's not what I've heard."

Meres looked up sharply at her sister-in-law. "What?"

"I've heard them tell Pharaoh. They admire you, Meres. They say you work hard and that you care about the gods as much as the priests, maybe even more." Pu's eyebrows crinkled in puzzlement. "Don't you know that?"

Stunned, Meres sat back. She'd had a good working relationship with the temple priests for the past ten years, ever since she'd been hired. But they'd never told Meres how they felt about her or her work. "No," Meres said. "I had no idea."

"You have far more power than you realize. If you can't change the route yourself, you can get it changed. Like you said, there's a solution to every problem. The trick is to find the solution." Pu folded up the map and offered it to her sister-in-law. "Will you help me?"

Meres hesitated. Not more than an hour ago she'd had a woman arrested because she'd failed to keep her young son from peeing on a statue of the Pharaoh. Defacing the Pharaoh's image was a sin, but on the grand scale of sins, it was a small one. What Pu had done was far more serious. First, she'd been unfaithful to the Pharaoh. Second, she'd let a foreigner impregnate her. And now she planned to leave the White-Walled City and possibly the Black Land itself. That meant Pu and her daughters—who were all bound to the Pharaoh by law—were likely to become foreigners themselves.

What would they do? Everyone knew that all foreigners hated Black Landers. If Pu and her girls weren't killed on sight by foreigners, how would they survive among them?

Pu had already committed acts of treason. Now she asked Meres to help.

The entire world seemed to grind to a halt. Meres felt as if she were frozen in a moment of time that she wished had never happened. Whatever she decided would change her life forever, and Meres didn't like the options. She could ignore what she believed to be true and right in order to help the people she loved the most: Pu and Ramose. Or Meres could do what she'd spent her life doing and play by the rules of the gods, which meant turning Pu over to the authorities. Those were the only two options Meres could see: one extreme or the other.

It was so easy to follow the rules, but for the first time Meres realized she'd never given the rules any real thought. She'd simply followed them because she believed they were important.

But Pu was important, too.

Meres took the map from Pu's outstretched hand and stuffed it in her pocket.

By the gods, Meres thought. *What am I doing?*

Chapter Three

As Meres walked home from her lunch with Pu, she kept her hand stuffed in the pocket where she hid the map.

What am I going to do? Meres thought. *I can't change the route of the Festival of Isis parade. Why did I tell Pu that I'd try?*

Meres knew her husband Ramose had gone out with his nets to fish on the Nile today. Like most Black Landers, Ramose earned his living as a farmer. Next week's festival marked the new season of Inundation, when the Nile rose each year to flood the farmland with the black sediment from the river bottom. Weeks from now when the river receded back to its banks, the black sediment would remain, acting as a rich fertilizer. The annual flood came every summer as a gift from the gods.

The Nile had already risen slightly, and like most farmers, Ramose wanted to take advantage of the fishing. He wouldn't be home until after dark.

Meres realized it would be wise to tell the priests about Neferita and her son before going home. By now, the priests probably had talked to Neferita and recorded her side of the story. Although Meres could wait to file her report until tomorrow, she'd rather be interviewed now while her memory was still fresh.

On this late Sunday afternoon, the city felt empty as Meres walked through it. The streets were narrow enough to stay shaded throughout most of the day, lined with courtyard walls of houses and public buildings, all painted white. Meres loved these streets during the week when simple colorful canopies shaded wares laid out on reed mats. Alleyways crammed with shops and vendors created a maze of a marketplace. But right now the only signs of life were an old man leading a donkey laden with stalks from a banana tree, trailed by dozens of geese and ducks.

The Temple of Our Lady of the Absolute loomed ahead. Two free-standing walls, known as pylons, formed the gate to the temple complex. Red banners waved at the top of a row of flagpoles attached to the pylons. Obelisks stood inside the pylons, decorated with painted hieroglyphs and historic scenes of war with evil foreign countries. Two enormous statues of the Pharaoh stood between the obelisks, creating a narrow passageway to the temple gates. Walking through that passageway, Meres paused at the entrance to the temple courtyard.

The guard looked at her in surprise. "What's a scribe doing at temple on Sunday afternoon?"

"I witnessed an incident in Pharaoh Park today. I'm here to file a witness statement."

He nodded and let her enter the complex.

Meres walked through the gates and crossed the vast courtyard in front of the temple. Enormous, painted hieroglyphs that illustrated the legend of Isis and Osiris covered the interior walls. Swallows and sparrows nested in cracks in the walls, and their chirps echoed nosily.

A 30-foot-tall statue of Isis, Our Lady of the Absolute, dominated the courtyard. She knelt on one knee, her arms and attached wings stretched out to each side. She wore a simple dress of fine pleats and the headdress that identified her as the goddess-wife of the patron god of the White Walled City.

Meres brushed a casual hand against the pocket holding Pu's map to make sure it was still hidden. Normally, she felt more at home in the temple than anywhere else. Now she felt like an impostor. She'd always come to the temple purely with the intent of serving Isis and the other gods.

Meres knelt on one knee in front of the statue, spreading her arms out to emulate Our Lady.

"Please give me strength and courage," Meres whispered. "Please help me keep my mouth shut so I may protect those who confide in me."

Meres trembled, surprised by her own words.

The statue of Isis seemed to stare back at Meres with a cold, stony silence.

Meres knew she was blessed. Only those who worked at the temple were allowed inside its gates. Likewise, only those who worked at the temple were allowed to pray before this holy image of Isis. The residents of the White-Walled City were allowed to glimpse inside the gates but never allowed to enter. All her life, Meres had longed to be one of the chosen few who were allowed this kind of proximity to the goddess.

The priests worked closely with Isis. They were the only ones allowed into the inner depths of the temple, where a golden image of Isis stood. The priests said they had conversations with the goddess. Meres would give anything to be a priest, but that was impossible. Only men were allowed to be priests.

She cleared her throat and spoke her daily prayer out loud. "I give you my absolute faith and trust. Grant me absolute knowledge and understanding, for blessed are those who are right."

She rose, bowing her head as she passed the statue and stepped through the temple door, careful as always to stay in the upper region.

First, she walked through the sun hall, an open, airy walkway in which sacred plants grew. The walls were painted with images of geese and lotus plants.

The sun hall led to the upper region of the temple, a large foyer lined with small storerooms for the vestments of the priests and items used in ceremonies and weekly festivals. Here, incense burned throughout the day. Meres spent much of her time in the temple library, nestled among the storerooms. The library's walls were lined with pigeonholes that stored rolls of papyrus. Every weekday of the year had its own pigeonhole, and it was Meres' job to retrieve the papyrus roll at the beginning of each day and help the priests carry out that day's rites and rituals, as well as the weekly festivals. Meres was also allowed down the hallway to the main offices of the priests, but not beyond. She had never seen the most important room in the temple, the sanctuary in which the golden image of Isis lived.

Footsteps echoed through the stone hallway.

Priest Hennet came into view as he turned a corner in the maze-like temple. Although he shaved his head, a requirement for temple priests, he didn't look like an average priest. Instead of staying fit like the others, Priest Hennet gave in to his sweet tooth on a daily basis. Middleaged, his belly hung like an enormous ball over the waistband of his white and finely-pleated kilt. He wore the skin of the leopard, legs draped across his shoulders and fastened by a gold buckle shaped like a leopard's head, which identified him as the head priest and therefore the most powerful.

He seemed lost in thought, frowning as he stared at the floor, clutching a stack of files to his chest.

"Good day, Priest Hennet," Meres said.

He jumped in surprise. Some of the files fell to the floor.

Meres dropped to the floor to retrieve them. "I didn't mean to startle you."

As she gathered a dozen papers that had fallen out of a folder, Meres couldn't help but notice the odd nature of them. She saw rows of numbers, a large "1040," and the words Capital Gains and Losses.

How odd.

"Those are not for your eyes," Priest Hennet said.

Meres looked up, startled by the cold way the priest's lips were pressed together. She'd never seen his face pale and crease with such concern before. His eyes darted like birds caught in a net.

For the first time in all the years that Meres had known him, Priest Hennet looked terrified.

Without looking at the papers again, she handed everything that had fallen to the floor back to the priest. "I meant no harm," Meres said. "I came to report the incident at Pharaoh Park today."

Priest Hennet smiled quickly and broadly, but Meres felt no warmth.

"We can always count on you to do the right thing, can't we?" he said, clutching the files to his chest again.

Meres swallowed hard and smiled, remembering her prayer just a few minutes to Isis outside in the courtyard. Again, she felt like an impostor.

At the same time, she remembered what Pu had told her: the priests had a far higher opinion of Meres than she'd realized. They trusted her.

Would it be so wrong to take advantage of that trust if it could protect Pu?

"How can I request an audience with Isis inside her chapel?" Meres said. She knew that anyone granted an audience with Isis received absolute privacy. Isis kept all conversations confidential. If Meres could ask Isis for help, no one else would ever know about it.

Priest Hennet laughed. "You know only priests are allowed to see her."

"Yes," Meres said, "but haven't I served her, as well? Isn't there some way I could earn an audience with her?"

Priest Hennet glanced at the folders in his hands. "Let's stick to the task at hand and worry about that later."

Frustrated, Meres struggled to stay pleasant. She knew from experience that whenever Priest Hennet suggested they "worry about that later," that meant "later" would never come. It was his way of saying "no."

She followed him to the secular office, just down the hallway. Even though only the priests were allowed into the depths of the temple, as their scribe, Meres had the freedom to work in a few designated rooms.

Priest Hennet gestured toward Meres. "Go ahead. Write down your experience with Neferita."

Meres sat cross-legged on a pillow on the floor and wrote on a yellow legal pad. She wished she could use a computer, like the one on the secular office desk. But only priests were allowed to use computers. Meres knew computers were imported from foreign lands, but the priests claimed they were the invention of the Black Lander god Thoth.

Priest Hennet plopped himself in a leather swivel chair. He stacked the files he'd carried onto the corner of his desk. Inside the chilly temple, he ran a sleeve of his white robe across his face, dripping with sweat. "We've already interviewed Neferita," he said. "She's being held in the guard house."

Meres kept writing, while Priest Hennet stared at his monitor and sorted through the paperwork in the manila folders. Finally, she handed the yellow pad to the priest.

After reading her statement, Priest Hennet raised his eyebrows and leaned back in his chair. "Neferita says she comes to the White-Walled City from Elephantine on a pilgrimage. A crocodile killed her husband last month."

Meres' own parents had been killed by a crocodile when Meres was very young. It was a common way of death in the Black Land. She couldn't help but feel empathy toward Neferita. No wonder the young mother had failed to control her son. She was still in mourning for her husband.

Meres realized Priest Hennet gazed at her a little too intently.

"Is everything all right?" he said.

"I'm wondering if I made a mistake," Meres said. "If Neferita is a new widow..."

"That matters not," Priest Hennet said. "Tragedy is no excuse for defiling the image of the Pharaoh."

"But she came here for help. Wouldn't it be better to give her guidance than punishment?"

Priest Hennet's smile struck Meres as chilly. "What an interesting thought." He turned back to his computer, adjusting the screen as if to make sure Meres couldn't see it. For the next minute or so, he tapped on the keys, studied the screen, and tapped on the keys some more.

"Neferita told us that she was in control of her son until you interfered," the priest said. "But thanks to your quick thinking, the Eye of Horus recorded the event. Your statement matches what we have already seen through the Eye of Horus. Neferita's version does not. We appreciate your statement today and you calling the attention of the Eye of Horus to Neferita and her son. We know the truth because of what you have done."

Meres knew Priest Hennet well enough to realize instantly that he had a secret.

The question is, Meres thought as she forced a smile, *what kind of secret is it?*

"We have passed your concern about Neferita to Isis," Priest Hennet said. "Isis has ordered us to send the woman's son to Our Lady's orphanage."

Meres' heart sank. She knew Our Lady's orphanage well. She'd grown up there after her parents' deaths.

The priest's smile widened. "And Neferita will be here soon to accompany you home."

"Home?" Meres said. "I don't understand."

"Clearly, the woman needs help. Isis has proclaimed that you can give Neferita the help she needs. Neferita must follow you in order to learn from you."

Meres suppressed her desire to stuff a hand in her pocket and clutch the map that Pu had drawn. How could Meres help Pu with Neferita at her elbow? "I'm sorry," Meres said, "but I'm sure my husband will object."

"Forever why?"

Meres flinched. When Priest Hennet felt the need to pressure anyone, he twisted old expressions into new ones. He'd flip "whatever for" into "forever what"—and then vary it, depending on the question.

Priest Hennet cocked his head. "Are you and Ramose having problems?"

A chill crept up Meres' arms. How did he know? "Yes. This is not a good time for us to entertain strangers."

"Not even if Isis requests it?" Priest Hennet's monitor beeped and he glanced at it. "I have just been authorized to offer you an audience with Isis inside her chapel—if you do her bidding and welcome Neferita into your home."

Why is he making me this offer now? Meres thought. *Just minutes ago he told me it would never happen. Why is it so important to him that I let Neferita into my home?*

The answer was obvious: Isis had asked for this. Meres couldn't imagine why Isis would do so—unless she had heard Meres' request for a private audience with Isis and created a way to make it happen.

"All right," Meres said. "I'll take Neferita home with me. When can I meet with Isis?"

"That," Priest Hennet said, "is something that only Isis can decide. I will let you know when she makes that decision."

Chapter Four

Meres walked out of the Temple of Our Lady of the Absolute as the sun began to set. She gazed at the reddening horizon. The sun was a symbol of the god Ra riding his chariot far away in the late afternoon sky, preparing for his nightly journey through the Underworld. Ra graced both worlds: the one Meres lived in now, and the one in which she'd live forever after this human life ended—the Underworld.

For a moment, Meres wished she already lived in the Underworld with Osiris and Our Lady, Isis. In that world, happiness and perfection reigned.

Meres turned at the sound of sandals plopping across the stone courtyard. A guard escorted Neferita around the corner of the temple and toward Meres.

Neferita's face flushed and her mouth looked pinched.

A wave of embarrassment washed over Meres.

Why did I make such a fuss about Neferita and her son? Meres thought.

She knew the answer: because it was expected of her.

All her life, Meres had done what was expected of her. Growing up, she'd learned her best interest meant obeying the priestesses who ran Our Lady's orphanage. Good behavior was rewarded with honey cakes, while bad behavior meant spending hours or even days locked up in a tiny room. Obeying the gods and doing their will paved the path to goodness, which required following the rules with absolute precision.

And following the rules with absolute precision meant turning in people who caused any harm, great or small, to the Pharaoh, the one man in the Black Land who symbolized all the gods. In fact, the Pharaoh *was* a god who had chosen to live among his worshippers in a human body in order to help them.

Without a word, the guard handed Neferita to Meres.

When Neferita's eyes met Meres', they blazed with indignation.

Meres wanted to apologize, even though she knew she'd done the right thing. As she looked away from Neferita's stare, a new thought struck Meres: *If I've done the right thing, then why does it feel so wrong?*

"Come this way," Meres said, turning her back on Neferita.

It's something I can ask Isis, Meres realized. *When I'm given an audience with her, I'll ask her why I feel I've done wrong. And if I somehow have done the wrong thing, I'll ask how I can atone.*

Meres led Neferita through the temple gates and out onto the streets of the White-Walled City. They passed old men wearing long white gowns. In the niche of a building across the street, a young man wearing slate-blue robes sat with his legs stretched out and a child enfolded safely between them in his robes. On a shaded street corner, a woman sat in solitude. She shucked corn in front of a small fire in a metal container, her face caught in the fire's glow. She placed the clean ears in a long, pointed wicker basket.

Neferita kept stride with Meres. "They took my son away from me because of you. A boy should be with his mother—not in an orphanage."

Meres tightened inside, quick to defend herself. "Where are you from?"

Neferita shot a sideways look at her. "Elephantine."

"You're not in Elephantine anymore," Meres said. "You're in the royal city, and you're expected to treat the Pharaoh and his image with respect."

"But I—"

"I don't care," Meres said. "When you are within the White Walls, you are expected to act appropriately. You are responsible for your son's actions, and you failed. When you prove that you can succeed, I'm sure your son will be returned to you."

"You—" Neferita clamped her mouth shut and struggled to keep it shut. Her face flushed deeper and anger burned in her eyes. A few moments and a few deep breaths later, she calmed. "I will do whatever is necessary to get my son back."

"Good."

As they walked down the street, a sudden whirring noise caught Meres' attention.

It was the sound of the Eye of Horus.

Meres often heard it in a crowd, but this was Sunday afternoon. Few people walked this part of the city on Sundays. In fact, other than the guard at the temple gate, Meres and Neferita were the only people in sight. So what exactly did the Eye of Horus have to look at?

Meres halted, suddenly feeling worried. *Is the Eye following us?*

Neferita stopped a few steps ahead of Meres and looked back at her. "What's wrong?"

Think, Meres told herself. *What's a good excuse?*

"There's something in my sandal," Meres said. She took off one sandal and pretended to brush a pebble from the sole of her foot. She took a quick glance behind her.

An Eye of Horus perched on top of a pylon at the temple gate, pointed directly at Meres and Neferita.

Someone was watching them.

On any other day, Meres would have made a joke of it by waving happily at the Eye.

But today was different.

Maybe the Eye was keeping track of Neferita. But that didn't make sense, considering that she'd been placed in Meres' care. Why would the priests bother to keep tabs on Neferita when they'd already asked Meres to do so? Just today, Pu had revealed how highly the priests thought of Meres. Why wouldn't they trust her now?

They know, Meres thought. *Somehow they overheard Pu when she told me she's pregnant.*

Meres swallowed the lump rising in her throat.

Or maybe they just suspect.

Act normal, Meres told herself. *Don't let them realize you're on to them.*

She knelt, examining her sandal as if there might be something wrong with it. Trembling, Meres felt her heart pound against her chest.

The heart was the container of all deeds, both good and bad. Meres knew that when she died, her heart would be weighed by the goddess Maat, whose realm was justice. If the heart weighed heavy with bad deeds, Meres' spirit would be devoured by a monster; she'd be eaten out of existence, dead to the world so that she could never meet the people she loved in the Underworld.

What if my heart has already recorded my bad deed of helping Pu instead of reporting her to the Pharaoh? Meres thought.

If Meres' spirit were devoured by a monster, she would never meet Isis in the Underworld.

I have to turn Pu in, Meres thought.

Sweat ran down her face as she pretended to struggle putting her sandal back on, still keenly aware that the eye of Horus studied her every move.

But her heart pounded even faster, and a sinking feeling in the pit of her stomach nauseated her.

How can I, Meres thought, *when I love Pu? When Ramose loves her?*

"By the god Osiris," Neferita said. "What's taking so long?"

"Nothing," Meres said. "I'm just making sure nothing has come loose."

Meres scanned the road ahead. If they took it, that road would lead to the Pharaoh's palace, where Meres could call Pu out and make her accusations in order to keep the unspoken promise that every citizen made to obey the Pharaoh and his laws.

Her hands shook as she wiped the sweat from her face.

I can't, Meres thought. *Isis help me. I can't.*

Neferita frowned. "You don't look so good."

"I'm fine," Meres said. "It's just been awhile since I've had anything to eat."

Instead of heading through the heart of the city, Meres led Neferita along the edge of the White Walled City. This way, Meres could stay close to the sun god Ra before he left this world for the day. Being close to the gods always calmed her.

A guard at the West Gate stopped them. "What's your business?" He yawned with boredom.

There are Eyes posted along the top of the city wall, Meres thought. *If I'm really in trouble, each of them will follow me as I walk past.*

Meres forced a nervous smile. "I'm the scribe at the Temple of Isis. I'm hoping to catch my husband on my way home. He spent the day fishing with his friends."

"Lucky bastard," the guard grunted. He pointed at Neferita. "Who's this?"

"A visitor from Elephantine," Meres said, rushing to speak before Neferita could answer for herself. "I've been charged with her safekeeping."

The guard nodded and indicated they could pass through the city gate. "Be careful. Folks have spotted crocs today."

Meres waved one hand in thanks as she pressed on.

Neferita shuddered. "Shouldn't we stay inside the city?"

"At this time of day, crocodiles lie low to blend in with the landscape until some unsuspecting fool walks too close," Meres said. She glanced back at Neferita, who lagged behind. "I know how to avoid them. I suggest you stay close."

Neferita hesitated, staring at the wide expanse of the Nile and its banks. When the wind kicked up and made the grass wave as if something were stalking through it, she rushed to Meres' side.

They stayed on the desert path near the city's high white wall. As they walked on the sand, its heat seeped through the soles of their sandals.

Meres kept her eyes on the nearby Nile and the clusters of tall, spiky papyrus plants lining its banks, ready to grab Neferita's hand and scramble up the wall at the first sight of trouble.

But there weren't any crocodiles stalking outside the city tonight. The Nile waters were calm as the last fishermen pulled in their nets and paddled their dried-papyrus boats toward shore.

Meres squinted as she scanned the river. She didn't see anyone who looked like Ramose.

She continued gazing toward the river as they approached the first Eye of Horus, pointed inward at the city. Whenever she'd walked outside the wall before, the Eyes either kept their focus on the city or spun to check the detected movement outside the wall for a moment or two before turning back toward the city.

Meres heard the Eye revolve toward them, followed by silence. Shifting her gaze to the path in front of her, she saw the Eye from the corner of her eyes.

It stayed locked on Meres and Neferita.

Every time Meres and Neferita passed an Eye of Horus on top of the city wall, the same thing happened.

The Eyes were watching them.

Meres stared at the sky above, thinking again of the sun god on his way to the afterlife in the Underworld. *Take me with you,* she thought.

If Ra would only swoop down long enough to catch Meres in his arms and lift her into his chariot, the sun god could take her directly to the Underworld. Meres wouldn't have to face Maat and the weighing of Meres' heart after death. And no monster could devour Meres and destroy her spirit forever.

Meres would be safe for all eternity in the Underworld, the magical place of sweeping, golden fields: the home to the dead and the gods.

Meres wished Pu had been faithful to the Pharaoh. She wished Pu weren't pregnant.

Most of all, Meres wished she didn't have Neferita at her side. Meres wished she could just have dinner with her husband. She dreaded Ramose's response to Neferita.

Up ahead, a baby donkey trotted out from a field of sugar cane. A little girl emerged from the field moments later, barefoot in the mud. She caught the rope around the donkey's neck, and they struggled, each pulling hard against the other, neither willing to budge.

Taking a deep breath, Meres led Neferita toward the South Gate that would admit them back into the White Walled City. It was time to go home and get this over with.

CHAPTER FIVE

Alone in his office, Priest Hennet retrieved the paperwork he'd dropped when Meres had shown up unexpectedly in the temple hallway.

She wasn't supposed to be there—it was her day off. Otherwise, he wouldn't have been so careless.

Sifting through the spreadsheets, Priest Hennet groaned. They contained very delicate information, and the fact that Meres had seen them—even if only for a moment—made him very nervous. He hadn't worked and sacrificed all these years for nothing. As the head priest of the temple, he was wealthy. He owned one of the most prestigious homes in the White Walled City. He could have anything he wanted. He couldn't let someone like Meres ruin it all.

Don't worry, he thought. *It's doubtful Meres knows what she saw, but even if she did, she's also provided the solution.*

Priest Hennet smiled. It had been obvious to him the moment he met Neferita that she was a foolish girl who would be easy to manipulate. Sighing with satisfaction, he locked the spreadsheets in the secret compartment in his desk.

He was a powerful man, and he resolved to let no one change that fact.

Especially not a woman.

❧❧

Meres led Neferita into her house. The air indoors was cool, a welcome relief from the sun's heat. She was proud of their home.

Inside the city walls, the Pharaoh's palace sprawled in the East, his wealthy administrators and the priests lived in the North, and the Temple of Our Lady of the Absolute dominated the West. That left the south side for everyday workers and farmers.

When Meres had worked as the scribe to a city official, she and Ramose had lived in a typical farmer's house: a single room in which they slept on reed mats. But working at the temple meant Meres needed and could afford a more upscale home. They now lived in a two-story white-washed mud brick home with bedrooms, a dining room with a low table and floor cushions, and a room for meeting guests, which included a few columns and carved wooden chairs. Instead of sleeping on mats, they now owned a bed.

The small windows near the ceiling let breezes in while keeping direct sunlight out. The white entry walls were decorated with blue zigzag lines that symbolized the Nile, punctuated with images of salmon. Meres kicked off her sandals. Neferita followed suit.

Ramose's sandals were already here.

"Ramose?"

No answer. If he wasn't within earshot, that probably meant he'd had good luck on the Nile today.

"Stay here," Meres told Neferita.

Neferita shrugged, resigned to obey.

Meres wound her way through the first floor. She found her husband out back, grilling fish wrapped in banana leaves over an open-pit fire near their shallow reflecting pool.

Ramose grinned. Like all working men, the sun had darkened his skin. Freckles splattered his nose, and a big dimple dented his chin. "Hello, my beautiful wife. Did you have fun with the gods today?"

Normally, Meres grinned at Ramose's standing joke. Like everyone else in the White Walled City, he knew that Meres' job allowed her inside the home of the gods but nowhere near them. Even so, everyone envied Meres.

Meres smiled slightly and shrugged his question off.

Ramose believed in the joy of living a simple life. He was happiest with dirt under his fingernails and enough of an ache in his muscles to remind him he'd put in a good day's work. Although he believed in the gods, Meres sometimes suspected that he could take or leave them. He certainly would rather be fishing or out in the fields than at any kind of religious event. Ramose frowned. "Rough day?"

Meres nodded, looking away.

"Are you all right?" he said.

When she didn't answer, Ramose gave the stuffed banana leaves a quick flip on the grill. He approached his wife, touching her shoulder lightly.

Meres recognized her good luck. Ramose was a rare man who stayed in tune with those around him—especially Meres. He knew how to read her, and he cared deeply about her feelings.

There weren't many men like Ramose in the White Walled City, and probably not many like him in all the Black Land. And yet, more and more she wondered if their marriage might be falling apart. But it wasn't her husband she doubted. Her best chance of having a child might require leaving him.

Tears welled in Meres' eyes. Without meeting her husband's gaze, she embraced him, resting her face against his shoulder. She struggled to stay calm as he held her.

"Tell me what's wrong, Meres," Ramose said steadily.

Backing out of his arms, Meres told him about the incident at Pharaoh Park, Priest Hennet's decision, and the fact that Neferita stood inside their house.

Ramose's lips pressed together. He said, "How many times have I told you not to stick your nose where it doesn't belong?"

When they were first married, Ramose had been annoyed by Meres' insistence on sticking to the rules. Over time, his annoyance sometimes got the better of him, especially when he tried to convince her that life meant more than simply following rules made by others.

He gave a sigh of resignation. "Guess I'd better put another fish on the grill." He plucked a fresh banana leaf from a squat tree in their courtyard. He filled it with a fish from the day's catch, plantains, beans, and rice. He wrapped the leaf into a bundle and placed it on the grill.

Meres watched in silence. *I don't want to fight,* she thought. *Pu needs me, and I have to figure out how to help her.*

Ramose didn't argue with his usual passion. He acted more tired than angry. "I know it's important to you to do whatever Isis and the priests say. I know you think other people are making disastrous mistakes when they don't live exactly the way you think they should."

"The way Isis says they should," Meres interjected. She clamped her hand over her mouth, wishing she'd said nothing.

Ramose gazed at her, long and hard. "You know how I feel. What you're really doing is trying to control other people."

"I just want to help them do what's right," Meres whispered.

Ramose crossed his arms. "How can you know what's right for anyone other than you?" His voice softened. "You're the only one who has lived inside your own skin. That means you're the only person who knows everything that has happened throughout the course of your entire life. That means you are the only one qualified to make decisions about your life. And that's why other people have to make their own decisions: because they're the ones who live inside their own skins, not you."

He used the back of his hand to wipe the sweat from his brow. Almost as an afterthought, he said, "Why is it so necessary for you to tell other people how to live their lives?"

"I don't know," Meres said. "I wish I'd never said anything today."

Ramose opened his mouth, ready to continue arguing. He hesitated.

"You've never said that before."

Meres hugged herself. "Something else happened today." *Be careful,* Meres told herself. *You promised Pu not to tell Ramose that she's pregnant and getting ready to flee. Watch what you say—you have to keep your promise.* "I had lunch with Pu. I'm worried about something she said."

Ramose gazed at Meres for a long moment. Tenderness crept into his eyes. "What?"

"Have you ever heard of a woman named Sekhmet?"

Ramose shook his head. "I know nearly everyone in the city, and I've never heard that name. Why would anyone name their kid after that kind of goddess? What does this have to do with Pu?"

Meres hesitated, choosing her words carefully. This conversation could become volatile at any moment. "She's scared, and I think it's because of a story they tell at the royal palace to keep the women of the harem in line."

Ramose snorted in disgust.

Many years ago, when Pu joined the harem, Ramose had fought Pu's decision long and hard. He'd argued that the harem was no place for anyone. He said it was degrading, that the women were no more than playthings at the Pharaoh's disposal. Of course, Ramose was right, but Pu didn't want to believe him.

Pu had claimed that belonging to the harem meant she'd have lifelong security—she'd never have to struggle to keep food on the table or a roof over her head. She'd be free to have as many children as she wished. Because her children would be the Pharaoh's children, they would be set for life. Her children would never have to struggle, because they would always have a home in the royal compound.

"It isn't security you want," Ramose had told his sister. "It's luxury. You're letting yourself be seduced by pretty, shiny things. It's the glamour of royal life you want, and you're willing to pay a price that's far too high. What about your dignity, Pu? Don't you want more from life than catering to someone else?"

Meres understood both Ramose's point and Pu's wishes. And now Pu finally realized that lifelong security would ultimately mean being demoted from a member of the harem to a palace servant. On one hand, Meres wished that Pu had married the man she loved, Jabari, a neighboring farmer. Pu claimed theirs had been nothing but a fleeting romance, but the man had been broken-hearted when Pu accepted the invitation to join the harem, an honor extended only to the most beautiful women in the Black Land.

At the same time, Meres understood Pu's reasons for joining the harem. What woman wouldn't want the chance to have as many children as she could, knowing they were all guaranteed to have a wonderful life?

Ramose had cut ties with his only sister. From the day Pu joined the harem, she and Ramose never saw each other again. Meres acted as a go-between, carrying news about Ramose to Pu, and vice versa.

"They say Sekhmet is a demon woman," Meres said.

Surprised out of his anger, Ramose laughed. "A demon woman? There's no such thing."

"Pu isn't someone who believes in monsters."

Ramose shrugged. "Don't be so sure."

"You know Pu better than that."

Ramose kept silent for a moment. "Maybe a better question is, what could she have to be afraid of? If the palace is using this legend to keep the harem in line, there must be a reason. What's the reason?"

The reason is, Pu has committed treason by sleeping with the enemy, Meres thought. *And I need to find out if there's any truth behind the threat of Sekhmet because I'm helping Pu get out of the country.*

Ramose's eyes narrowed with suspicion as he searched his wife's face.

Meres hadn't bothered to ask Pu why Ramose should be kept in the dark, because the reason was obvious. The year before Ramose met Meres, he'd been in love with another woman and planned to marry her until he learned she was having another man's baby. To this day, Ramose still spoke bitterly about any woman who cheated on the man she claimed to love.

The only way to let Ramose know that Pu planned to leave the Black Land was to tell him why—and there was no guarantee that Ramose wouldn't turn Pu in as a traitor.

Out loud, Meres said, "You know the Pharaoh. He's done odd things before that don't make sense."

A sudden wind whipped the flames of the cooking fire, lighting up the doorway behind them.

"Neferita!" Meres said, spotting the young woman as she stood just inside the house. "How long have you been there?"

"Only for a second," Neferita said, watching Ramose lift the fish off the grill. "The smell came into the house—it's wonderful."

"I'm Ramose. Welcome to our home." His voice held little warmth. "I'm sure you've had a long day. You'll feel better after a good meal."

They all sat by the edge of the reflecting pool. The walls of the small courtyard glowed amber from the light of the small oil lamps Ramose had placed nearby.

Meres opened the banana leaf Ramose had placed on a plate for her, mindful of the escaping, fragrant steam. The three of them ate in silence.

By the time they were finished, the stars had come out.

Ramose folded his empty banana leaf around the fish bones, gleaming amber like the walls in the lamp light. "We have a small guest room," he said to Neferita. "You can sleep there." He collected the other banana leaves and fish bones. He took them to the compost pile in the far corner of their home's courtyard.

While Ramose cleaned up, Meres escorted Neferita to the guest room.

Minutes later, Meres and Ramose blew out the last oil lamp in the house and went to bed. They whispered to each other in the dark.

"How long is she staying with us?" Ramose said.

"That's for the priests to decide. They think we can teach her how to be a better citizen and a better parent."

"What? We've never been parents. What kind of idiot made that decision?"

Meres had just assumed that because she and Ramose were older than Neferita that they could give her guidance. She'd assumed they were smarter and wiser.

Ramose is right, Meres realized. *We have no experience raising children. Why would the priests want us to teach Neferita?*

"I don't know," she said, answering her husband's question. "Maybe it's temple policy. Maybe in a case like this, Neferita must be assigned to someone who works at the temple."

"It doesn't make any sense. I want her out of here."

"I agree. I just don't know how to make it happen."

"Why not try some magic?"

His suggestion startled Meres. "I thought you didn't believe in magic."

Ramose stretched and yawned. "I don't. But you do. And you have access to the priests who have assigned her to us. Why not work some of your magic on them? And maybe even on her."

Meres hesitated to consider the thought because it seemed like such a defiant act.

But Isis herself had been defiant. She'd been audacious and daring.

"Magic," Meres whispered, rolling the possibility around in her mind.

Ramose kissed her. He rested one hand against his head while he ran the other over her body. "Magic."

CHAPTER SIX

Meres sat across the table from Pu at the *Cleopatra Cafe*. They each had a bottle of beer.

Meres frowned. This wasn't right. "Should you be drinking?" She whispered to Pu, not wanting to raise suspicion among anyone who might overhear. Beer-drinking farmers, streaked with sweat and dirt from a hard day's work, crowded the cafe. Right now, only Meres knew Pu's secret and the importance of keeping it.

Pu's dark hair looked striking against her red linen dress. She laughed. "That's a funny question. What's wrong with having a few beers?"

"You know," Meres said. "What you told me yesterday, first in Pharaoh Park, and then here in the cafe."

Pu laughed again. "You must be dreaming."

Is that all it was, Meres wondered. *Just a dream?* "So you're all right?"

Pu drained her bottle, tilting its bottom high. She threw the glass bottle hard against the nearest wall, and it shattered. Pu grinned. "Never better."

No one noticed the broken bottle.

Strange.

Meres took a swig from her own bottle. Her beer tasted like bittersweet syrup. "How's the Pharaoh?"

"He's an idiot, as usual." Pu waved to the waitress, signaling for more beer. "Honestly, Meres, you need to get the stars out of your eyes. They're clouding your vision."

Meres choked on her syrupy beer, startled by Pu's words.

The waitress slammed two fresh bottles on the table.

"Thanks, Hon," Pu said to the waitress.

Meres' jaw slackened in shock as Pu popped the bottle cap off with her teeth.

Pu took a long swig and belched. "To be more specific, you act as if the Pharaoh is a god."

Meres stared at Pu in disbelief. "But the Pharaoh *is* a god."

Pu threw her head back, laughing loud and long. She shook her hair, and it lightened to a tawny color. Her face transformed, becoming cat-like. Her laugh ended with a roar. She shouted, "He's no god—but I am!"

Meres shrank in terror. The woman across the table wasn't Pu anymore.

She was the lioness goddess, Sekhmet, the daughter of the sun god Ra, who served as his eyes. She was the most confusing of all gods: as the Mistress of Life, Sekhmet protected anyone who needed her help. At the same time, Sekhmet the Destroyer could just as easily kill.

"Please, Mistress, forgive me." Meres jumped out of her chair as if it were on fire. Meres kneeled, touching her hands and forehead to the floor.

"Have some self respect," Sekhmet said, kicking her. "Get back in your chair."

Dumbfounded, Meres obeyed but kept her gaze cast down.

Sekhmet snorted. "Why is it you people can't see the forest for the trees? Why do you insist on black and white? Don't you understand the meaning of gray?"

The farmers' voices rose in the cafe, punctuated by the clink of bottles and the ring of the cash register.

After several long moments, Meres wondered if Sekhmet had left. Tentatively, Meres looked up.

Sekhmet's large green eyes stared back, the irises narrowed to black, vertical slits. Tawny fur covered her face, and round ears rested on top of her head. But the rest of her body was human. "I ain't going nowhere, Hon," Sekhmet said. "Not until our business together is done." Her chest rumbled loudly.

Sekhmet purred.

Meres blinked back anxious tears. "What business is that?"

Sekhmet's smile revealed long, sharp teeth. "You."

The goddess sprang across the tabletop with a roar, mouth open to devour Meres.

Meres woke up screaming.

Ramose wrapped his arms around Meres, pulling her close. "You were dreaming. It's just a dream."

Meres' heart pounded. *Of course. What had Pu said in the dream? That's right. Pu had said, "You must be dreaming."*

But Meres trembled. "It wasn't just a dream," she whispered.

In the middle of the night, Meres saw nothing but black. She held on to Ramose.

He groaned sleepily. "What was it? Another one of your prophetic visits with the gods?"

"I think so," Meres whispered. "Just talking about magic made it happen."

"Go back to sleep," Ramose muttered. "You can sort it all out in the morning." Moments later, he snored.

But Meres' mind raced, trying to understand the meaning of her dream.

～～

Meres stayed in bed while Ramose showered that morning.

Ramose was right about one thing: whenever Meres dreamed of the gods, some part of that dream always came true. It had happened since childhood, and it was one of the reasons she'd landed the coveted position of scribe in the Temple. The perplexing thing was, Meres usually dreamed about Isis or Osiris. She had never dreamed about Sekhmet before.

So why had she dreamed of Sekhmet now?

Ah, Meres thought, believing she understood the meaning of her dream at last. *When Pu and I were in Pharaoh Park yesterday, she worried about being watched by the Eye of Horus. That's why I dreamed of Sekhmet—she's the Eye of Ra. One Eye made me think of the other.*

A freshly showered Ramose walked naked into their bedroom. He selected a white linen kilt from a basket of clean clothes, wrapped it around his waist, and tied the ends in a knot. "What happens to our guest today?"

Our guest. Neferita.

Meres groaned. "I don't know. Priest Hennet said she should stay with us. Beyond that, I don't know what to do."

"Will she go with you to work?" Ramose said. "Or stay here all day?"

I can't have her following me around, Meres thought. *Not when I don't know what to do about Pu yet.*

Out loud, she said, "Can she go with you?"

"To the construction site? What would she do there?"

Like most farmers in the White-Walled City, he tended his crops during the season of Summer. During the season of Harvest, he collected the fruits of his work and distributed them as dictated by the Pharaoh. During the third and final season of Inundation, the Nile flooded all crop land, making it impossible for farmers to work. During this time, farmers became construction workers: they paid their taxes by voluntarily working on whatever project the Pharaoh wanted to build. This year, the Pharaoh had decided to revamp the marketplace in the center of the city.

"Let's find out," Meres said. "If we leave soon, we can all go to the construction site. If there's no place for her there, I'll take her with me to the temple."

Chapter Seven

"This woman—Neferita—is my responsibility by the priests' order," Ramose explained to the foreman at the construction site, shouting above the thunder of hammers and the screeching of saws.

While the royal palace stood as the head of the city and the temple acted as its heart, the marketplace was the blood that gave it life. Awnings of solid bright yellow, red, and green covered the stalls lining the Avenue of the Rams that ran through the center of the city. Fresh fruits, vegetables, spices or meat piled high in each stall. The normally heady scent of citrus and curry now mixed with sawdust and cement mix.

Meres recognized the foreman as one of the Pharaoh's men. The foreman, a heavyset man, adjusted his hard-hat, as bright as the yellow awnings in the marketplace. He crossed his arms. "What do you expect her to do here?"

It was a good question. Neferita looked like a lost child among the construction workers hauling lumber and setting up scaffolding behind the stalls.

"Maybe she can haul water for the workers," Ramose said. "Or carry equipment."

"There's no need," the foreman said. "I already have people for that."

The Pharaoh sanctioned a new construction project each year during Inundation. Ramose had often grumbled that it was never anything more than an excuse to collect taxes by coercing the city's residents to give the Pharaoh free labor. Meres had always argued that the Pharaoh had everyone's best interest at heart, and this year was no different. In the past, each farmer drove his own cart to market and stocked his stall. The Pharaoh's new construction involved building storage buildings behind the stalls. That way, each farmer could leave any unsold produce in storage instead of carting it back home at the end of each day.

At this time of year, almost everything in the marketplace came from foreign countries. Likewise, the new storage areas would make it easier to store imported food, meaning less would be lost to spoilage.

By nature, Meres enjoyed watching people, a habit she'd acquired growing up in the orphanage. Keeping an eye on everyone surrounding her and trying to figure out what they might be thinking had come in handy, especially when it came to keeping out of trouble and the punishment bound to follow.

As she scanned the construction site, Meres noticed several men staring at Neferita.

Of course. Here, everyone knew almost everyone else, at least in passing. Neferita was young and pretty and new to the city. It was likely that none of these men had seen her before.

"Isn't there something she can do?" Ramose said. "Couldn't you use an assistant? Someone to run messages?"

"No," the foreman said gruffly.

His tone caught Meres' attention. When she looked back at the foreman, she saw him regarding his workers' interest in Neferita.

Oh, no, Meres thought.

"Get back to work!" The foreman yelled.

"But—" Ramose said.

The foreman paused just long enough to glare at Ramose. "That includes you." The foreman jerked a nod at Meres and Neferita. "And get rid of the distractions."

Meres exchanged a knowing look with her husband. Taking Neferita by the hand, Meres said, "Let's go. You can come with me to the temple."

The women snaked their way through a maze of equipment that stretched for blocks along the street. A group of women passed by, balancing baskets of lettuce, cucumbers, and figs on their heads.

Across the street, a group of brick makers mixed dirt, water, and chopped straw. They'd soon mash it with their feet, fill up a matrix of wooden-slat brick molds, and leave it in the sun to dry. Other workers roofed a small new storage house with palm branches, insulating them with mud.

As they walked down the street, Neferita said, "This is so beautiful. There's nothing like this in Elephantine."

Meres frowned. To her, the Avenue of the Rams looked a mess, compared to its normal glory. "What's so beautiful about it?"

Neferita pointed at the row of life-size ram-headed sphinxes that lined each side of the street. "There must be hundreds of them!"

Meres smiled, and something inside her softened toward Neferita. Maybe Neferita wasn't the best mother. Maybe she hadn't learned how to control or teach her son right from wrong yet. But Neferita had the ability to see beauty shine through, even when surrounded by chaos.

Neferita was right. It had taken decades to create hundreds of stone statues that were set every ten feet apart and faced the street. Walking down the Avenue of the Rams and passing by all those sphinxes had sent chills of delight down Meres' spine the first time she had done it. Considered sacred, the street connected the Pharaoh's palace to the temple. No children were allowed on the Avenue of the Rams, except on special occasions.

Suddenly, Meres saw something else shine through. Gazing at the rows of sphinxes, Meres felt hope.

She saw the solution to Pu's problem.

Chapter Eight

"We need to change the route of next week's festival parade," Meres said while she took notes, sitting on the floor at the foot of Priest Hennet's desk. "None of us thought about the construction going on at the vendor stalls on the Avenue of the Rams."

"Forever what?" Priest Hennet's chair squeaked as he leaned back, hands resting behind his head. "It's been considered. All the construction is off-road. There is nothing wrong with the avenue itself."

"It's so beautiful," Neferita said wistfully. Like a shadow, she sat next to Meres on the floor.

Meres said, "There's no problem for the parade. The real problem is there's no place for people to watch the parade. The construction stretches for blocks. Do we really want that much of the parade to go on in isolation?"

Neferita looked worried and fidgeted.

"I see," Priest Hennet sighed. He took another honey cake from the platter on his desk. So far, by Meres' count, he'd devoured a dozen honey cakes. He hadn't offered any to Meres or Neferita, but that was nothing new. Meres had often worked in his office with a rumbling stomach, watching him eat platters heaped with food. It had never occurred to him to share, as far as Meres could tell. Or maybe he just didn't care to.

Meres rose to her knees, facing Priest Hennet and the desk between them. She reached up and across to point at the map spread open on the desktop. "Here's an easy solution. Instead of going straight down the Avenue of the Rams, we can send the parade off to the side, down a few small streets."

Priest Hennet's chair groaned again as he leaned forward to follow her logic. He frowned. "That's a peculiar route."

Meres shook her head in disagreement. "Not at all." She drew a loop to the side of the Avenue of the Rams, exactly as Pu had requested when she'd drawn a make-shift map for Meres. This route would let Pu and her daughters take their place on the sidelines to watch the festival parade, only to slip away and escape through the one gate in the city with a broken Eye of Horus. "If we swing the parade around this way, we can spread out the crowd that normally lines the Avenue of the Rams along these other streets. It creates a longer route, which means we have more room for the crowd."

Priest Hennet grunted as he studied the map.

Neferita rose to her knees. She shuffled over to kneel next to Meres. Neferita pointed to the opposite side of the Avenue of the Rams. "Or we could re-route over this way," she said, helpfully.

Meres concentrated on showing no reaction, although she silently kicked herself for ever getting involved with Neferita. She should have just turned her back and walked away when Neferita's son had peed on the Pharaoh's statue. "It's not as attractive on that side."

"Why should that matter?" Neferita said, growing more inter-ested in the conversation by the moment. "Everyone will be watching the parade."

"That's a good point," Priest Hennet said.

Meres ground her teeth in anger. Who did Neferita think she was? Until now, Meres had been the only commoner allowed inside the Temple of Our Lady of the Absolute. Meres had been the only one in all of the Black Land to work with the priests who served Our Lady. Neferita was supposed to be undergoing humiliation and punishment, not trying to give her advice on an event that didn't concern her!

Calm down, Meres told herself. *This is about helping Pu, not about feeling insulted.*

"It's a good way to create ill will between us and the Pharaoh and his palace," Meres said. She pointed at the area Neferita suggested. "The royal stables are on this side of the palace. If we place the crowd here, they'll smell the manure." Meres dragged her finger to the opposite side of the Avenue of the Rams. "On the other hand, if we place them here, they're near the royal gardens. And remember, the onlookers at the beginning of the parade route are always those most favored by the Pharaoh."

Priest Hennet nodded his approval as he popped the last honey cake in his mouth. When his phone rang, he answered while still chewing. He listened for several long moments and then hung up. "Work out the details, girls. Duty calls. There's been another crocodile attack."

Like everyone else, Meres first thought of the ones she loved. "Where?" She said faintly. "Who?"

"No one you know," Priest Hennet said as he stood, straightening his office on his way out. "Just a royal cook and her husband. Thank the gods their children are safe."

As he left the office, Meres sank back on her haunches. Neferita followed suit.

"Are you all right?" Neferita said.

"That's how my parents died," Meres said softly. "But it's common."

Neferita's eyes widened. "Not in Elephantine."

Meres shrugged it off. "But we're right on the Nile."

"So is Elephantine," Neferita said. She lowered her voice and glanced behind her, as if checking to make sure no one listened. "I brought my son here because we needed help and my husband had relatives here. But I found out they died last week. Killed by crocodiles."

"Like I said, it's common."

"Before we left Elephantine, people warned me not to come. They told me about the crocodiles and the sacrifices at your festivals."

"What?" Meres stared at Neferita in disbelief. "What sacrifices?"

Now Neferita look surprised. "They say you sacrifice men so you can act out the story of Isis and Osiris."

Meres laughed. "No! Everything we do is symbolic. Like next week's festival. It's the Festival of Isis, so the parade is about the story of Isis and Osiris: thousands of years ago, Osiris led Egypt out of war and into a state of civilization. As the great-grandson of the Almighty God Ra, Osiris became Pharaoh of Egypt and married his sister, Isis."

"Yes, I know," Neferita said.

Ignoring her, Meres continued. "But envy consumed their brother Seti. When Seti tricked Osiris into stepping into a sarcophagus made exactly to his measurements, Osiris became trapped in it, and Seti threw him into the river Nile to his death."

"But what you said about it being symbolic. That's not what I heard," Neferita whispered. "They say it really happens here."

"Oh," Meres said, standing up and stretching her legs. "It happened once, decades ago. A man committed a crime, and they did it to punish him."

Tentative, Neferita stood and stretched, too. "So it just happened once? Not all the time?"

Meres nodded. "It's very rare that anyone commits a crime here. And it's always a small crime. They punished a bad man."

"What did he do?"

Meres paused, realizing she'd never asked that question herself. "I don't know."

CHAPTER NINE

By the time the whistle blew to signal the lunch break, Ramose felt starved. Thanks to Neferita's unexpected presence since last night, he felt out of whack. Ramose spent a few minutes searching for his lunch box before he realized he'd been so discombobulated this morning that he'd not only forgotten to bring it, but he'd forgotten to make his lunch as well.

While most of the others settled down in whatever shade they could find to eat their bag lunches, Ramose headed down the Avenue of the Rams toward one of his favorite sandwich shops.

"Ramose!" A familiar voice called.

Ramose turned and grinned at the sight of a heavyset man with a baby face framed by curly red hair. "Jabari!" Ramose called in response.

Jabari had been Ramose's neighbor and best friend growing up. Their friendship had cemented when they were nine-years-old on a day when a crocodile had slipped past a drowsy guard at one of the city gates and found its way into their neighborhood. They'd heard little Pu's terrified screams and raced to find her cornered in the family courtyard by the beast. At that time of day, the adults either worked or went to market, so there was no one to call for help. Before Ramose could think, Jabari had smashed a boulder against the crocodile's snapping jaws until he'd killed it. Feeling shame at having frozen in terror when he first saw the crocodile, young Ramose had felt a burst of admiration for Jabari and decided to be more like him. Never again would Ramose hesitate when he saw someone in danger.

After the two men embraced, Ramose stepped back, beaming at his friend. "I thought you were working at the palace these days. What are you doing here?"

"Looking for lunch!" Jabari clapped a hearty hand on Ramose's back. "Once I saw you, I figured I could follow you to find the best sandwich in town."

Ramose laughed. He led Jabari down the street. "I haven't seen you in months."

Jabari sighed. "The one thing you can always count on with Pharaoh is he keeps you hopping. I've been doing a bit of everything these days."

"That's why you're here? Are we so short-handed that Pharaoh's sending his own men to help out?"

Jabari shook his head as Ramose led him down a side street toward a small food stand labeled *Sacred Scarab Sandwiches*. "I switched places with my oldest son. He struck out on his own this year. Thinks he wants to farm. But he's still a kid, and lately he's been under the weather. He knows it's time to do Pharaoh's work to pay his taxes, but the boy wouldn't last a day in this heat."

Ramose smiled. "So you're here in his place."

"Just until he feels better." Jabari looked down in silence for a few moments.

Ramose braced himself. He knew what to expect. It happened every time they talked, like some strange unspoken ritual. Usually, Ramose hated what would happen next. But this time he realized that Jabari might be in a position to help him.

"How's Pu?" Jabari said softly.

All these years, and he still loved her. Never mind that Jabari had a wife and three kids. Pu never left his thoughts, even though she'd rejected him in favor of living the high life as a member of the Pharaoh's harem.

Ramose gave his standard answer. "You should know better than me."

It was true. Although Jabari's duties changed often, working for the Pharaoh meant his path often crossed with that of the harem. He probably did little more than exchange pleasantries with Pu, but he saw her on a regular basis.

On the other hand, Ramose hadn't seen his own sister in years. He knew Meres had lunch with his sister on a weekly basis, but that was Meres' choice, not his. As long as Meres kept her conversations with Pu to herself, Ramose found it easy to look the other way. Between the way Pu had treated Jabari and Ramose's own experience in being jilted by his own first love— before he met Meres—he no longer had any use for Pu.

If Ramose spent the rest of his life without seeing his sister again, he would not grieve.

What typically would come next was a report from Jabari, usually about Pu's health or about her daughters, who weren't allowed to mix with commoners outside the royal palace. And since Ramose had no reason to visit the palace, he'd never met his nieces.

Instead, Jabari said, "I'm worried about Pu."

They ordered sandwiches and made small talk while they waited. *There's probably nothing to worry about*, Ramose told himself.

Jabari would worry about Pu if she stubbed her toe.

But he remembered what Meres had told him last night.

When their orders arrived, wrapped in white paper, Ramose led Jabari to an isolated bench at the far end of the park next door. Once they settled on the bench, Jabari said, "I can't pinpoint anything specific, but she's been acting strange. There's something wrong. I wish you'd—"

"Has Pu ever mentioned the name Sekhmet to you?"

Jabari paled. Even though he'd just unwrapped his sandwich, he didn't take a bite. Instead, he stared at Ramose, looking as scared as Ramose had felt all those years ago when the crocodile had cornered Pu. "Why do you ask?"

Ramose hesitated. What if Jabari felt more loyalty to the Pharaoh than to Pu? What if Jabari had come here on a mission to find out what troubled Pu? What if Pu had good reason to be scared?

Nonsense. No one in the world loved Pu more than Jabari.

The same sense of shame he'd felt watching Jabari kill the crocodile while he stood frozen washed over Ramose again. The Black Land prided itself on the high value it placed on love. Family came first. Community came next, because every man mattered as much as one's own brother. Every woman was as important as one's own sister.

So what does that say about me? Ramose wondered.

"Ramose? What's wrong?"

Choosing to trust Jabari, Ramose plowed ahead. "Pu said something strange to Meres yesterday. She said there's a demon woman named Sekhmet who lives beneath the city. Have you ever heard Pu or any of the other harem women talk about this?"

The sandwich slipped through Jabari's fingers and splattered across his lap, but he didn't seem to notice. "Sekhmet is real," Jabari whispered. "I've seen her with my own eyes."

Chapter Ten

Pu worried.

She strode down the East corridor of the royal palace, deep in thought. Her leather sandals squeaked across the pale green marble floor, flanked by white marble walls supporting a high ceiling leafed with gold.

She breezed through the atrium, a large, circular room where all four corridors met. Its domed glass ceiling filtered light to nourish the small indoor garden of palm trees, spiky papyrus plants, and hibiscus flowers in the center of the atrium, walled by a stone bench, where a few high ranking officials sat in heated debate.

As Pu turned sharply down the South corridor, she second-guessed herself.

What if Meres tells? Pu wondered. *What if I'm arrested and tried before judges? If I'm sentenced to death, what will happen to my children?*

Pu crossed her arms and picked up her pace.

Don't be foolish, she told herself. *Meres has never let you down before. She's always done what she said she would do, and yesterday she promised to help you. Meres keeps her word. Everyone knows that.*

Pu stepped through an open doorway into the nursery. She would never get used to the strangeness of that term. It made sense for Pharaoh's youngest children, but not for the older girls, left behind while the boys attended school. Here, the girls helped take care of the youngest while learning social graces.

"Good afternoon, Pu," a matron said. White streaked her black hair.

Pu smiled hastily. "How are my girls doing?" The more Pu's certainty of escaping the White Walled City grew, the more anxious she felt about keeping tabs on her children.

"Same as usual. One sullen, one a screaming terror, and the twins on a destructive rampage." The matron was the calmest person Pu had ever met. Sighing, the matron said, "I blame myself. By now I should know it's time to lie when Pharaoh's children ask me the meaning of 'pillage.' Why is it a concept that children always embrace so easily?"

"Good to know," Pu said, "just in case I end up joining your ranks in the near future."

The matron offered a sympathetic gaze but nothing else.

Pu swallowed nervously. So her suspicions were true. As the oldest member of Pharaoh's harem, Pu suspected he'd lost interest in her, thanks to the harem's newest, young members. She knew her options were limited. Once kicked out of the harem, she could work in the nursery, become a housemaid in the palace, or join the ranks of seamstresses in the royal garment factory. None of those choices appealed to her. Like every woman who joined the harem, Pu loved beautiful clothes, jewelry, and being pampered. Knowing she had no good options made it easier to leave.

She spotted her eldest daughter, fifteen-year-old Zalika. Pu threaded her way through dozens of rambunctious children playing in the nursery.

Zalika had tucked herself into a quiet corner, sitting with a sketch pad in her lap and a tray of colored chalks on the floor next to her. The spitting image of her mother, Zalika had the uncanny ability to block out the rest of the world and live inside her own tiny bubble when it suited her. Zalika focused her complete attention on the portrait she created, even when Pu knelt beside her.

Pu caught her breath when she realized Zalika's portrait was of Pharaoh. And it wasn't a flattering image.

"What happened?" Pu said softly. "Did you do something wrong? Did Pharaoh punish you?"

Zalika kept her gaze on her art. "He doesn't know I exist."

Pu's heart sank. Pharaoh had many children, and girls easily found themselves lost in the shuffle—and all of Pu's children were girls. One more good reason to leave. Pu bit her lip, knowing she couldn't tip her hand to any of her children in advance. As recently as a week ago, Pu would have tried to offer some kind of comfort to her daughter. Now, she wrestled to keep her mouth shut to protect them all.

Zalika continued the conversation as if Pu had actually tried to reason with her. "Why should he? I'm nothing but some bauble he's going to give to one of his scummy old friends someday."

Impulsively, Pu wrapped her arms around her daughter and held her close.

Zalika tensed, holding her breath at her mother's touch.

Pu understood. If she were Zalika, she'd feel the same way. Too late, Pu had realized that girls born to a harem mother have limited options. She let go, kissed Zalika's forehead, and whispered, "I love you.

And that's not going to happen."

Zalika laughed bitterly, staring at the portrait.

A clock chimed.

Pu glanced up. Three o'clock already. There wasn't much time. "I'll see you later," Pu said, rising as she scanned the room to check on her other daughters. The other girls looked fine. Pu had no time for them now.

She didn't see Zalika give her a curious glance.

Pu hurried out of the nursery, leaving her children behind for now.

Chapter Eleven

In Priest Hennet's absence, Meres drew up the new parade route for tomorrow's festival while Neferita complained.

"I don't see why everyone in this city thinks they're so superior to out-of-towners," Neferita said, sitting on the edge of the priest's desk. "We're all Black Landers. Shouldn't that count for something?"

"Of course," Meres said absent-mindedly. She sat on the floor as she marked up a fresh map and wrote a new security list.

"But no," Neferita said, putting her hands on her hips. "I might as well be an evil foreigner plotting to overthrow the Pharaoh. People stare at me on the street. They stare at my son..."

"He's too young to wear his hair in a sidelock," Meres said automatically.

"Kids grow up fast. You know how it is." Neferita paused. She spoke with an undertone of cruelty. "Sorry, I forgot. You don't know, do you? You don't have children, so you can't possibly understand the pressures I'm under."

Neferita's words stung, but Meres ignored her. As Meres drew up the new plans, she suddenly understood Pu's confidence in escaping the city during tomorrow's parade. Meres recognized a few of the guards' names as men who'd been friends of Ramose and Pu since childhood. One name in particular stood out: Jabari.

"It's hard enough to become a widow when you least expect it," Neferita said. "But what do you think it's like to travel with a young child to your nation's capital city to ask your dead husband's relatives for help, only to find out they're dead, too, and now you've got nobody in the world except yourself and your child?"

"Mmm," Meres said, hearing nothing Neferita said. Meres assigned Jabari and any other guards she recognized as likely to help Pu to new details on the parade route. After all, thanks to the route change, their old positions had become obsolete.

When Priest Hennet returned, Neferita slid off his desk and inched away from it, as if hoping he hadn't noticed her sitting there.

"Neferita," he said. "You can visit your son today."

Neferita brightened. "Thank you, your greatness."

"Meres, have you finished with the changes?" he continued.

Meres nodded, handing the paperwork to him.

Priest Hennet didn't bother looking at it. "You may speak with Our Lady now. You have fifteen minutes. Then you must return to work."

Stunned, Meres would have collapsed were she not already sitting on the floor. Elation and terror washed over her in sickening waves. No one but the priests had ever been allowed to speak directly with a god. Now, Meres would be the first commoner to do so. It didn't seem real. Was it actually going to happen?

"Well?" Priest Hennet said. "Are you going to keep Isis waiting or waste your time gawking at me?"

"I don't know..." Meres stammered. "I mean, I don't know where to go. I've never been that deep inside the temple—I don't know where to find Her."

After sending Neferita toward a guard at the end of the secular hallway, Priest Hennet led Meres into the sacred depths of the temple. The passageways were narrow and flanked by towering columns. Faint light made the temple dark and mysterious. As their footsteps echoed from the cold stone floor, Meres realized that she'd originally asked to talk to Isis in order to ask for help for Pu. Now that Meres had solved the problem on her own, what would she ask the goddess?

As they made a couple of sharp turns, Meres caught quick glimpses of priests on the other side of the columns that separated the passageways from the inner rooms.

I've cleared a path for Pu, Meres thought. *Maybe now I can find out the truth about any other dangers she might be facing.*

Priest Hennet halted in front of a tiny sanctuary.

As Meres peered through the open doorway, she saw a life-size statue of Isis in the center of that sanctuary.

Priest Hennet gestured toward it. "You have ten minutes left. Someone will be waiting here to escort you back to the office when you're done." He walked briskly down the hall, disappearing into the shadows.

Meres gulped. This was a moment she'd always dreamed of but never believed could really happen. Tentatively, she entered the sanctuary. She swung the wooden door shut behind her, locking it in place.

She turned to face the gold statue of the winged goddess. Feeling light headed, Meres decided to kneel. "This means everything to me," she said. "You mean everything...my whole life, all I've ever wanted is to be like you."

Meres stopped suddenly when she heard someone else breathing. Looking behind, Meres made sure the door was still locked in place. She gazed around the sanctuary. She leaned to one side to glimpse behind the statue, but saw no one.

Meres' spine went cold as she realized she stood alone in the sanctuary of Isis.

"Meres," the statue whispered. "Why have you come to me? What is it that you seek?"

CHAPTER TWELVE

Her heart racing with the fear of being found out, Pu strode into the office of the Governess of the Royal Harem with as much confidence as she could muster.

You're the senior member of the harem, Pu reminded herself. *You're the right hand of the Governess. There's no reason why anyone should question your walking into her office, even when everyone knows she isn't there.*

The Governess had left late that morning for a luncheon honoring members of the Royal Palace helping with tomorrow's festival. Even though the luncheon had probably ended, the Governess's afternoon meeting would probably keep her away from the palace until this evening.

Even so, Pu breathed a sigh of relief once she entered the Governess's office and closed the door behind her.

Cobalt-blue silk covered the office walls, and a tent-like canopy of sheer white gauze hung from the ceiling. Several tall statues of the Pharaoh circled the office perimeter, all facing toward the center and holding up the canopy. A circle of red and gold silk pillows dotted the floor, and a single lounge chair rested on marble lion-clawed feet.

Pu dug into the pocket of her dress, panicked until she found the small slip of paper that had been in her possession for the past several weeks. Even though she'd hidden it deep in the pocket, from the moment she'd put it there this morning, she'd been terrified that it would somehow fall out and get lost.

She stared at the ten precious numbers that could mean the difference between escaping the Black Land, or facing the deadly Sekhmet. She'd hidden this slip of paper on the day she received it. Pu shuddered at the thought that she'd nearly destroyed it, assuming she'd never have reason to use it. Thank the gods she'd listened to a small voice inside that told her to hide the numbers and protect them with her life.

Pu slipped through the opening of the gauze canopy and into the heart of the Governess's office.

She saw what she needed on the floor beneath the lounge chair. Pu sank to the floor and pulled out the telephone.

Of course, she'd never had reason to use one. Devices like this were reserved for gods and their most trusted servants. But Pu had witnessed the Governess place several calls, so she knew it was just a matter of pressing buttons, speaking into the phone, and listening to it.

She picked up the receiver, put the paper on the floor in front of her but stared at the phone in dismay.

The first three numbers were grouped inside parentheses, but there were no parentheses signs on the keypad. Likewise, the next three numbers and final four were separated by a hyphen, and she saw no hyphen sign on the keypad.

They must not matter, Pu thought. Disregarding these marks, Pu entered the ten-digit number and placed the receiver to her ear.

But she heard nothing. Mimicking what she'd seen the Governess do when she placed calls, Pu said, "Hello?"

Again, silence.

Pu hung up. She'd assumed the number would work. Why wasn't it?

Don't panic, Pu told herself as she trembled, her thoughts threatening to race out of control. *You can figure this out.*

Pu closed her eyes, thinking back to every time she'd been here when the Governess had placed calls. Pu replayed each instance in her mind, trying to recall every detail.

Sometimes she used a book, a small one with a simple black cover. It was probably in the Governess's small desk in the corner.

Pu found it in the first drawer she opened. She flipped it open to the center. Sure enough, names and numbers filled the book but all were the same kind of ten-digit number.

Don't give up. Think. What else do you remember?

Pu focused, trying to rewind each memory and replay it slowly. But she couldn't remember anything that looked like a clue.

This can't be happening, Pu thought, feeling faint. *If I can't call this number, we'll be completely lost. The girls and I won't stand a chance.*

But she remembered what Meres had told her, just yesterday: There's always a solution to any problem—we just have to figure out what that solution is.

"There's always a solution," Pu said. "And it's likely to be here in this room, probably right under my nose."

The book. Pu flipped through it until she found instructions in the Governess's writing: "9 for outside line then 1 and number."

That's it, Pu realized. *That's the secret key.*

She put the book back where she found it. She scrambled back to the phone and dialed. This time, Pu's heart leapt when she heard a ringing sound in response. Moments later, she heard his voice.

"This is Bruce—"

"It's me, Pu—"

"...can't answer right now, but if you leave your name and number at the beep, I'll return your call as soon as possible."

That's right, she realized. He'd told her this might happen. But he'd also told her what to do if she couldn't reach him directly.

She listened carefully and spoke calmly after hearing the tone. "This is Pu. I'll be leaving the White Walled City soon." She wanted to tell him the depth of her love and fear. But she knew better. Everything he'd warned her about made sense now, and she had to follow his advice.

Without another word, Pu hung up the phone.

Making sure everything looked the same as she'd found it, she turned to leave and gasped when she saw the Governess standing in the doorway.

The Governess was a petite woman who had the presence of a giant. Her steel-colored hair, short and curly, covered her head like large metal shavings. Her black eyes stared hard and long at Pu. "What are you doing here?"

In return, Pu wanted to ask the Governess how long she'd been standing there but didn't dare. The Governess had a sharp mind and a long memory. If Pu asked any questions, she'd do nothing but raise suspicion. Although Pu was a member of Pharaoh's harem, her value was no greater than any of his other possessions. But the Governess was in charge of keeping the harem women in line and would not hesitate to report any questionable activity to the Pharaoh himself.

"I apologize," Pu said. "I needed a quiet place for a quick nap. I knew you were at a meeting this afternoon, and I thought you wouldn't mind if I rested here for awhile."

The Governess didn't waver. "What were you doing with my phone?"

She heard me, Pu thought, fighting back a sudden wave of terror. Feeling the color rise in her cheeks, knowing she'd been found out, Pu decided to tell a certain degree of truth. "Sometimes I pretend I'm more important than I am. I'm getting older, and my days in the harem are numbered. I know I'll end up working as a maid in the palace or maybe in the clothing factory. When I'm feeling sad about my future, I pretend I'm you."

"Don't do that again."

Pu nodded and bowed. "Yes, Ma'am. I'm sorry, Ma'am."

Finally, the Governess stepped aside.

Pu darted out the door before the Governess could change her mind.

❧❧

As Pu's footsteps echoed down the hallway, the Governess picked up her phone and pressed two numbers.

Moments later, she spoke into the phone. "Something strange just happened."

CHAPTER THIRTEEN

A wave of fear washed over Ramose. Had his childhood friend gone mad? Struggling to keep his composure, Ramose decided to dig gently for information and gauge Jabari's response.

"You've seen Sekhmet," Ramose said conversationally, as if seeing nothing unusual in discussing a demon woman who lived below the White Walled City. To appear casual, Ramose took a bite from his sandwich.

Jabari brushed the sweat from his forehead, but new beads popped up. His hands trembled as he reassembled his own sandwich that he'd dropped on his lap moments ago. "I know how this sounds. I know you think I'm crazy. But when you work in the Royal Palace and you refuse to look the other way like you're told, you find out there's a lot of strange things going on."

Ramose nodded slowly. Pu had shocked everyone when she rejected Jabari's proposal and joined the Royal Harem instead. Jabari had been a farmer who offered Pu a simple but comfortable life. They'd been inseparable since the day Jabari had saved her life, first as childhood friends and then as teenage lovers. Everyone assumed they'd get married. Her rejection had shaken Jabari to the core.

Jabari had made excuses about selling his farm and becoming one of the Pharaoh's guards. He claimed the long hours of farming made him weary. He said he needed a change. He said he'd rather work in the comfort of the Pharaoh's shadow than alone in his fields.

But everyone knew the real reason. Like Ramose, he worried about her decision. While Ramose shunned her, Jabari changed his life so he could put himself in a position to protect hers, should she need it.

Ramose absorbed what Jabari had just told him. "Strange things? What kind of strange things?"

Jabari gazed deeply into Ramose's eyes. "You can't tell anyone."

Ramose nodded. "Of course. You have my word."

Jabari searched for the truth in Ramose's eyes. "If you repeat anything I tell you, then all our lives will be in danger."

A new chill raised the hair on the back of Ramose's neck. He swallowed hard, suddenly nervous. "I promise."

"Pharaoh is supposed to be a god on Earth, but he is no god. He's just a man with many flaws."

"All gods have flaws. They're not so different from us. They just have more knowledge and power." Ramose shrugged and took another bite.

"You don't understand. It's not just that Pharaoh has flaws. He's a bad man with bad intents. Look at Ra. He willingly sacrifices his life at the end of each day. He spends the night on a horrific journey with peril around every corner. If not for Ra, we'd live in a world of eternal night. Without Ra, no crops could grow, and we'd starve. Look at Osiris. Ra sent his son to us so we could learn how to tend crops and feed ourselves, and live together in peace. Look at Isis. When Seti murdered and dismembered her husband and scattered his body across the nation, she walked across all of the Black Land to collect his remains and convinced the gods to give him life for one more day. These are extraordinarily people who care about others. Pharaoh is not like them. Pharaoh cares only about himself."

Remembering his conversation with Meres, Ramose gave the benefit of his doubt. "The new construction project is improving storage for food in the market."

Jabari laughed bitterly. "Think about it. Every season of Inundation means farmland is flooded for several weeks. Pharaoh can't afford to have so many people idle for such a long time. They might begin to see the truth behind the royal facade. Sure, every year's Inundation project is worthwhile—but it also keeps all the farmers occupied during a period when they have nothing else to do."

The world looked normal enough. Squirrels scampered across the grass in the park. In the distance, women walked down the sidewalk, carrying bundles of fresh produce. A few other workmen from the construction site perched on the curb, eating and laughing. The gold cap of Pharaoh's pyramid gleamed in the sunlight. The tallest structure in the nation, the pyramid's brilliant gold cap could be seen from anywhere in the Black Land.

"You've never worked in the palace," Jabari continued. "You've never seen how Pharaoh bribes his officials. You've never seen how he keeps everyone else under his thumb by scaring them into silence."

Ramose remembered what had begun this conversation. "With Sekhmet? The demon woman?"

Jabari nodded. "They say she's the spawn of the goddess Sekhmet herself. She can take the form of woman or lioness and lives underground."

Ramose laughed. "That's absurd."

"I've seen Sekhmet," Jabari insisted. "Everyone who works in the palace gets a glimpse of her and what she can do."

"You've seen her with your own eyes."

"It was just a glimpse, but it was enough. When I first started working for Pharaoh, the guard I replaced had been caught stealing. I saw him go into a room where a woman waited for him. The door was closed and locked. An hour later, the guards outside the door opened it. That's when I saw her, crouched in a corner and licking the blood from her hands."

"Blood?"

Jabari nodded. "They removed what was left of him. It looked like he'd been ripped apart by a crocodile."

"There was a crocodile in the room with them?"

"No. Just the guard and Sekhmet."

Ramose looked blankly at Jabari.

"Haven't you ever wondered why the major cause of death is by crocodile attack?" Jabari lowered his voice to a whisper. "I don't think it's always a crocodile that kills someone. Sometimes I think it's Sekhmet."

Ramose gazed in horror at Jabari, realizing the kind of danger that his sister Pu faced just by living in the palace.

Jabari nodded as if reading Ramose's expression. "Something is wrong with Pu. If she's in danger, we have to figure out how to protect her from Sekhmet."

Chapter Fourteen

Still kneeling, Meres stared in astonishment at the statue of Isis, which had just spoken aloud.

"Meres, why have you come to me? What is it that you seek?"

She stood alone with the statue in the Sanctuary of Isis, deep inside the Temple of Our Lady of the Absolute. No one else could have said those words. Even though the statue's lips hadn't moved, the words came through its slightly parted lips.

What did I think would happen? Meres thought. *That Isis would speak to me in a vision? Or that I'd hear her words in my head?*

Meres trembled. She'd been faithful all her life, but suddenly Isis felt very real and present. It was one thing to have faith. It was another when what you believed in suddenly came to life and wanted to have a conversation with you.

"Please," the statue of Isis whispered. "Tell me what you need of me."

I can't, Meres thought. *How do I tell a goddess that I needed help figuring how to change the parade route for Pu's sake, but I figured it out myself? If I tell her that, it'll sound like I think I'm as smart as she is. Or that I'm wasting her time.*

Meres remembered what she always told herself when she was scared: Don't be afraid to tell the truth. It will make you free.

An idea occurred to Meres. There was still something she needed and wanted to know. And it might even help Pu. "I need you to tell me about Sekhmet," Meres said.

The statue whispered, "Forever what?"

Meres flinched as if she'd been slapped. No one but Priest Hennet used that strange expression. Why would Isis use it?

The statue continued, "You already know everything there is to know about that goddess. Why do you ask me about her?"

Meres remembered a rumor she'd heard many years ago, before she'd come to work in the temple. She'd heard someone say that when the Pharaoh held counsel with Isis that there was a secret shaft from the room where he met with her to another room inside the temple, where the priests would eavesdrop. That way, they could stay one step ahead of the Pharaoh.

Now, Meres stood to face Isis, stepping as close to the statue as she dared. There was a small but deep open space between the statue's lips. A slight breeze seemed to flow from the statue's open mouth.

It had a faint scent of honey cakes.

It's true, Meres thought. No longer elated, she only felt terror. She'd never believed the rumor and had forgotten all about it. But now she was convinced that she was looking straight into the priests' greatest secret. And if they realized she knew their secret, they might do anything to make sure that secret never left the temple.

"Speak, Meres," the whisper said. "No need for shyness."

My dreams! Meres suddenly realized. *Everyone knows I dream of the gods!*

"I dreamed of Sekhmet," Meres said, realizing all she had to do was tell the truth.

"Sekhmet?" The statue said. "I thought you only dreamed of me."

"Last night," Meres said, "I dreamed of Sekhmet."

"What happened in your dream?"

Meres had asked Sekhmet about the Pharaoh, and she had answered: *He's an idiot, as usual. Honestly, Meres, you need to get the stars out of your eyes. They're clouding your vision.*

"Sekhmet challenged the Pharaoh's power," Meres said.

To be more specific, you act as if the Pharaoh is a god. He's no god—but I am!

"Forever how?"

Have some self respect. Why is it you people can't see the forest for the trees? Why do you insist on black and white? Don't you understand the meaning of gray?

Meres had screamed herself awake from the dream about Sekhmet. She'd assumed it was a nightmare.

But maybe it wasn't. Maybe it had been a warning from the gods. Maybe even from Isis herself.

Meres' terror melted away, replaced by anger. How dare the priests use Isis? How dare they use her temple and her image for their own personal gain?

It was time to get creative.

"Sekhmet says she will attack the Pharaoh and the White Walled City," Meres said, consciously keeping an edge out of her voice. "And you know my dreams are prophetic. After all, you're the one who sends them to me. I'm surprised you don't already know about this one."

The statue took a quick, deep breath. "Sekhmet has dared to enter your dreams directly. You were right to demand an audience with me. I will stay on guard to protect the city. I will keep a special eye upon you."

Meres bowed and thanked the statue of Isis profusely. As she left the sanctuary, Meres thought, *I'm sure you will.*

CHAPTER FIFTEEN

That night, Meres, Ramose, and Neferita made small talk during dinner. Seated outside, Meres lit more oil lamps. The new moon made the night sky less bright than usual. It wasn't until the end of the evening, when Neferita went to her room and all the lamps were blown out that Meres and Ramose had a chance to compare notes in bed.

"I never should have let Pu set foot in the palace," Ramose said quietly.

"It wasn't your decision to make," Meres whispered. "It was Pu's. I understand why she did it. Working in the Pharaoh's harem means security for life. Not just for you, but for all your children. Look at how many men die in the fields or when they're fishing. Pu had to consider that if she married Jabari, she could end up becoming a widow when she least expected it. That's something she never has to worry about in the palace."

Even in the dark, Meres sensed Ramose gazing at her. She could even imagine his expression softening as he spoke. "So why didn't you go into the harem? Why did you marry me?"

"I've always wanted to be close to Isis," Meres said. "If I'd gone into the harem, I never would have been able to work in the temple. I'd rather be a scribe."

"You're not afraid I might die?"

"I try not to think about it," Meres said. "Pu and I are different. I already know what it's like when you lose the people you love. She doesn't. Besides, if Isis can keep living after her husband died, then I could, too. Pu's the kind of woman who doesn't know that's possible. She probably assumed she'd curl up and die if her husband were killed."

Ramose sighed. "What's done is done. We can't change the past. All we can do is try to get Pu and her kids out of the palace. Maybe we could get a house for them."

Pu had made Meres promise not to tell Ramose about her plan to escape the White Walled City, because Pu had been afraid of his response.

But now everything had changed. Jabari had claimed truth to the story Pu told about the demon woman who lived beneath the city and speculated it might be the real cause behind some deaths that had been reported as crocodile attacks.

And for the first time in many years, Ramose took more interest in helping his sister than judging her.

Meres prided herself on keeping her word. But the situation had become far more dangerous than she could have imagined. Pu's safety was more important.

"There's one thing I haven't told you yet," Meres said. "Pu's getting ready to leave the Black Land and take her children with her."

"That's impossible. Pu belongs to the Pharaoh."

"That's why she's leaving."

"But that could be seen as treason. If she's caught, she could be executed."

"That won't happen," Meres said. "I'm helping her."

Ramose stayed silent for so long that Meres normally would have wondered if he'd fallen asleep. But she recognized his labored breathing. She knew his mind must be racing.

Finally, Ramose said, "What can I do to help?"

≈≈

As soon as the last oil lamp had been extinguished, Neferita crept along the wall between her room and their bedroom, trying to find the best place to eavesdrop.

It had been three days since she'd first arrived in the White Walled City, and in those three days her life had turned into a nightmare.

It was bad enough that her husband died last week. He'd been an old, fat bastard, but he'd also been a high vizier of Elephantine, making him rich and powerful. Neferita had cried when he dropped dead of a heart attack, but her tears were for the lifestyle she feared to lose. She had saved some money, probably enough to keep the house, but not enough to keep the servants.

Neferita had brought her only child with her to the White Walled City, because her dead husband had always bragged about his cousin who held a powerful position in the royal city, thanks to his friendship with one of the Pharaoh's sons. As fate would have it, the cousin had died the same day as her husband. She'd come to terms with this fate, but her son decided to tinkle on a statue of the Pharaoh at an unfortunate time, and that bitch had caught him in the act.

Being arrested had been humiliating. Hearing her son scream when they'd carted him off to the local orphanage had ripped her heart open.

But the next day when Priest Hennet had taken her aside and offered security for her son and safe passage out of the city, Neferita didn't hesitate to take it.

Why should she feel bad about spying on the bitch who'd turned her life into a living hell? She had no qualms about reporting what she'd learned to Priest Hennet.

It had been easy enough last night. Instead of staying in the foyer, Neferita had slipped up on them while they were talking in the back courtyard. It had been easy to hide in the shadows of the house. And from Priest Hennet's reaction, she'd overheard some juicy tidbits.

But tonight Neferita could only catch a few words here and there. She'd have to find a better vantage point.

Slowly and carefully, she tiptoed down the length of her room, trailing one hand lightly against the wall to steady herself. But when she set foot into the hallway, a floorboard groaned.

Neferita froze, holding her breath.

All she heard was silence.

Don't worry, she told herself. If one of them catches you, just say you have to go to the bathroom.

She heard the man's voice, clearly this time and deep in their room. Either they hadn't heard the floorboard groan or they'd assumed the house creaked as it settled.

Boldly, Neferita slipped closer to the doorway to their bedroom, careful to stay out of sight. She leaned lightly against the hallway wall to settle in for a long time.

As she listened, Neferita smiled. Priest Hennet would be very happy indeed to hear her report tomorrow morning. With any luck, this nightmare would end soon.

Chapter Sixteen

The next morning, Meres breathed deeply to calm herself as she walked down the Avenue of the Rams in the festival parade. Thousands of people who lived in the White Walled City lined the streets, cheering as soon as they saw Meres and Ramose.

Because Meres was the temple scribe, she and Ramose played the parts of gods in at least one parade each year. They'd committed to this one months ago.

Priests led the parade, decked in their finest robes and necklaces that covered their chests. They were followed by musicians playing reed pipes and beating small drums. Behind the musicians, barefoot dancers shimmied in time to the drumbeats. Finally, Meres and Ramose marched, followed by Priest Hennet and the youngest priests.

Dressed as Isis, Meres wore a simple white linen sheath dress, ankh earrings and feathers attached to her shoulders and arms. Having already marched two miles from the Temple of Our Lady of the Absolute, where the parade had begun, her muscles ached from the weight of the wings and her naked feet burned from the hot sand that covered the street.

Ramose walked by her side, smiling and waving as the crowd cheered. He wore a white linen kilt, a turquoise and gold broadcollar, and the royal headdress. In one hand he carried the royal scepter and flail. Today he represented Osiris, the first and greatest Pharaoh in the history of the Black Land.

Last night, Meres and Ramose decided that today—the Festival of Isis—would take on a new meaning for them. Today would be the day they set Pu and her daughters free. "I couldn't do it when we were children," Ramose had said. "That day the crocodile almost killed Pu, I froze. I was so scared that I couldn't move. Jabari saved her life, not me. Now I've got a second chance, and I'm not going to waste it."

The royal palace loomed ahead, a white pyramid rising seven stories tall. The sun baked down from a clear sky.

Far ahead, Meres saw Pu standing at the front of the royal crowd.

Four girls stood nearby, looking bored.

Pu's girls.

Meres caught her breath. Like Ramose, Meres had never met her own nieces. Royal protocol dictated that Ramose had to meet the girls before Meres, simply because of blood ties. Because Ramose had refused to see Pu after she'd decided to join the Pharaoh's harem, he'd given up the chance to meet his nieces.

Keeping her focus on the crowd around her, Meres snuck glances at the girls. It was easy to recognize them as her nieces. They all looked like Pu.

If we succeed, I'll never know them, Meres suddenly realized. *This may be the only time I'll get to see them—and it's from a distance.*

Once more, Meres felt left out. Everyone else belonged to large families, but all Meres had was Ramose and an occasional lunch with Pu. As an only child and orphan, Meres had grown up dreaming of belonging to a family, surrounded by people who loved her. Meres had urged Ramose from the day they were married to mend his relationship with his only sibling, and now she felt proud of Ramose, even if Pu would never know.

෩෨

Pu willed herself to breathe slowly and deeply as she stood in the front row of the festival crowd. *Almost time,* she told herself. *It's almost time.* She fidgeted with the necklace the Governess had given to her this morning—a smaller version of the broadcollar the Pharaoh himself wore—relaying that the Pharaoh wanted to see Pu wear it for the festival today.

Her teenager, Zalika, managed to whine while blowing pink bubbles with her gum. Zalika wore the same necklace as her mother. The Governess had provided one for each of Pu's children. "Why do we have to be here? None of our brothers or sisters have to."

They're your half-siblings, Pu thought. *All Pharaoh's other children by his other mistresses.* "If they jumped into the Nile and were surrounded by crocodiles, would you do it, too?"

Zalika rolled her eyes. "That's different. This parade is stupid. Why are we the only ones who have to come?"

Pu squinted, trying to focus on the approaching figures as they marched down the Avenue of the Rams toward the royal complex. There— she saw them at last. A lump rose in the back of her throat when she saw Meres and Ramose dressed as gods. For a moment, she remembered how she'd once followed her brother everywhere. She'd always tagged along, wanting his friends to be her friends, wanting Ramose to adore her as much as she worshipped him.

She jumped in surprise when tiny hands grabbed her leg. Her toddler sat on the ground at Pu's feet, babbling gleefully as she slapped Pu's bare leg.

What am I thinking? Pu scolded herself. *There's no time to think about the past. I've got to make sure my girls have a future.*

Pu scooped her toddler up in her arms. Turning to Zalika, Pu said softly, "You're right. Let's get out of here."

Heaving a sigh of relief, Zalika turned to head back to the palace.

Pu grabbed her teenager's arm with her free hand, struggling to hold the toddler with one arm.

Zalika spun, her face scrunched with disgust.

Thinking only of the danger they'd face if they stayed much longer, Pu tightened the grip on her teenager's arm and pulled her close.

"Ow!" Zalika tried to wrench free until she looked up at her mother's face. Zalika's eyes widened in fear.

Pu whispered. "Do exactly as I say. If you don't, they will kill me. They might kill you, too."

Zalika laughed nervously. But when her mother's grip on her arm tightened to the bone, tears welled in the girl's eyes. "Stop. It hurts."

Good. Zalika looked scared enough to obey.

Pu eased her grip. "Get the twins and follow me."

Zalika pulled free. "I know how to get back to the palace. I'm not an idiot."

"We're not going back to the palace. This is no joke, Zalika. If you don't get the twins now and stick by my side, we could all die."

Zalika crossed her arms and raised her voice. "Why? Who's going to kill us?"

Pu recognized some of the men standing near them in the crowd as royal administrators. They turned to look at Zalika and Pu in surprise. She met their gazes, gave them a slight smile, and shook her head as the exasperated mother of a teenager.

One of them smiled back in sympathy. Another narrowed his eyes in suspicion. Her toddler felt like a bag of sand ready to drop to the ground. Pu held her close with both arms. "Get the twins. Now."

Pu and Zalika were startled when the hundreds of people around them gasped in unison. A loudspeaker broadcast a man's voice, saying, "You are hereby charged with treason against the Pharaoh and the White Walled City."

CHAPTER SEVENTEEN

Before the festival parade began, Meres hadn't thought twice about the changes in this year's event. The priests were always making changes to keep the festival fresh. But when the parade stopped in front of the royal palace, she felt confused.

The temple's younger priests carried a wooden sarcophagus directly ahead of Meres and Ramose—one of this year's additions to the parade. When she'd questioned them, they claimed it was a relic from a sanctuary inside the temple.

Now that the parade had stopped, the young priests stood the sarcophagus up on one end.

Priest Hennet stepped from the sidelines into the parade. Holding a microphone, he said, "You are hereby charged with treason against the White Walled City and the Pharaoh himself."

They know, Meres thought, suddenly dizzy with fear.

Startled, Ramose turned to Meres and whispered, "I'm no traitor!"

Meres caught her breath in surprise. Of course! "Don't worry," she whispered to her husband. "It's just something they've added to the parade."

Priest Hennet had dressed like Seti, the evil brother of Osiris who committed the most heinous crime of all: murder. Normally, people portraying the gods simply marched in parades or made other public appearances on festival days. But it looked like they were about to re-enact the beginning of the myth of Isis and Osiris, the gods who first ruled the Black Land.

Seti, Osiris, and Isis were the great-grandchildren of the one Almighty God, Ra, the god of the sun. While their great-grandfather carried the sun across the sky in his chariot every day, they walked upon the Black Land. By teaching the Black Landers how to farm and fish, Osiris created civilization and ended the turmoil that had previously torn them apart. By marrying his sister Isis, he taught them that all people are brothers and sisters and can live together in harmony.

But Seti was jealous. He wanted Isis for himself, and he wanted the power of ruling a nation. Seti learned the exact measurements of his brother's body and built a sarcophagus to those measurements. Seti tricked Osiris into trying the sarcophagus on for size, with a fit so tight that Osiris couldn't escape.

Priest Hennet gestured to the sarcophagus, and the young priests removed its lid. "A gift for you," Priest Hennet said, winking at Ramose. "Please honor me by showing us how you look wearing it."

Now Meres felt a pang of jealousy at her husband's proximity to a precious relic from the temple.

It's only fair, Meres told herself. *You get to work at the temple every day. You may not see much of the temple, but you get to walk where other citizens can't. Be happy for Ramose—he'll never have a chance like this again.*

Ramose hesitated, casting a questioning look at Meres. When she nodded her approval, he stepped toward the sarcophagus, made in the traditional shape outlining the human figure and carved from a rich, dark wood. Images of Isis with her wings spread decorated each side, meant to protect the body inside, its lid painted in gold with the image of Osiris.

"No!" Someone shouted from the crowd. "Don't be tricked, Osiris! Seti's trying to kill you!"

Meres turned toward the crowd to see others embracing the moment. Onlookers raised their voices and fists, calling out with the intent of protecting the god Osiris. But no one stepped forward. After all, it was just play acting.

Ramose turned his back to the sarcophagus, and the crowd eased a sigh of relief. But they gasped as Ramose backed into the sarcophagus.

Priest Hennet said, "How do you like it?" He held the microphone up to Ramose.

Ramose smiled, playing along. "It's a perfect fit."

Priest Hennet turned toward the crowd with a smirk. "Good. Because it's where you'll spend eternity."

Quickly, the young priests slapped the lid back on the sarcophagus and screwed its nails to secure it in place.

From inside, Ramose banged on the lid, his voice muffled but laced with anxiety.

Meres stepped forward. Enough was enough. Acting out myths was fine, but this had gone too far.

Priest Hennet stopped her with one hand on her shoulder.

Meres recoiled, stepping back from his touch. "Let my husband out."

The royal guards pushed their way through the surrounding crowds to help the young priests raise the closed sarcophagus with Ramose inside. As the crowd screamed in protest, the priests and guards carried the sarcophagus toward the closest city gate.

Meres panicked, but as she tried to run after them, Priest Hennet held her back.

Once the sarcophagus vanished out of sight, the crowd cheered its approval, and the parade resumed.

✌︎❧

"You are hereby charged with treason against the White Walled City and the Pharaoh himself."

Like the crowd surrounding her, Pu felt riveted by the priest's words, broadcast over loudspeakers.

Oh, no, she thought. *They're talking about me!*

But when the young priests carrying the sarcophagus set it upright, she realized what had to be the truth. It wasn't real. It was just part of the parade. She was still safe, after all.

Pu felt like a little girl again, cornered in the garden by a crocodile. It had been a hot summer day, and she'd come out into her family's garden for a dip in their reflecting pool.

Like all reflecting pools, the long and shallow rectangle acted as the focus of the garden. "It's not a place for swimming," her mother had often lectured. "The garden should be a place for peace and quiet. The pool's water should be calm, like a mirror."

But one day, little Pu couldn't resist. A few tall palm trees in their garden kept the reflecting pool shaded most of the time. When her father worked and her mother had gone to the market, Pu slipped into the garden. Ramose and Jabari were playing inside the house, so she knew they wouldn't notice her absence. She slipped through a row of papyrus plants and sat on the edge of the reflecting pool, easing her feet into the cool water.

But one of the many lily pads floating at the far end of the pool moved.

Excited, little Pu had stood up, hiking up her little linen sheath dress, ready to wade. She'd seen plenty of frogs in the pool and now she finally had a chance to catch one!

But a wave rippled through the lily pads.

Little Pu froze in her tracks. No frog could make lily pads move like that. Only something big could do it.

As the crocodile shot out from underneath the lily pads, little Pu dived back on land and through the papyrus plants. "Mommy!" she'd screamed, forgetting that her mother was miles away by now.

Before she could race back into the house, where she'd be safe, the crocodile launched itself from the reflecting pool, now blocking her path. Water slid off its leathery skin. Sharp teeth crammed its open jaw.

For the first time in her young life, Pu felt completely alone in a dangerous world. Terror made her feel like her heart had stopped and turned to ice. She looked into the crocodile's tiny eyes and saw its determination. The muscles contracted beneath its skin, which rippled like lily pads on water.

Pu screamed and ran the other way to a palm tree on her left. Realizing she couldn't climb it, she jagged sharply to her right.

The fort!

Just last week, she'd helped Ramose and Jabari build a fort from rocks in the garden, much to their parents' dismay. It wasn't much more than a few piles of large rocks with a slab on top. But the entrance backed up to the mud brick fence surrounding the garden, and each of the children could barely squeeze between the fence and the tiny entrance to their fort.

Still screaming, Pu squeezed between the back of the fort and the mud brick fence. But as she tried to crawl into the fort, her foot stopped her. It was wedged between two boulders on one side of the fort.

The ground shook beneath her. Pu looked up to see the crocodile's snout peeking from the edge of the stone slab inches above her head.

The crocodile had launched itself on top of the fort's stone slab roof.

But she'd heard a boy yelling, and the crocodile's snout disappeared. She sobbed for what seemed like an eternity, while the boy kept yelling over horrible crunching sounds.

Finally, human hands had freed her foot from the boulders and pulled her out. Jabari had lifted her into his arms, and she'd latched onto him with all her might, crying now with relief. She'd seen the crocodile, its head bashed open with a boulder pulled free from the fort. Jabari's arms and face were streaked with blood, and she later learned he'd been bitten after grabbing the crocodile's tail and hauling it off the fort roof.

She clung to Jabari as he held her in his arms and, in that moment, fell in love with him. At the same time, she'd seen Ramose standing on the other side of the garden looking as terrified as she still felt. Ramose had looked like a statue, incapable of moving.

Now, as the crowd surrounding them began shouting, Pu thought she caught Ramose's gaze as he turned toward the sarcophagus. He stood a stone's throw away, but when he smiled, the feeling that the smile was directed at her flooded Pu.

No, Pu thought. *It's impossible. Meres promised she wouldn't tell him I'm leaving, and Meres never breaks a promise.*

"Mama?" Zalika said.

Pu turned to see fear on her teenager's face.

Tears welled in Zalika's eyes. "What's happening? Why's everyone so mad?"

"Get your sisters now," Pu said. "And follow me."

She took one final look at the parade. When she saw Ramose disappear inside the sarcophagus, she remembered the same terror she'd felt when her foot stuck between stones as she'd tried to crawl into their fort.

Pu didn't have time to wonder about the sarcophagus or what it meant. She'd learned to keep moving. Otherwise, the crocodile would get you.

CHAPTER EIGHTEEN

What just happened? Meres thought as she marched in the festival parade through the White Walled City. She felt so confused and numb that she no longer noticed the hot sand burning beneath her feet.

She kept waiting for Ramose to return to the parade, followed by the young priests who had carried him out in the sarcophagus. After all, everyone else in the parade acted as if it had been planned. Chances were that no one had told Meres and Ramose so that they would respond in the same way as Isis and Osiris. That way, the horror of Seti's betrayal would seem real to the festival crowd.

That's why festivals were held weekly in the White Walled City and throughout the Black Land: to remind all Black Landers of the ordeals endured by the gods and the dangers of forgetting that all Black Landers were brothers and sisters at heart. This festival in particular reminded everyone that murder is the most heinous crime of all. And other than the ancient murder of Osiris by his brother Seti, no murder had ever been committed in the Black Land. Not counting the killings by the gods, of course, who were entitled to make such decisions about the lives of mere mortals.

As the parade passed by the royal complex, Meres cast an even gaze across the crowd of administrators and royal workers standing in front of the Pharaoh's pyramid.

She saw no sign of Pu or her daughters.

Meres stood straighter, feeling the weight of worry fall from her shoulders. Relief washed through her. They must have escaped—changing the festival route had worked. Doing it may have even saved their lives. Meres still worried about what would happen once the palace realized Pu and four of the Pharaoh's many daughters had disappeared, but maybe they'd have enough time to get to a safe place where the Pharaoh couldn't reach them.

An elderly woman on the sidelines called out in a creaky voice, "Find him, Isis! Bring Osiris back to us!"

Meres smiled and waved. Of course. She knew the legend well. Once Osiris had been trapped and locked inside the sarcophagus, Seti's men had thrown it into the Nile, and Isis had begun her long mission to bring the body of her husband back to the Black Land. Thanks to Isis, Osiris became the god of the Underworld, the heavenly world to which everyone crossed over after death.

But the elderly woman didn't wave or smile back. Her face sagged with deep wrinkles and scrunched with intense concern. "Hurry! He'll drown if you don't help him!" She pointed toward the city gate.

The elderly woman's sense of urgency scared Meres. She saw no indication that the woman played a role in the parade. Suddenly, the legend felt real.

Meres followed the elderly woman's pointing hand. As the parade rounded a bend in the street, Meres could see past the white-washed mud-brick buildings and through the open Northeast gate, flanked by two guards. From here, she could see the Nile. The young priests waded back onto shore, and the sarcophagus floated into the middle of the river, its lid still nailed shut.

That's impossible, Meres thought as confusion washed over her. *That would be murder, and no one commits murder. Not here—not in the Black Land. Only foreigners commit such evil deeds.*

"Go!" The elderly woman called out as her shriveled arm shook in the warmth of the light cast upon them all by the one and Almighty God Ra. "Before it's too late!"

Meres hesitated, wondering what the priests would think if she suddenly bolted from her duty of playing Isis in the parade. Wouldn't she be breaking the rules? Wasn't it the wrong thing to do?

A sudden wind pushed the hair back from her face and rustled through her costume wings.

It's what Isis would do, Meres realized, feeling as if the Almighty God Ra had just kissed her forehead and given her wisdom. *It's what Isis had already done.*

Meres bolted, pushing her way through the dancers and drummers and temple officials. The crowd cheered and parted for her to pass through. Moments later, the guards hesitated as she approached. They blocked the gate.

She slowed to a walk, clenching her hands by her side. "I am Isis," Meres said in a guttural voice. For the first time in her life, she felt primal, ready to rip each guard's throat out with her teeth if necessary. "Do not make the mistake of standing between me and my husband."

One guard backed away in response, looking down at the ground. The other's face froze in surprise.

Keeping her eyes locked on his, Meres strode through the gate. She ran toward the river, ready to take on the small army of young priests walking toward her, their kilts dripping wet. "Where's my husband?" Meres shouted at them. "Where's Ramose?"

They were little more than boys. Most of them looked away, and the emotions Meres read on their faces ranged from guilt to shame.

She stopped short on the sandy river shore, but the young priests ignored her as they walked past.

The sarcophagus had reached the center of the river and floated downstream.

"No," Meres said in disbelief, staring at the sarcophagus. "Tell me you have not committed murder."

She turned and watched their backs as they headed toward the Northeast gate. She thought she heard one of them cry.

Her own voice choked as she shouted, "Tell me you have not committed murder!"

Cheers and drum beats rose from the White Walled City as the festival continued in the distance. As the young priests walked through the Northeast gate, one of the guards snuck a scared peek at her.

Surely Ramose would jump out from behind a tree any moment now. This was a joke. It had to be joke. What other explanation could there be?

But Meres thought she heard his distant, muffled voice call out from inside the sarcophagus.

Forgetting about the crocodiles that riddled the Nile, Meres stripped off the wings she wore and ran into the river. She'd always been a good swimmer—a strong swimmer.

Now she was her husband's only hope.

She had to catch up to the sarcophagus and break its lid open before the Nile currents swept it away forever.

Chapter Nineteen

Priest Hennet huffed as he climbed the shallow stone steps, steady-ing himself against the walls of the narrow stairway, a secret path inside the temple's pylon gate that led to its roof. Shadowed away from the sun rays and sight of the Almighty God Ra, the stone walls were cool to the touch. Priest Hennet coughed after breathing in the dust he kicked up. It tasted like chalk.

Normally, Priest Hennet wouldn't bother climbing—he'd have them bring her to him. But considering everything he'd learned in the past few days, he wasn't taking any chances.

He couldn't afford the risk.

Minutes later, he staggered to the roof of the pylon, surrounded by walls just high enough to peek over. With enough discretion, no one in the city would ever realize that the sacred pylon gate also served as a lookout point for the priests. And today he'd made sure plenty of guards were here to keep this woman in her place.

Priest Hennet leaned forward and placed his hands on his knees, trying to catch the breath he'd lost. At the sound of a clearing throat, he looked up to see the young woman standing before him with her arms crossed.

"I've held up my end of the bargain," Neferita said. "If you'll give my little boy back to me, we'll go back home to Elephantine now."

She'd been useful, he'd grant her that. But he had no intention of taking her to the orphanage where her son had been placed the day they came to the White Walled City. Priest Hennet had other plans for Neferita, but he saw no reason to tip his hand. "Of course," he said jovially. Taking a deep breath, he stood and wiped the sweat from his face. "I've come to escort you. Follow me."

The journey back down the stairs proved to be physically easier but far more painful, thanks to the incessant babbling of the woman trailing behind him.

"I saw everything—well, almost everything because some of the construction by the Avenue of the Rams blocked my view. I told my guards that I saw a woman and some children run out one of the city gates, but they didn't listen! It happened when everyone watched you put Ramose into the sarcophagus. I bet I was the only one keeping an eye on the crowd, and I know what I saw. I'm sure it was Ramose's sister—and she took the Pharaoh's children with her!"

Priest Hennet didn't tell her that he knew Pu and her children had escaped. In fact, he'd done everything within his power to ensure their success. It would make it easier to make an example of them once they were captured. Although he had every intention of keeping Ramose and Meres from ever returning, the royal wife and children must be returned to the Pharaoh. Unlike Ramose and Meres, Pu and her children were the Pharaoh's property, and it was Priest Hennet's sworn duty to protect that property.

Once they reached the bottom of the stairs, Priest Hennet took Neferita by the arm and led her around a corner and into another staircase that led below ground.

It wouldn't be long now. Soon, Neferita would get exactly what she had coming to her.

≈≈

Neferita paused, staring at the steps leading below ground, disappearing into black. "This can't be the way to the orphanage."

Priest Hennet fished a flashlight from the pocket of his white linen robe and flicked it on. He pointed a strong beam of light down into the dark, illuminating nothing but the stairs and what appeared to be an underground passage. "It's a shortcut. Anyone who knows you've been living with Ramose and Meres might get suspicious if they see us together."

"But there's nothing to be suspicious about," Neferita said. "Everyone thinks what happened was just an act."

"We'll make a public announcement soon—after all, Meres and Ramose won't be returning. It may be necessary for me to name you as a source of information, and some people might see you as a threat. Should that happen, I cannot guarantee your safety or the safety of your son."

Neferita swallowed hard. Despite the propaganda that all Black Landers were brothers and sisters, in truth every city in the country embraced a different god. Of course, everyone accepted Ra as the one and only Almighty God. But Ra had many children, grandchildren, and great-grandchildren who were gods in their own right. Here in the White Walled City, the goddess Isis reigned. But in Elephantine, everyone worshipped Hathor, the cow-eared goddess who represented motherhood and nurturing. Being from Elephantine made Neferita a known worshiper of Hathor, and that made her different. Being different and being suspected of exposing two important citizens of the White Walled City—the sole scribe of the Temple of Our Lady of the Absolute and her husband, brother to a royal wife—could put Neferita in a bad position, maybe a position bad enough to keep her little boy in the orphanage.

"All right," Neferita said. "Lead on."

But as they descended into the unknown, the hair on the back of Neferita's neck stood on end.

∽∾

A large tomb was carved into the ground below the Temple of Our Lady of the Absolute—a secret tomb that only the priests knew about. For anyone walking into the tomb for the first time, it felt like walking into a forest made of stone. Rows of seventy-foot high columns supported the stone-slab ceiling. Each row stood five columns wide, and twenty rows sank into the depths of the room. Small lights were recessed into the capital of each column, shaped like a hefty stem with a lotus flower on top. The lights were always on, making it impossible to tell day from night. It was also impossible to know when one day ended and the next began, making time cease to exist.

Thanks to the many columns and the way the lights were angled, the tomb was a place of shadows.

Pale yellow stars shaped like skinny starfish crowded the indigo ceiling as if it were the night sky. The stone walls were washed white and decorated with life-size images of all the gods and their stories.

Beyond the forest of enormous lotus columns lay an alcove housing a sarcophagus made of white alabaster. The sarcophagus stood four feet high with an interior carved three feet deep. Sekhmet stretched and yawned as she slowly came awake inside the white alabaster sarcophagus. She slept alone inside the smooth stone surface. This tomb was her home.

Sekhmet had long lost track of her age, remembering only that she'd been sentenced to live here when she was a little girl. She had vague memories of once having had parents, but they were difficult to remember. Her life had once been very different, but that was before she'd become a god.

Naked, she climbed out of the sarcophagus. Her blonde hair hadn't been cut or washed in many years and had evolved into a mass of dreadlocks that looked like a lion's mane. She opened a wooden door in her alcove and slipped into the bathroom, which included a flush toilet and a small sink with running water. After using the toilet, Sekhmet filled the sink with water and lapped it up with her tongue.

Every day, she tried not to think about her past. Some days were successful. No matter how many times she'd tried, she couldn't remember exactly why she'd ended up here or what had happened to her parents. She remembered the priests asking her if she'd like to play with a kitty that lived in a special part of the temple. Her parents had been with her. Some days she thought she remembered happily walking away with the priests ignoring her parents while they called out in protest. Maybe in defiance. Maybe in obliviousness. She wasn't sure. That memory changed all the time.

Some days she thought she remembered hearing her father having a heated conversation with a group of priests while feeling the soft touch of her mother's hands push her toward a different priest. Had the priest given her mother something in exchange? It was hard to remember.

And some days she thought she remembered looking back and seeing herself standing alone in the shadows of a temple.

It was easy to remember the moment she'd first set foot inside this tomb. The first time, just one priest had joined her, and what he'd done had been confusing and disgusting. But even worse, when he finished, he'd left and locked her inside. Every day since that first time blurred together. But everything had changed on the day she had become a god.

After lapping the water from the sink, Sekhmet decided to get dressed, slipping on clothing that fit her like a second skin, the same color as her hair. Sometimes she stayed naked, but a chill sliced through the air today.

Back in the alcove and on the other side of her sarcophagus stood a stone altar. The priests had filled it with fresh shredded meat, bananas, figs, dates, and flat bread. Good. Sekhmet devoured the meat by the handful.

Some time ago, everything had changed. One day all of the priests had come, and she'd been terrified of what all of them could do to her at once. She had grown used to one at a time, or maybe two or three. But on that day, the priests filled the tomb like its columns. Even though her body trembled with fear, she'd stood her ground. But one priest had stepped forward, explaining that her long years of initiation were over and that the time had come for her to begin her reign of revenge. He'd given a cup of blood to her, insisting she drink it all. She'd been suspicious, thinking they were going to poison her first and use her dead body. She'd overheard priests talking and knew that some people did that. She'd fought the priests but they'd succeeded in forcing the blood down her throat. But instead of dying, she'd gone into a rage, relishing the chance to hurt someone who'd hurt her. To this day, she couldn't remember much, but the priests told her that was normal. They said when it ended, three priests had been torn apart and she'd been covered in their blood.

That was the day she'd become a god. She'd become Sekhmet.

The priests helped her transform by tattooing her nose black, as well as framing her eyes with thick black lines. She'd seen herself once in a mirror and that was enough. Seeing what she looked like had scared her.

She'd acquired a taste for killing. Every so often—not nearly often enough—the priests would bring someone to her. Someone bad. Someone who deserved the wrath that only Sekhmet had the power and will to exact. She didn't care about the identity of her victim or what that person had done. It didn't matter. The only thing that mattered was the joy of the hunt among the stone forest of shadows and the relief that someone else's death brought.

Every day she felt as if her entire body screamed with thousands of demons trying to escape. But when she killed, something opened up inside and let one of those demons out. Every time Sekhmet killed, it brought a moment of peace. It was the only time when Sekhmet felt real. For a while, her own pain stopped. It was the only time when she could feel her own breath and the pounding pulse of the blood rushing through her body.

It was the only time when she thought she remembered what she used to be like when she was a little girl, long before she knew this tomb existed.

The rest of the time, Sekhmet felt as cold and dead as the stone surrounding her.

At the opposite end of the tomb, its door creaked open. Sekhmet crouched behind her alabaster sarcophagus, licking her fingers, greasy from the meat.

Muffled voices and footsteps were followed by the sudden slam and click of the temple door locking shut. The same door she'd hated for imprisoning her now gave her pleasure with the promise of a new hunt.

"Wait!" A woman called out on the other side of the stone forest. "This isn't the orphanage! Where's my son?"

Sekhmet licked her lips and smiled.

CHAPTER TWENTY

They drove out into the desert.

Once Pu and her children had escaped, she found Jabari outside the city wall with one of the Pharaoh's black Jeeps, bought from the foreign lands where they were manufactured. Only the Pharaoh owned vehicles that needed no animals to pull them. It was one of the many royal privileges, and the most trusted guards were the only people in the Black Land who knew how to drive.

A single paved road led out of the city and paralleled the banks of the Nile. After a few miles, the road forked; to the left it continued to follow the Nile. They took the road to the right, heading deep into the desert. Several minutes later, Jabari turned onto a road of gravel mixed with red dirt, flanked by high-grown yucca and sagebrush. A low range of red rock hills stretched before them, and a larger range of gray mountains stood in the distance.

Sitting next to Jabari, Pu rocked her youngest girl, who had alternatively screamed and cried since they'd left the city. In back, Zalika kept her arms crossed and head down while the twins jumped up and down next to her, squealing with delight at this new adventure.

Jabari brought the Jeep to a halt in front of twin sandstone columns that blocked most of the road. He looked up at the Almighty God Ra, whose sun chariot descended toward the west horizon, the land of the dead. Daylight would last for just another few hours.

"What are we doing here?" Zalika said.

The twins vaulted out of the Jeep and chased each other in circles. Turning to Zalika, Pu said, "Keep an eye on your sisters."

Zalika leaned forward, elbows resting on her thighs. "And what was that parade about? Why all the drama? That guy—how could they nail him into a coffin and throw him in the river?"

Startled, Pu held her youngest daughter closer, pressing her little body against her chest. "It was just for show. Nobody was thrown into the Nile. No one could survive that."

Zalika groaned in disgust. "Pay attention. You didn't watch the whole thing. I did."

The sweat running through Pu's scalp and down her back suddenly felt like ice. Pu shivered hard. "That's impossible," she said.

"I know what I saw. Somebody had better explain what's going on."

Jabari turned in the driver's seat to look back at Zalika. "Your mom's in trouble because she did something the Pharaoh wouldn't like if he found out about it."

"Jabari!" Pu said. "She's my daughter, not yours. She should be hearing this from me."

"So why haven't you told her yet?"

Pu stared at him blankly. It was a good question. Zalika could handle the truth. Pu turned her attention toward her eldest, looking her squarely in the eye. "I'm pregnant," Pu said. "You and your sisters are Pharaoh's daughters—but this baby isn't his."

Zalika leaned back and laughed.

"This is no joke," Pu said. Part of her wondered what Jabari would think of her. She hadn't told him why she needed help, and she felt as guilty as if she'd cheated on him. Pu didn't care about Pharaoh. She never had. But she still cared as much about Jabari as she had on the day he saved her from the crocodile in her own backyard.

But this wasn't about her and Jabari. The only thing that mattered now was taking care of her children, and that included helping Zalika understand. "The baby's father—"

Zalika laughed so hard that tears rolled down her face. "I don't care about him," she said and wiped the tears from her face. "What you've done, he deserves it. I don't like the way he treats you or me or any of us. We're just playthings to him, and I'm sick of it." Abruptly, she jumped out of the Jeep.

"Wait!" Pu said in a panic.

The teenager glanced toward Jabari as if she were embarrassed he might overhear, and leaned in close to whisper to her mother. "I've got to pee."

Pu nodded her approval.

"We can set up camp here," Jabari said. "We're hidden from the main road. No one will come looking for us at night, even if they realize we're gone. Our best bet is to get a good night's sleep and plan on an early start in the morning."

"But that gives them time to catch up with us tonight," Pu said. "We should keep driving until dark."

"I took care of everything. I made arrangements so no one will think twice about our absence for another day or two. No one saw us leave; you know that as well as I do."

That was true. Jabari had promised that no guards would be any-where near the gate because he'd convinced his superior that he could handle that gate alone. No one had seen Pu or her daughters leave, because everyone had been watching the parade. Pu had checked as they were leaving. And once outside the gate, no one could have seen or heard them leave in the Jeep. The city gates were too high and the festival had been too loud. Pu had turned and watched as they'd driven away and never saw anyone. If she'd seen no one, then no one saw them.

Maybe Jabari was right. The young girls needed rest, and it made sense to set up camp before sunset.

And maybe Zalika was right, too. Pu had always assumed Pharaoh's children had no reason to be unhappy, but for the first time she realized they had just as much reason to be as unhappy as Pu. Maybe all this was for the best, after all.

A black tarp covered the back section of the Jeep, behind its back passenger seats. Jabari said, "I brought along some gear. Why don't you go stretch your legs while I set everything up?"

Pu placed the toddler on the front seat, letting her curl up with her thumb in her mouth, overdue for her afternoon nap.

Pu walked away from the Jeep, keeping an eye on the giggling twins who were now chasing a tumbleweed. She loved this time of day, when the light took a low angle and a golden glow. Colors looked dif-ferent—warmer and magical.

For the first time in many years, Pu's spirit lifted with the new promise of hope.

She heard Jabari call out to the twins, "Come back in the Jeep. I've got a present for you." Pu smiled at the sound of the twins squealing with delight and the sound of their footsteps thudding across the desert floor.

She jumped at the sound of a loud bang. Spinning toward the Jeep, she saw the passenger seat covered in red. Glowing in the afternoon light, it dripped onto the sand below.

Looking up, she saw a rifle in Jabari's hands. Standing next to the Jeep, he aimed and shot at the twins, now in the back seat.

"No," Pu murmured in disbelief.

Rage rushed through her like the Nile on fire. Screaming, Pu ran toward him, only to hear a fourth bang and what felt like a hard blow to her chest.

Pu stopped short, gasping for air.

Jabari walked toward her, emptying the gun as he fired at her chest.

Her legs trembled, unable to hold her weight any longer. Still gasp-ing, Pu collapsed to the ground. She felt something sticky and looked down to see her chest and hands covered in blood.

The last thing she saw was Jabari's face, reddened and streaked with tears.

≈≈

When Pu lost consciousness, Jabari knelt by her side. This was his chance to get the one thing he'd wanted since the day she'd joined the royal harem.

Jabari touched his lips to hers, closing his eyes and visualizing what he imagined every night when he slipped into bed next to his wife. Jabari imagined a world where Pu had married him.

As he ended the kiss, Jabari choked back his sobs and steeled himself. His job had just begun. Reaching into a pocket, he withdrew a baton of rolled-up papyrus and put it into one of Pu's hands, curling her fingers around it. He pushed the hair from her forehead and kissed it. "May the gods keep you safe," he whispered.

Then he remembered Zalika.

He spun slowly, scanning the area, and realized she'd disappeared. Zalika must have wandered off. But where had she gone? And why?

"Zalika?" Jabari called out.

No one answered.

Maybe she'd run away. Teenage girls were always talking about running away. Maybe her reaction to hearing the truth had been a put on. Maybe she'd headed back to the White Walled City. Maybe Zalika felt loyal to her father, the Pharaoh, when push came to shove.

Jabari crept through an opening in the vegetation and onto a parallel dirt path, lined with desert bushes and trees towering eight feet high. She wasn't on this road either. "Zalika?"

He didn't like the last option. If she'd seen what he'd done, she should be taken care of immediately. On the other hand, who would believe a teenage girl who said she'd witnessed the murder of a royal wife and three of the Pharaoh's children?

He stepped through another opening between the plants and found himself at the base of a sandstone mountain that had been partially quarried years ago to build the pharaoh's palace. Blocks the size of the Jeep had been cut out of the mountainside, leaving its front looking like stairsteps for a giant. Smaller blocks were still scattered in piles, as if that same giant had played a game of pick-up sticks with them. Tall desert plants surrounded the small quarry area. He'd planned to take care of them all quickly. Too late, he realized that he'd brought them to a maze where anyone could get lost easily.

Or hide.

Jabari sighed as if all the weight of the world rested on his shoulders. If Pu had married him instead of joining the royal harem, he would have given his loyalty and devotion to her gladly. Although he'd married someone else, the marriage was one of convenience, not love. Jabari married and had children because that's what every good citizen of the Black Land did. The day Pu rejected him for a life of leisure had been the worst day of his life.

It had also been the day that Jabari resolved to give the loyalty and devotion he felt for Pu to the Pharaoh instead. He cast one last look at Pu as he left her on the empty desert. Jabari drove back to the White Walled City, the royal heart of the Black Land, ruled by its Pharaoh and the one Almighty God Ra.

CHAPTER TWENTY-ONE

Hours after she'd jumped into the Nile to swim after the sarcophagus drifting down river, Meres dragged herself out of the water. Here, miles outside the walls of the city, the banks were deep and made of concrete. Climbing out of the banks and onto the desert floor, Meres collapsed. Her chest heaved and ached. Her hair, arranged in dozens of tiny braids, weighed so heavy that it made her head hurt. Looking up, her worst fear came true.

She saw no sign of the sarcophagus in the river. No matter how hard and fast she'd swum, Meres couldn't catch up.

She'd lost Ramose.

Tears welled in her eyes. He'd been nailed into the sarcophagus, right before her eyes. Inches away. If she'd stepped forward, she could have stopped them. She could have saved her husband's life.

The tears spilled down her face. "Why was I so stupid?" Meres asked the desert. "Why did I just stand there and do nothing, like an idiot?"

She shivered, even though her drenched clothing felt good in the intense heat of the day. "I've failed my husband," Meres prayed. "Punish me or tell me how to make amends."

Slowly, the hot sun warmed her skin. Meres sobbed, convinced that Ramose couldn't have survived. Suddenly, all the years she'd spent mourning their inability to have children felt like wasted time.

"What have I done?" Meres said. "We didn't have children, but I had him. I had Ramose."

And now she was alone. Without her country. Without friends. And without her husband.

At the sound of sudden rustling, Meres sat up sharply. Several feet away, a falcon wrestled with a snake, flapping to avoid contact while seizing it behind the neck with its sharp talons. Mesmerized, Meres watched as the snake grew still.

For a moment, the falcon looked directly at Meres. It flew to the top of a nearby tree with the snake grasped in its feet.

Every day the Almighty God Ra guided his solar boat across the sky. At the end of each day, his daughter the sky goddess Nut swallowed him whole. The absence of Ra turned day into night—in essence, his absence meant his death. But he traveled through Nut's body at night, which was the Underworld, the world under the surface of the Black Land and all the other countries in the world. Through every hour of the night, Ra had to battle a different demon or monster. Every morning, Nut gave birth to him, and Ra was reborn as a new day.

But in the seventh hour of each night's journey, the terrifying roar of the evil serpent Apophis rocked the Underworld as he attacked Ra and his ship. Even though Ra traveled with many gods and goddesses, the giant snake's undulations hypnotized them into a state where they were as still as stone. At that moment Apophis struck at Ra, but Isis always defeated the dreadful snake monster.

"Apophis," Meres said, staring numbly at the tell-tale signs of the struggle left behind in the sand.

The snake had been heading toward Meres. It could have struck her before she knew of its presence. If poisonous—if this snake had come to her as a minion of Apophis—it could have killed her.

And a falcon saved her.

Meres looked up at the sun. She'd prayed to Ra, and he'd sent his great-grandson in response: Horus, the falcon god.

When Osiris had been nailed inside his own sarcophagus and thrown into the Nile by Seti, Isis had searched throughout the Black Land and into other countries until she found her husband's body. But when she brought it back home, Seti stole the body of Osiris, dismembered it, and spread the pieces throughout the country. Isis had gone on a mission to find the pieces and reassemble them by wrapping strips of linen around them to keep them together.

Isis had prayed to the gods, begging them to give Osiris life again. They agreed, but they limited his new life to a single day. After that, they named him ruler of the Underworld.

Before Osiris's murder, Isis and Osiris had no children. When the gods gave him one more day of life, they conceived their one and only child, Horus, who had the magical ability to change himself into a falcon.

It's a sign Meres realized.

She had to keep looking for Ramose, even if it meant finding his dead body.

Of course. Suddenly, she understood her own mission. She had failed her husband by not protesting when she saw him nailed into the sarcophagus and thrown into the Nile. She had failed him when she couldn't swim fast enough to catch up to the sarcophagus, swept away by the river's current.

But if Ramose was dead, it would be impossible for him to get to the Underworld unless priests prepared his body properly for burial. If buried properly, his spirit would travel through the realm of the Underworld, where he would offer his heart to be weighed. Ramose had a good heart. Meres had no doubt that his heart would weigh true and Ramose would be welcomed into the Underworld by Osiris himself. But if Ramose's body wasn't found and buried properly, his spirit was destined to wander alone in confusion for eternity.

For a moment, Meres wondered about her own heart. Would her heart weigh true when she died, or would she have to face the waiting monster and be devoured, her spirit destroyed forever?

Meres shook off that thought. It didn't matter now. She wasn't the one who had died.

Meres walked along the east bank of the Nile, following the downstream flow. Unlike any other river, the Nile flowed North. She realized she faced a long journey, but she didn't care. She loved Ramose, and he needed her now more than ever.

Meres would find his body and make sure his spirit could find its way to the Underworld.

CHAPTER TWENTY-TWO

Sekhmet opened her eyes slowly and found herself slumped on the tomb floor in the heart of her stone forest.

The body of the woman she'd hunted and killed lay bloody before her.

It was always like this after one of Sekhmet's feeding frenzies. She'd stalk her victim for fun, which could last for hours. Sekhmet knew every inch of her tomb intimately. For most of her life, it had been her only home. She knew its perfections and its flaws. She knew every shadow and how to hide inside them. She understood every line of sight within the forest of stone columns and how to move among them without being seen.

Like always, the priests had given the victim a vial of sacred blood as an offering to Sekhmet—one of Sekhmet's favorite parts of the ritual killing. Each time, Sekhmet's acceptance—when she drank the blood from the vial—convinced the victim that a release would follow. That Sekhmet would let the victim run to safety.

But that was just the beginning of Sekhmet's fun.

Now, Sekhmet licked the sweet taste of blood from her lips as her eyes adjusted.

As usual, a few priests surrounded the body of the dead, ready to dispose of it. But this time, Priest Hennet stood among them.

Sekhmet growled low in her throat. She didn't like Hennet. He'd been the first to use her, all those years ago, and she still wished he'd been the first they'd let her kill. More than anyone else, he deserved it.

"Good day, Goddess," Priest Hennet said, his voice as smooth as polished stone. "Did you enjoy your treat?"

Sekhmet couldn't help but grin. "She was a meek, timid thing. Hardly worth my effort."

In truth, the woman had been a pitiful coward. Most people brought to Sekhmet had the good sense to try to save themselves. Most tried to find a way to escape, which was impossible, and others stood up and fought to defend themselves or tried to bargain with Sekhmet, once they recognized her as a god. But this poor excuse of a woman had given up! When this victim realized she wasn't alone inside the tomb, she'd frozen, unable to speak or move.

At first, Sekhmet had enjoyed toying with her. It was too easy to stalk her, staying out of sight while using the natural echoes inside the tomb to scare her. Sekhmet even grew so bold as to cast whispers at the woman, terrifying her until her knees buckled and she sank to the floor in hysterics. When Sekhmet had finally grown tired, the woman didn't have the sense or presence of mind to remember what the priests must have told her: that offering the vial of blood would save her. Like always, it hung on a leather thong around the victim's neck, and Sekhmet had to yank it free and take matters into her own hands.

The victim had been disappointing, but a kill was a kill.

And any blood was good blood.

Sekhmet hesitated, frustrated as always that the details of the kill were so fuzzy. After every hunt ended, the priests explained that the horrific violence of her frenzy muddled her memory. She supposed it made sense, but she hated having to be told about the exact moment of the kill because it made her feel less powerful than she knew herself to be. She could tell the priests expected her to be thankful, but she found herself resenting them instead.

Priest Hennet cleared his throat.

Sekhmet's grin widened. She knew all his nervous habits.

"Perhaps the next one will be more satisfactory," Priest Hennet said as his colleagues picked up the victim's body and headed toward the tomb entrance. "The next one is unusual. Special."

Sekhmet tried not to let him see her excitement. She enjoyed toying with Priest Hennet, too. "Is the next one elsewhere? Will others watch?"

Sometimes the priests took her outside the tomb and through the underground catacombs to the house of the Pharaoh, another living god. She'd help the Pharaoh by hunting someone bad in another underground place. Usually, others would watch from above, and Sekhmet felt a rush of pleasure with every gasp and cry of terror she heard.

For far too many years, Sekhmet had been the one in pain, and no one had ever come to help her. It was only fair and right that she had a turn to give back the pain she'd received, and if she could give back fear at the same time, so much the better.

"No," Priest Hennet said.

He stepped closer, and Sekhmet could smell the scent of honey cakes on his breath.

She gazed at him evenly, knowing he hated that. "I like it when they watch."

He shook his head. "Not this time." He handed a photograph to her. "You need to find her and bring her back to us. Then you can play with her as much as you want."

Sekhmet stared at the photograph, not sure if she wanted to take it. "Bring her back? What does that mean?"

"She's left the White Walled City, but she needs to be found and brought back by someone who won't be missed."

Sekhmet understood what he meant, but she felt a pang of hurt anyway. At the same time, the meaning of his words dawned on her. "Do the passageways reach so far?"

Priest Hennet cleared his throat again, and the photograph trembled in his hand. "No. You will go out into the day and track her down. When you bring her back, we will make an example of her."

Sekhmet brightened with hope. "In the places under the palace? Where others can watch?"

"If you wish."

Sekhmet wavered between the joy at the thought of terrifying an audience and a small pang of fear at the idea of going out into the day. She had no real memory of her life before this tomb, and she wasn't sure exactly what "the day" meant. And yet, she suspected it was a place where she could find other gods and prove her own power to them as a hunter. That would be worthwhile.

But what if she got lost? How would she eat? Would there be altars heaped with fresh food every day?

But she couldn't let Priest Hennet see her fear. If that happened, she'd be giving him the upper hand. She'd suffered too long and too much to risk losing her ability to scare him.

Taking the photograph from him, Sekhmet said, "As you wish."

"Thank you, Goddess," Priest Hennet said, stuffing his trembling hands in pockets. "The name of the woman you seek is Meres. Follow the Nile, and you will find her."

CHAPTER TWENTY-THREE

As Pu slowly regained consciousness, her hands opened and a sudden gust stole away the small scroll of papyrus that Jabari had carefully left for her. It rattled along the hard desert sand and stopped near the base of a cactus.

The world came into focus, and Pu's head pounded. Sitting up, she saw herself covered in blood. Her ribs ached and throbbed.

My blood, Pu thought, remembering what had happened. *Jabari shot me. But I'm alive.*

A wave of nausea overwhelmed her. *Lean forward, head between your knees*, she told herself. She shuddered as her chin brushed a bloody spot on her clothes, still slightly tacky, and it made her gag. *Don't think about it. Pretend there's no blood. Don't look at it. Just breathe through your mouth.* After several long moments, she felt better.

Pu struggled to her feet and hurled herself across the desert floor to where the twins had been chasing each other. Here were their footprints and scuff marks where they'd slid and tumbled. But there were also dark splatters on the sand.

Their blood. Jabari had shot them, too. Pu had seen it with her own eyes.

Feeling faint, she sat down hard on the ground. Everything she saw went dark for a moment, as if the sun had suddenly set. She breathed faster. What was happening? Why couldn't she see?

Light came back into the world as quickly as it had left, and the light-headed feeling vanished. Pu felt as if she'd just stepped out of her own body for a few moments and stepped back in.

The blood-stained sand was still there.

Pu shook her head. "This can't be real," she said out loud to herself. "Jabari would never hurt the girls. He'd never hurt me. I must be dreaming."

She pinched her arm hard, but nothing happened. She didn't wake up.

She remembered Zalika. Pu's teenage daughter had gone into the desert to find a place to pee. Where was Zalika now? Filled with new energy, Pu ran to the tire tracks and noticed a small spray of blood by them.

Jabari had put Pu's toddler in the passenger seat up front by the driver. Several minutes later, he'd shot her, too.

A shadow passed over her. Looking up, Pu saw a vulture circling in the sky above.

A sense of dread ran down her throat like ice water. The vulture served as one of Pharaoh's most treasured allies and protectors. Along with the sacred cobra, the Pharaoh's royal crown included the image of the vulture. In fact, Pharaoh's favorite piece of jewelry was an enormous necklace that covered half of his chest: the image of a vulture with its wings spread open.

Why did this vulture circle above her now? Did it mean the Pharaoh could see her?

But the vulture wasn't alone in the sky. The Almighty God Ra continued to sail his sun boat across the sky.

Pu turned toward the sun, standing tall. "Almighty Ra," she called out. "I ask you for your help. Help me find my daughter Zalika."

As if in answer, a sudden gust of wind blew toward her. She closed her eyes as the sand kicked up around her and she kept praying silently. Finally, the wind died down, and something touched her bare feet.

Looking down, Pu saw a papyrus scroll tied with a black ribbon to keep it shut. She looked up and around, turning slowly to scan the desert surrounding her. She was alone.

She looked up, her heart warmed with gratitude. To the sun, she said, "Thank you."

Sitting down, she removed the black ribbon and opened the scroll, which read: "Make no mistake, Pu, you are dead, as are all of your children. Because they are innocent, they have been mummified and have been welcomed into the House of Osiris in the Underworld. You, however, have betrayed the Pharaoh, the gods, and all of the Black Land. Your heart will never weigh true, and you are doomed to be devoured by the monster Ammit upon the judgment of Osiris. You are doomed to remain where you are now, lost and alone in the Underworld, for all eternity."

Pu understood immediately what she held in her hands. Everyone knew that when you died, the gods delivered written instructions.

And the scroll verified the death of her children, as well. If they had already been mummified, that meant their bodies had been found and carried back to the priests in the White Walled City.

Feeling stiff and sore from where she had been shot, Pu looked around and saw nothing but the desert, sky, and sun. It was true. The children's bodies were gone. Even the vulture had disappeared, probably flying back now to the White Walled City to tell Pharaoh that it had seen Pu. That meant Jabari had succeeded in killing Zalika, too. And now Pu would never see any of them again.

Why did I let myself fall in love with someone else? she thought, rubbing her hand over her flat but pregnant belly. *Why didn't I just accept my place in the harem?*

As the sun dipped toward the horizon, Pu felt chilled. She thought about everything in her life that she regretted. Suddenly, she understood why Ramose had been against her joining Pharaoh's harem.

Watching the sun set, Pu thought, *I could have married Jabari. We could have been happy together. The girls could have been our children, and we could have had Ramose and Meres in our lives.*

Instead, she'd let herself be tempted by the glamour of living with royalty, even if it meant only seeing Pharaoh on his whim and spending most of her life with his other women and the royal administrators.

Pu rubbed her face with her hands. *What have I done? How did I end up throwing my life away?*

She thought about Ramose and Meres. By comparison, they were poor, but they seemed happy most of the time, even though they'd never been blessed with children. And even though that seemed like a slap in the face from the gods, Meres had remained loyal to them, going so far as to work in the Temple of Our Lady of the Absolute as the scribe.

She's always followed the rules, Pu thought, as if realizing the implication of that fact for the first time.

Of course. Meres understood the world was black and white. Those who followed the rules were rewarded. And those who did not—like Pu—were punished. It was so easy. So simple. Why did Pu have to die to figure that out?

She picked up the scroll before it could blow away, clutching it to her chest. Her fate had been cast. Her sins weighed too heavy in her heart, and she understood she could do nothing to lighten that burden and save her own soul.

But a thought struck her. What if she journeyed in the path of her children? It would be dangerous to walk through the Underworld, but if she arrived at the House of Osiris, she could ask for one last look at her children before the destruction of her soul took place. It would give her the chance to see all her children once more and make sure they were safe and happy.

And maybe she'd be granted the opportunity to apologize to them for her failure as their mother.

Pu watched the exit of the Almighty God Ra as day became night.

Her body was dead, and she now existed as a spirit. To follow Ra now would be folly. She would stumble in the dark. Better to sleep now and wait until she saw Ra rise in the East again. When that happened, a new day would begin.

And when that happened, like everyone who had died before her, Pu would go forth into the day, beginning her own personal journey into the Underworld.

CHAPTER TWENTY-FOUR

As they walked through the catacombs beneath the White Walled City, Sekhmet held her head high and focused on exuding confidence and serenity. Her skin was as pale as the alabaster sarcophagus she'd left behind in the tomb she knew as home. By contrast, the dozen priests surrounding her had skin ranging from brown to blue-black. Priest Hennet had warned her that she'd see the Almighty God Ra in the sky but staring at him for more than a few moments would hurt her eyes, maybe forever. Priest Hennet also explained that her father had the power to light up and heat the world, sometimes unbearably so. For that reason, he'd given Sekhmet a turquoise linen sheath dress to wear.

Sekhmet knew every image on her tomb walls. She'd had a lifetime to memorize them. The gods often wore knee-length kilts, while the goddesses wore dresses down to their ankles. Although as short as a kilt, her new turquoise dress was the dress of a goddess, nonetheless, complete with pockets.

Ever since Priest Hennet had given the photograph of the woman Meres to Sekhmet, she'd struggled to control her nerves. It wasn't the excited anticipation she felt before or during a hunt among the stone columns in her tomb. Instead, it tapped into her memories of Long Ago, before she became a goddess and had been nothing but a toy used by the priests.

Don't be afraid, Sekhmet told herself. *Your father will be there to protect you.*

Ever since becoming the goddess Sekhmet, she'd wondered about her father, the Almighty God Ra. There were pictures of him on her tomb wall, and she'd prayed to him often, even as a child. The day she'd become a goddess, he'd answered her years and years of prayers. But why hadn't he come down and rescued her when she needed him? Why had he let the priests hurt her?

Still walking, Sekhmet looked down at the photograph in her hand, illuminated by the lights lining the passageway ceiling. This wasn't the time to think about her father. This was the time to think about the hunt.

Finally, they arrived at a door at the end of many interconnected passageways. Sekhmet had paid attention to every turn, but she jumped at a flurry of wings that flew past them from a doorway.

"Bats," Priest Hennet said. "They're just bats."

Sekhmet stood steady, determined to show no sign of fear. "How will I get back inside when I bring the woman back?"

"I'll have someone waiting for you." Priest Hennet opened the door to the outside world.

Sekhmet cried out, blocking her face to protect her eyes from the blinding white light. The brightness terrified her and she stood frozen in place. She wanted to turn and run back as fast as she could to her tomb. She wanted to crawl into her alabaster sarcophagus, curl up, and go to sleep. It was safe inside her sarcophagus. She knew what to expect when inside her tomb. But she couldn't afford to let Hennet or any of the other priests see her fear. If she failed to keep her control over them, they'd take back control of her.

"Here," Priest Hennet said. "I have a pair of sunglasses for you."

Sekhmet squeezed her eyes shut as Priest Hennet pulled her arms away from her face. She felt something slide next to her head above her ears and rest on the bridge of her nose.

"Take your time," Priest Hennet said. "Open your eyes slowly."

Sekhmet took his advice. She'd seen some priests wear clear glasses before, but these had dark lenses that made the brightness more bearable. Bracing herself for the answer, Sekhmet said, "Where is my father?"

Priest Hennet took a few steps from the safety of the underground passageway out into the brightness. He pointed up to the sky.

Sekhmet followed Priest Hennet outside and followed his pointing finger. She let out a startled cry when she saw the vastness of the brilliant blue sky above. And far, far in the distance she saw a brilliant ball of light. "Is that my father?" Sekhmet whispered in awe.

"That is the sun that your father carries in the solar boat that he sails across the sky," Priest Hennet said.

Sekhmet struggled to comprehend a world so much larger than her tomb. The wall paintings made the sky look close enough to touch, making it easy to see the boat and her father's face. But in real life, he was so very far away. Even though her heart sank at not being able to see him or his boat, the brilliant ball in the sky warmed her not only with its heat but with the comfort that she felt close to her father at last. Maybe he had the power to see her from his solar boat in the sky.

Maybe he had the power to protect her, now that he could see her.

"The Nile is there," Priest Hennet said.

Sekhmet looked away from her father to see the priest pointing toward an enormous ribbon of rushing water. At least, she believed it must be water, even though it looked nothing like the Nile in the paintings, always shown as three zigzag lines of blue. "The Nile," Sekhmet said, trying to wrap her head around the concept of the river.

"Follow it away from the city and you are bound to find Meres."

Sekhmet fought off a final yearning to go back into the catacombs. Looking back at the exit door, she saw the other priests hovering inside, waiting for Priest Hennet to return. The door had opened from a large white wall.

The White Walled City, Sekhmet thought. *There really is a wall surrounding it.*

She turned slowly, taking in everything around her: the desert, the Nile, and the great big sky above her that made up most of this outside world. She jumped at the sound of a slamming door and turned to see that Priest Hennet had vanished and the door had shut.

Sekhmet fought the urge to panic by taking a deep breath. She looked up toward the sky and smiled. "Hello, Father."

❧

Just outside the city, Sekhmet ran along the banks of the Nile with joy. Her father had seen her and was bringing his solar boat down to land on the ground! Before long, she knew she'd be running into his arms, truly safe at last.

But she noticed he sailed toward the opposite side of the Nile.

A roar came from far up ahead on the road by the Nile. Her father still sailed in the sky—it couldn't be him. The best course of action was to hide. Sekhmet ducked down between the yucca and blackbush dotting the desert sand.

As the chariot drew closer, she saw that it had no horses drawing it, so she assumed it must belong to another god, or perhaps to a powerful magician.

One man guided that chariot, which carried blood-drenched bodies of children. As part of her heart sank, remembering what had happened to her underneath the White Walled City in childhood, Sekhmet wondered what had happened to them. Was there greater danger on the other side of the Nile? Was this why the priests had sent her to bring back the woman Meres? Had Meres murdered these children?

As the chariot sped past Sekhmet's hiding place and disappeared into the city, she ground her teeth in determination. She would find Meres, no matter how long it took or what she had to do.

As she slid down the hard east bank and paddled across the river to follow her father to the west side of the Nile, Sekhmet reminded herself that she was a powerful goddess who had the help of a more powerful father. Once in his arms, she would ask for his help in finding Meres. After all, from his solar boat in the sky, surely her father could see everything and everyone.

But as the solar boat came closer and closer to the horizon, Sekhmet grew anxious as the brightness of day dimmed, and her father still seemed so very far away. Panicking, she ran away from the Nile that she'd been told to follow and into the desert toward the setting sun.

She ran until darkness made her trip and fall, landing hard on the desert floor. Just as the brightness had overpowered her when she first encountered it, now darkness overwhelmed her.

"Father!" Sekhmet cried out into the dark. "Where are you?"

She realized what must have happened. She knew from the tomb paintings and what the priests had told her over the years that the Nile separated the worlds, with their world on the east bank and the Underworld on the west bank.

"I've run into the Underworld," Sekhmet whispered. "And there is nothing here but danger."

Now that her father had once again abandoned her, Sekhmet shivered, no longer warmed by his distant touch. She curled up on the sand, wrapping her arms around her legs.

Just like always, she was lost and alone in the world.

CHAPTER TWENTY-FIVE

Meres walked through the night, its sky clear and with a new moon. But once her eyes adjusted to the dark, she could see by starlight. She walked alongside the Nile, careful to avoid sharp-edged or thorned plants, scorpions, and other night creatures.

Her mind raced. First, she blamed herself. She shouldn't have helped Pu. But that didn't make any sense—how do you turn your back on people you love when they've done no real harm and have no malice in their hearts?

Meres blamed herself for telling Ramose that Pu needed help escaping the White Walled City. But that wasn't fair. Pu was Ramose's sister. Even if they hadn't spoken since Pu had joined the royal harem, Ramose had the right to know that she needed help.

Someone must have told the priests about Pu and that Meres and Ramose planned to help her escape during the festival parade. But who?

"Not Jabari," Meres said as she walked. "He loves Pu and Ramose. He'd never betray them."

Maybe Pu hadn't been careful enough. Maybe someone in the royal palace had become suspicious and notified the priests. But that didn't seem likely. After all, Meres had seen Pu and her daughters watching the parade. Nothing had looked out of place. After Ramose had been sealed in the sarcophagus and carted away, Meres had glanced at the crowd again and saw that they had vanished. She'd assumed they'd made their escape.

Meres had been careful when working in the temple. Nothing she'd said or done could have possibly given them away. But a new thought dawned on her.

"Neferita," Meres said. "She was by my side day and night."

Because Meres had caught Neferita's young son peeing on a statue of the Pharaoh, Meres had reported the offense. Of course Neferita would be angry, especially when her son had been placed temporarily in an orphanage at the same time she'd been ordered to learn how to become a better citizen by shadowing Meres.

What if Priest Hennet was already suspicious of Pu and had promised to waive further punishment if Neferita agreed to spy on Meres and Ramose?

Meres breathed heavy and hard with anger. Of course. Neferita had turned traitor.

By the gods, Meres thought. *If Neferita stood before me now, I'd wring her neck. I know it's wrong to kill another. I understand Neferita is my sister because all women are my sisters. But I'd give anything to feel her neck in my hands right now, even if only until she passed out.*

Like a pendulum, Meres spent the night swinging between the hope that her husband had somehow survived being swept away by the Nile and the certainty of his death. All the while, she blamed Neferita.

As the sun rose, Meres followed the Nile as it wound through a narrow valley between the bases of two mountain ranges. Soon, she saw thin strips of crops along the river and a town up ahead. Small boats lined the bank, and white-washed mud-brick houses dotted the river's edge. Behind the houses, mountain rock walls jutted straight up into the sky.

She brightened with new hope. Someone must have noticed the sarcophagus. Fishermen, perhaps. Meres ran toward the town. But as she drew close, she saw something that stopped her cold.

Next to the boats lined up on the river were the shattered remains of Ramose's sarcophagus.

≈≈

Sekhmet believed the worlds were spinning around her. Even though she stayed in one place, she'd witnessed the land of living mortals become the Underworld—the land of the dead—and now it had become the land of the living again, as her father Ra guided his solar boat carrying the sun into the sky again.

Although she'd laid down on the desert floor and tried to sleep, she'd stayed awake all night, shivering in the cool desert air, knowing that the Underworld overflowed with monsters and danger and that she could be attacked at any moment. She didn't know much about her father or the other gods. The priests had told her little over the years, and she based her knowledge on her own interpretation of the paintings on the walls of her tomb.

Obviously, all gods were vulnerable. Even the Almighty God Ra.

When she'd seen the first glimpse of her father's return, Sekhmet had raced toward him, shouting his name and waving her arms to get his attention. But no matter how loudly she called, he steered his boat farther and farther away from her.

Finally, Sekhmet stood still, willing herself not to cry. She'd dreamed of meeting her father for years. She'd imagined the way his face would light up when he saw her for the first time and how he'd race toward her, oblivious to everything else in the world. She'd comforted herself with the hope that maybe someday she'd find him, and that he'd weep tears of joy in finding her at last. She'd thought that he sailed his solar boat across the sky in a constant search for her, lighting up all the world with the sun so he could recognize her once he found her.

Sekhmet crossed her arms and turned her back to the sun, staring at the long shadow of herself stretching across the sand. He could see her now. How could he not?

Her father snubbed her only because he didn't recognize her as a goddess. He'd seen nothing of her powers, because she'd spent her life locked away from his sight. If he could have seen her hunt in her forest of stone columns, Ra would have recognized her immediately as his daughter.

But now she had her chance. By hunting and killing Meres in the open, right underneath his solar boat, Sekhmet would prove herself to him. And then, at long last, she'd know the embrace of a father who loved her.

"I am Sekhmet," she told herself quietly and calmly. "I am a goddess." She took a long, deep breath. "I am a killer."

She withdrew the photograph of Meres from her pocket.

Sekhmet believed that being a goddess gave her special hunting powers. Over the years, as she'd hunted dozens of victims in the stone forest of her tomb, she'd become aware of what seemed to be the heat coming from their bodies. Sekhmet could hunt with her eyes closed, thanks to the power of their body heat, making it easy to know where they were and how they moved.

As easy as watching the sun cross the sky.

And their scents were potent. Each victim had a unique odor that changed depending on emotion. Just by the way they smelled, Sekhmet had no trouble identifying one victim from another. She knew when any given victim was afraid or desperate or without hope simply from their scent.

Now, Sekhmet stared long and hard at the image of Meres. The scent of the photograph was useless—it simply smelled like a photograph. But when Sekhmet concentrated, she imagined what Meres might smell like. The woman probably understood Priest Hennet wanted her. She must have run away. She would smell scared or desperate or determined to escape. Whatever Meres' feelings, they would smell strong.

As a light wind blew across the desert, Sekhmet raised her nose and breathed deeply. The sharp tang of sagebrush accented the dry, dusty air.

She smelled the cool water of the distant Nile, laced with the flesh of fish.

As the wind shifted, Sekhmet turned to face into it. She felt herself go cold inside, caring about nothing but the hunt. Eventually, she picked up a mortal scent on the wind—a strained scent, as if its owner had already endured a great deal.

Smiling, Sekhmet walked toward the direction from which that mortal scent had come. Yesterday she had promised to bring Meres back alive to Priest Hennet, but since then the world had changed.

No one had told Sekhmet that the worlds of the living and the dead would revolve around her. No one warned her that she'd suddenly find herself in the Underworld and might have to face monsters at any moment.

And no one had explained that her own father wouldn't recognize her unless she showed him how well she could kill.

She trembled with a new thought. What if he found it impossible to love her when he realized who she was and what had happened to her? If the Almighty God Ra found it impossible to love his own daughter, that would mean Sekhmet was impossible to love. She would never know what it felt like to be embraced by someone who truly cared for her.

Just as well. Killing was easier that way. Once she showed her father how well she could kill, he would recognize her as his rightful daughter. If he couldn't love her, the least he could give her was his approval.

Just the thought of it gave Sekhmet a cold, hard happiness. She kept a steady pace as she walked through the desert, looking forward to finding Meres and ripping her apart.

Chapter Twenty-Six

"Almighty God Ra: bringer of light and light, I pray to you for help," Pu said as she knelt before the rising sun. Her voice trembled because she had never taken the time to memorize all the spells in the Book of the Dead, meant to guide souls safely through the Underworld and the next eternal life.

Everyone said only those with evil hearts needed to memorize the spells. People who lived their lives with the best of intentions would magically know the spells whenever they needed them on their journey to the afterlife.

But which one am I? Pu wondered. *Do I have an evil heart because I committed treason against Pharaoh? Or does the way I lived my life before betraying him count?*

She tried not to blame herself for failing to memorize the spells. After all, she'd never expected to die so young.

Speak from your heart. That was the advice she'd heard all her life about what to do when the time came to make the journey. Right now, that's all she could do.

"I know I've done wrong," Pu said to the sun. "When my heart is weighed against my sins, I know it will weigh heavy. I am willing to be destroyed by the god Ammit. All I ask is to see the souls of my dead children and ask their forgiveness before it happens. That's why I ask you to give me protection and guidance through the Underworld."

She studied the papyrus given to her by the wind yesterday. Below the instructions were markings. Pu hadn't noticed them at first, but now that she studied them, it seemed to be a small map. She compared it to the landscape surrounding her. The map showed the rock columns that stood before her, blocking the road—it had to be where the Jeep had stopped. An arrow pointed to the road that continued behind the stone columns.

What comes first? Pu struggled to remember the details of the path in the Underworld that every soul must travel.

Of course!

Pu rose and said the spell out loud. "I am Pu, and I ask for protection as I go forth into the day. Osiris, guide me to your house in the Field of Reeds. Open a path for me to travel, and open up the Road to Rosetjau that will lead to you. Keep me safe from monsters and anything that would do me harm or lead me astray. And when I arrive, let me enter and face my destiny."

Behind the stone columns, she discovered a narrow gravel path cutting through the desert, as well as a simple wooden sign. She read the sign over and over again, making sure she made making no mistake. "It's real," she said, suddenly feeling numb with grief. She sank to the sand before her knees could buckle beneath her. "It's all real."

The sign read: "The Road to Rosetjau."

≈≈

In the early morning hours, on the banks of a small city on the Nile, Meres searched frantically among the shattered ruins of the sarcophagus. "Ramose!" She cried out, looking everywhere for his body.

This was not the proof she'd hoped to find, but it was proof, nonetheless. Clearly, the sarcophagus had shattered against the river bank. No one inside could have survived that kind of impact.

The wooden sarcophagus now looked like little more than a pile of kindling. Meres paused when she saw a large chunk. The entire sarcophagus had been painted with images of the gods and hieroglyphs. During the festival parade, Meres had been too happy and excited at the beginning to look at it closely. When Ramose had been nailed inside, she'd been too startled and confused. But now she took a very close look.

Only the priests knew how to read hieroglyphs, considered to be the sacred language of the gods. Hieroglyphs were nothing more than pretty drawings of people and nature to everyone else. But Meres wasn't everyone else. The nature of her job required her to learn hieroglyphs. Now she frowned, chilled by the hieroglyphs she read on the shattered fragment of the sarcophagus: "... and send him to Osiris."

Those were not words that were found on any sarcophagus she'd ever seen. It was each soul's responsibility to travel through the Underworld. No one—not even a god—could send anyone to Osiris.

"Madame," a man's voice said behind her. "Do you need help?"

Meres turned to see a pale stranger with close-cropped red hair. Instead of a Black Lander's white linen kilt, this man wore brown pants rolled up to the knee and a short-sleeved blue shirt. Other men, dressed like him, approached the boats lined up on the shore next to the ruins of the sarcophagus. They appeared to be fishermen, getting ready to go out on the river in the early morning hours.

Meres' skin prickled with fear. "Where am I?"

The red-headed man studied her carefully. "You must be a Black Lander."

Meres nodded gingerly, wondering how far she would get before he could catch up with her if she made a sudden dash into the desert.

"You crossed the boundary between our countries," he said. "You're now in the land of Punt."

Meres froze. Without meaning to, she'd stumbled into a foreign land.

And as all Black Landers knew, foreigners committed rape and torture and murder just for the fun of it.

CHAPTER TWENTY-SEVEN

Every so often, Pu glanced up in the sky to check on the progress of the Almighty God Ra's solar boat. She'd been walking on the gravel road to Rosetjau all day, and now she wondered if she'd been walking in the wrong direction.

Pu knew very little about the Underworld and what the journey through it would be like. As she walked, she wondered how long it would take. Was it a journey she could complete in one day? In a week? In a year? And how would she know her location at any given point? Would there be more signs, like the sign she'd found that marked this road? She knew there would be many dangers, but how and when would they manifest?

Pu's stomach grumbled. At first, she'd been surprised. Somehow, she'd assumed she wouldn't desire food or drink anymore. Of course, souls welcomed into the Underworld by Osiris would be given all the sustenance they wanted, but Pu knew she was different. She had no hope of being welcomed, so she'd assumed she had no need of food or drink.

Or maybe she just assumed she didn't deserve any.

Something rose out of the desert sand ahead, and Pu stopped in her tracks.

It looked like a jackal but had a coat the color of sand instead of black. The pale jackal stood, as if emerging into existence out of the sand itself, and stepped onto the road directly in front of Pu. Of course. This had to be Wepwawet, the guard of the Underworld who stood by its entrance.

Strange. This stretch of desert looked no different than any other she'd encountered this morning. She'd always assumed she'd recognize the entrance to the Underworld when she saw it. But her only clue was the presence of its guard, Wepwawet.

What do I do now? Pu wondered as she and Wepwawet stared at each other.

Part of mummification involved tucking magical amulets into the linen strips wrapped around the body. Those amulets were used by souls in situations like this. But Pu knew she wouldn't be mummified because of her crime. There were no magical amulets. Traitors didn't deserve amulets.

But could she make her own?

She looked all around her, hoping for inspiration, but the desert offered none. She winced when a sharp edge of stone dug into the bottom of her foot. She pulled her foot back, stepping away from the sharp stone.

Inspiration hit.

Picking up the stone, Pu studied its edge. She used it to cut into the bottom of her dress, cutting a narrow strip loose. She folded, twisted, and tied the strip into a shape similar to an ankh.

The knot of Isis.

But in order to empower its magic as an amulet, she needed to color the white linen red. Again, Pu looked around the desert, its yellowish brown sand, and it dark green sagebrush. She saw nothing even remotely close to the color red. And it had to be red to symbolize the blood of Isis.

Pu stared at her own skin. As a soul, she wasn't surprised that she took the shape of the body in which she'd lived her life. That was to be expected from all she knew about the soul and the afterlife. What did surprise her was how real this body felt. She felt aches and pains from having walked all morning on this gravel road. Even more surprising, she was hungry and thirsty. Could it be that her soul body was more similar to her mortal body than she ever could have guessed?

Pu used the sharp edge of the same stone to slice the pad of one of her fingers.

The pain startled her, but several moments later that finger began to bleed. Overjoyed, Pu caught every precious drop with her homemade knot of Isis, and the linen transformed from white to red.

When the bleeding stopped, it had thoroughly drenched the knot of Isis. Holding it in the palm of her hand, Pu held it up to the sun to dry. She hoped she could work magic in the same way that she'd been told she would know any spells she needed in the Underworld by looking into her heart.

Pu focused on her daughters, remembering their smiles and the way they smelled when she held them close. Looking up at the sun, she said, "I call to you for help and guidance, Almighty God Ra. I hold the knot of Isis. Turn my blood into hers. Make the spells I speak as powerful as hers. Let this amulet protect me as I walk through the Underworld."

She let the sun bake the knot of Isis until her hand grew weary of holding it high. Letting her hand drift down, Pu saw that the blood had dried, stiffening the linen.

Holding up the knot of Isis, Pu said, "Welcome me into the Underworld, Wepwawet. Let me pass so that I may find my way to the Field of Reeds and the House of Osiris."

Wepwawet's ears pricked up, and he stared at her intently. He opened his jaw wide, his pink tongue curling as he yawned. Staring beyond her, he seemed newly interested in something in the distance. Wepwawet rose and bounded off in that direction.

Holding onto the magic amulet she'd created, Pu shook her head in confusion and forged ahead. She glanced over her shoulder to see the jackal-like god run across the sand. Out loud, she said, "This just isn't anything like what I thought death would be like."

CHAPTER TWENTY-EIGHT

Two fishermen escorted Meres from the riverbank where she'd discovered the shattered ruins of the wooden sarcophagus to a small mansion built into the base of the mountain wall, surrounded by cottonwood trees and silktassel bushes. A single row of columns stood like sentinel guards across the expanse of the first storey. Those columns supported a second-floor balcony. A stone walkway surrounded the mansion. Water filled a depression in one of the stones, and a large blue bird drank from it.

Although the fishermen weren't armed, Meres felt threatened. All her life, she'd heard stories about foreigners, and now that she'd stumbled into the land of Punt she set her first goal as staying alive. Foreigners were constantly killing their own kind but were equally happy to kill others who crossed their paths. They were incapable of understanding that murder wasn't allowed in the Black Land. The concept of brotherhood could not be explained to them. The Pharaoh and priests were experienced with foreigners, and they knew of what they spoke. No Black Lander with an ounce of common sense would ever dream of having anything to do with another country or its people.

The pale redhead led them up to the front door and knocked. When a servant answered, Red said, "I've got a Black Lander with me. She found the sarcophagus."

"My husband!" Meres said to the servant. "Is he here?"

The servant looked long and hard at the fishermen until the redhead said, "Don't look at us. Nobody tells us anything."

Looking down, as if avoiding Meres, the servant finally said, "No."

Meres closed her eyes. It was too late. Ramose was dead.

Ushered inside, Meres and the fishermen waited in a high-ceilinged entrance with a polished marble floor and gold-leafed walls. Light streaming in from a skylight bounced off the walls, casting a warm glow. "Sorry, Ma'am," the redhead whispered. "He was alive when we found him. Like I said, nobody tells us anything."

After disappearing for a few moments, the servant returned and led them into another room.

Lush plants lined the walls surrounding a long and narrow pool in which a naked woman swam. The servant gestured for the fishermen and Meres to sit in simple white chairs by the pool.

They're going to drown me, Meres thought. *They probably drowned Ramose.*

The woman in the pool stopped swimming and came up for air. Even with her gray hair slicked back—or maybe because of it—she was a handsome woman with strikingly sharp features. Unlike Black Landers, she didn't use kohl to darken and extend her eyebrows or line her eyes. Instead, her eyelids shimmered with a metallic copper that seemed to repel water. And yet, her earrings were simple turquoise ankhs, the kind a little girl would wear. Looking toward her unexpected visitors, she rested her forearms on the edge of the pool and bobbed slightly, as if she were barely tall enough to reach the bottom with her toes. "What brings you here?"

Red cleared his throat. "This here's a woman from the Black Land."

"Any fool can see that," the woman said softly. "She's dressed like Isis."

Meres gasped in surprise.

The naked woman laughed. "Just because you know nothing about us, doesn't mean we know nothing about you."

Meres started to speak but caught herself. She knew the simple act of opening her mouth could get her killed.

"No matter what you've been told, no one's about to harm you. I won't allow it. And what I say, goes."

Still, Meres kept quiet.

Giving Red a pointed look, the naked woman said, "You've told her who I am—yes?"

Looking down at his feet, Red muttered something incomprehensible.

"Apparently, no." She shook her head slowly in disappointment, as if Red were a toddler who had painted the walls with mud, having no idea he'd done anything wrong. To Meres, she said, "I am Queen of the land of Punt. As an act of good faith and friendship, I will allow you to call me Angelique."

Queen Angelique flattened her palms on the curb of the pool. Using her feet to spring off the pool floor, she hoisted herself up and turned to sit on the curb. Dripping wet, she rose to her feet with the grace of a dancer. Standing nude before them, her body looked as trim and toned as a woman half her age. Judging from her regal posture, Queen

Angelique took pride in it.

Startled, Meres looked away. Although common in the White Walled City, public nudity symbolized a lack of social status. Children were often naked, as were dancers and other entertainers. Most men wore only a kilt, as did some women, such as professional mourners and members of the royal harem. But the higher a woman's rank, the more clothes she wore. The Pharaoh preferred a harem to a wife, but if he had a wife she'd never present herself naked to anyone but the Pharaoh.

"I've offered friendship to you," Queen Angelique said. "Now what is your name?"

Meres looked up to see the queen studying her closely, as if reading Meres' thoughts. Guilt washed through her, and Meres felt her face warm, ashamed that she'd judged this woman. "I'm Meres. I'm from the White Walled City in—"

"The Black Land. Yes, we've established that." Queen Angelique waved one hand at Red and the other fisherman, shooing them away in a way that made it clear they were free to leave the mansion and return to their boats.

Meres watched the men bow repeatedly as they backed their way out of the room.

Queen Angelique picked up a plush white robe folded neatly near the edge of the pool and shrugged into it. Sitting next to Meres, Queen Angelique patted Meres' knee. "There! Now it's just us girls. I imagine you've come about your husband."

The queen didn't look like a murderous barbarian. No longer feeling outnumbered, Meres could stop focusing on her own survival and return to her search for Ramose. "I've every right to his body," Meres said.

Queen Angelique laughed. "I dare say you do. That's every wife's right."

Confused, Meres tried to understand her meaning. Foreigners didn't believe in Isis, Osiris, or any of the other gods. To the best of Meres' knowledge, foreigners didn't believe in the Underworld, so they didn't practice the rituals needed to ensure each soul's safe journey through it. Still trying to decipher the queen's words, Meres shuddered, remembering that some barbarians didn't necessarily rape their victims before killing them. Sometimes that came after.

"Now, now. What must you be thinking, dear girl?"

Something inside Meres snapped. She'd spent her lifetime safe inside the walls of the royal city, terrified of the outside world and all that it held. But now she felt tired of being afraid. Until she could recover Ramose's body and deliver it to the priests who would prepare it for burial, his soul was lost and alone in unknown chaos. No one should have to suffer like that, and Meres had the power to help him. As a new determination arose within her, Meres realized a willingness to fight for her husband's soul in a way she'd never known before.

"I want to see my husband," Meres said calmly. "Now."

"That's not possible. He's no longer here."

"Where is he? What have you done with him?"

Queen Angelique shrugged. "We could do nothing except take him west, back across the border to Annu."

"But why?" Meres knew about Annu. Legend had it that every 1000 years, a magical bird would fly to the city of Annu and build a nest of dry sticks. The Almighty God Ra would shine the rays from the sun he carried in his solar boat upon those sticks until they caught fire, burning that magical bird into ashes. But the power from the embers brought the bird back to life, reborn from its own ashes. Did the people in the land of Punt believe that people could be revived in the same way?

"No!" Meres said before the queen could answer the question. "If his body is burned, his soul will be lost forever."

For the first time, the look in the queen's eyes softened. "My darling girl, no one is going to set your husband on fire. Annu is a city of healers. Don't you know that?"

Meres didn't dare let herself feel hope. "I saw the sarcophagus smashed into bits. Ramose couldn't have survived. He was nailed inside."

Queen Angelique pressed her lips together into a thin line of anger. "How do you think we felt when we found him like that? I didn't simply give permission for the men who found him to destroy that cursed thing—I gave my blessing." Taking a deep breath, she continued. "It was never my intention to mislead you, and I apologize if that has happened."

Meres gripped the armrests of her chair before the world spun out of control. "Ramose—"

"He's alive."

CHAPTER TWENTY-NINE

By mid-day, Sekhmet felt exhausted, parched, and starved. Normally, she had water at her fingertips and food placed on the altar in her tomb every day. The desert was vast, and she'd long since left the Nile. She'd seen nothing that looked remotely like food since she'd left the White Walled City yesterday.

As her father traveled high in the sky above, Sekhmet had thought long and hard. She wondered if he truly did recognize her but chose to reject her because she had failed to prove herself as a huntress. Did he blame her for letting the priests do as they wished with her when she was a child? Deep in her heart, she'd always felt ashamed for believing them. She remembered little about her childhood, but she did remember the lies they'd used to lure her into the depths of the underground catacombs. Could her faint memory of guilt be real? Did she actually remember her parents warning her to wait at the temple gate? Or did she only want to believe she'd once had parents who wanted to protect her?

But none of that explained the Almighty God Ra's refusal to come face to face with her. After all, she'd once been nothing but a mere girl. A mortal being.

Now she was the goddess Sekhmet.

Her nostrils flared, catching a fresh whiff of the energy left behind by her prey, the woman Meres. And Sekhmet convinced herself to keep trudging forward through the heat and the dust. Some time ago, she'd spotted a blip on the horizon, and now she'd come close enough to see a small town.

Sekhmet walked through a wide and long valley, and the town stood above her on a gentle rise. As she walked up to the town, its emptiness struck her. Buildings lined a wide dirt street, some made of brick and others of wood. A lone tumbleweed rolled down the street, but she saw no people.

Did they see me coming? Are they all hiding in fear?

At first, Sekhmet thought to slink alongside one of the buildings to try to catch a glimpse through its windows in case people were cowering inside.

No, Sekhmet thought. *That's no way for a goddess to behave. What would my father expect me to do? How can I prove my worth?*

Fighting off the dizziness from hunger, Sekhmet stepped onto the center of the street and raised her arms to the sky. "Welcome me! For I am a goddess!"

She expected people to come rushing out of the buildings, ready to help her find her prey, ready to appease the daughter of the Almighty God.

Silence.

Sekhmet took a few steps forward, gazing at the buildings. Many had broken windows. "I am the lioness, Sekhmet!"

The tumbleweed rolled into her, pausing as it bumped into her legs. It rolled past her.

Angry at its insolence, she turned. "Stop! No one touches a goddess without her permission!"

Ignoring her command, the tumbleweed kept rolling away.

Sekhmet pounced on it, crushing it underfoot and ripping the tumbleweed apart. As the wind kicked up again, she tossed the many severed limbs of the weed into the air, letting them scatter in many directions.

A surge of power rushed through her. "Let that be a lesson," Sekhmet said grimly.

She walked down the length of the street but sensed life nowhere.

Suddenly, an elderly woman rounded the corner of a pale yellow house, her arms full of sunflowers. She'd arranged her white hair into a bun, and cat-eye glasses perched low on her nose.

"You!" Sekhmet called out.

Startled, the woman looked up. Crying out, she let the sunflowers fall to the ground as she hurried toward Sekhmet.

Sekhmet braced herself. People were supposed to run away from her, not toward her. They were supposed to flee in terror, and then Sekhmet would chase them down. True, she only wanted to get information from this woman—find out when her prey had been here. Perhaps the woman ran to throw herself at Sekhmet's feet and pray for help of some kind. Or mercy.

But the woman's face creased with concern. "Oh, child," she said. "You're sunburned!"

Sekhmet frowned, puzzled by the woman's words.

Gently, the woman took Sekhmet by the palm of her hand, pulling it forward. "Haven't you noticed how red your skin is?"

Sekhmet's eyes widened in horror. Yes! Now she could see it, comparing her skin next to this woman's. Sekhmet's skin had turned from white to pink, as if her entire body had become flushed with anger. And when she touched her own skin, it hurt.

"No," Sekhmet said in disbelief, staring at her skin. "How could this happen to me?"

"We've got to get you out of the sun—"

The sun. Was it possible her own father had hurt her?

"—and into a tub of cold water. It'll suck the heat right out of you."

"No." Not her father. Why would he want to hurt his own flesh and blood?

The world spun out of control, and Sekhmet collapsed into the arms of the stranger.

❧

The cool, smooth surface of Mrs. Dempsey's bathtub reminded Sekhmet of her own sarcophagus back in the tomb, and that gave her comfort. The cold water, chilled by ice cubes, shocked her at first but ultimately felt soothing.

And after Mrs. Dempsey had asked enough questions to learn that Sekhmet had gone for a full day without much water and no food, she brought a large pitcher of iced tea up to the bathroom, along with a small metal table she unfolded and set up next to the tub. After giving a large glass to Sekhmet, Mrs. Dempsey brought as much food as the goddess could eat. Finally, Mrs. Dempsey brought a large vase of sunflowers and placed it in an empty corner of the bathroom.

"You should be good for awhile," Mrs. Dempsey said. "I'll come back in an hour with more ice, but if you need anything at all, just holler." She took a quick glance at everything in the bathroom, as if checking to make sure she'd missed nothing. Mrs. Dempsey smiled and left, closing the door behind her.

For the first time in many years, Sekhmet cried. She breathed evenly and made no sound. Tears streamed steadily from the outside corners of her eyes and dripped from her jaw into the icy water.

Staring at the sunflowers, Sekhmet realized that the care Mrs. Dempsey had shown her today was what she'd hoped to get from her father. For the first time in her life, Sekhmet felt loved. How could a stranger be so kind to her? Especially when that stranger showed no recognition of Sekhmet?

Sekhmet cried for a long time. She wished Mrs. Dempsey had left her alone. Now, it was going to be difficult to kill her.

CHAPTER THIRTY

Queen Angelique had had enough.

Breathe, she told herself. *Take this one step at a time.*

Still wrapped in a plush white robe, she sat next to Meres in the pool room, her favorite place in the house. When Queen Angelique glided through the pool, lap after lap, she escaped the world and all its troubles. She loved the rhythm of swimming, stroke after stroke, kick after kick. She loved the rhythm her own breath fell into. But most of all she loved the way the water filled her ears, blocking noise so she could enter her own private world. She swam every morning for at least an hour, pacing herself like a marathon athlete. She'd walk the perimeter of the pool room to check each plant and to water those in need.

But this morning, the servant had interrupted her halfway through her swim with news of the woman from the White Walled City. Because her routine had been changed, Queen Angelique couldn't help but gaze around the room, wondering which plants needed water today.

Returning her focus to Meres, Queen Angelique said, "There's plenty more, if you want."

Meres looked up from a plate of fruit and pastries. She was a strange bird. On one hand, she cowered as if expecting that she'd be attacked any moment. On the other hand, her eyes shone with fierce courage. She looked like a woman on a mission.

Queen Angelique sighed. This wouldn't be happening if her son had simply named this a new town in the Black Land. Instead, he'd been so angry with Angelique that he'd created the land of Punt just to turn her into one of the foreigners that all Black Landers feared.

Meres dropped her gaze and shook her head, looking afraid of asking for more because she thought she'd be punished. Or poisoned. Or afraid to appear greedy or ungrateful for what she'd already received and then be punished or poisoned.

"I've learned one important thing about traveling," Queen Angelique said. "Whenever there's food, eat as much as you can, because you don't know when you'll have the opportunity to eat again. Do you like meat?"

Meres looked up hopefully and nodded.

"Bacon!" Queen Angelique called out, even though they were alone in the room. "Hash browns! And waffles!"

Minutes later, the servant appeared with more plates of food and another table. After laying out the spread, the servant disappeared again.

As Meres inhaled a handful of bacon, Queen Angelique said, "We've got all day. Slow down. Enjoy."

Meres relaxed as she chewed, and her cowering aura evaporated.

Good. Queen Angelique like her better this way. In fact, Meres began to remind Queen Angelique of herself twenty years ago. Life had been good when her husband had been alive. Together, they'd ruled and nurtured a world that embraced humanity. Queen Angelique had been proud to be part of this family tradition. Every day she felt that she made a difference in the world. When her husband died young, their only child should have taken over the throne, but Queen Angelique worried about him. Unlike his father, he focused his efforts on creating a harem for himself. He'd exhibited more interest in acquiring fine things for himself than in nourishing his people.

Although Queen Angelique had exercised her right to rule, in time her own son had secretly banished her. And these people of her town—including the fishermen and her own servants—worked for her son, keeping him posted on her every move. But she had no desire to challenge his authority. All she wanted was to swim every morning, water her plants, and look forward to the day she'd be reunited with her husband.

As Meres slowed down her feeding frenzy, Queen Angelique helped herself to a plate of waffles and strawberries.

"I have to find my husband," Meres said. "I have to go to Annu right now."

Queen Angelique nodded her understanding. She'd already told Meres how a fisherman had spotted the sarcophagus floating down a calm stretch of the Nile yesterday and steered it to shore. Hearing muffled cries, he'd pried the lid off to find Ramose inside, injured, battered, bruised, and drenched to the bone from the water that had seeped in and nearly drowned him.

The act of locking a man inside a sarcophagus and casting him into the Nile was an act that had gone too far. Was the Pharaoh assuming Angelique would find the mess he'd made and clean it up? Even if the Pharaoh knew nothing of it, this stunt reeked with the stench of the high priests. Queen Angelique had spent years wallowing in self-pity and anger. She'd finally made peace with herself and her life, and she would let no one destroy that.

Meres would have been a child when Angelique ruled. Odds were that Meres had never seen Angelique, so she didn't recognize the woman who had once been her ruler. It would be easy to just let Meres walk away.

But Queen Angelique knew that if she watched Meres walk away now without saying another word, this moment would haunt her forever. Maybe even enough to tip the scales the wrong way when the gods weighed her heart.

As Meres stood, Queen Angelique grabbed her by the wrist.

"How much do you love your husband?" Queen Angelique said.

Meres frowned as if it were the most stupid question she'd ever heard.

Good. Queen Angelique had hoped for that kind of answer.

Putting her breakfast aside, Queen Angelique rose and held onto both of Meres' wrists. "You will follow him wherever they tell you he's gone?"

"Of course."

"When you find him, promise me one thing. Follow the beam of light that connects the earth and sky."

Meres shuddered and tried to pull away, but Queen Angelique's grip held tight.

"You think it's in foreign land, and that's true. But that light will lead you to the greatest truth of all."

Meres stopped struggling. "How is that possible?"

Queen Angelique's nerves felt as tight as her grip on Meres. The wise knew when to whisper. "Tell no one except your husband. Look at what happened to him. Do you think you'll be welcomed back into the White Walled City with open arms? Of course not! You can never go back. Your home is gone forever."

Staring at the Queen, Meres' eyes watered.

"Don't let anyone know that I've told you to follow the light," Queen Angelique said. "If you do, they'll kill me, you, and your husband."

Meres looked as stunned as if Queen Angelique had just slapped her. "What?"

Without another word, Queen Angelique let go of Meres, shrugged off her robe, and slipped back into the pool, shuddering despite the fact that the water felt warm enough in which to bathe. She swam for hours and wasn't surprised to find herself alone in the pool room when she finally looked up.

Queen Angelique didn't know the truth herself. She only knew it existed and where to find it.

For many days, she couldn't stop thinking about Meres and the dangers she'd likely face.

CHAPTER THIRTY-ONE

Queen Angelique's servant had provided directions and drawn a simple map from the land of Punt to Annu, the city of healers. Meres simply had to follow a trail to the South. The Queen's men had driven Ramose there, but the Queen's only car had broken down on the way back. Her men believed it would take a week to repair it. Given the choice, Meres decided to walk instead of wait. The distance wasn't far, but the trail wound through and over the low rock mountains that walled in the Land of Punt.

Meres had been walking toward Annu for hours now and found herself once again surrounded by desert. As the sun blazed high above, she felt grateful for the queen's advice to eat whenever she had the opportunity. After all, Meres had no idea how long it would take to get to Annu or if she'd be able to find food between now and then. She was equally grateful for the small container of water the servant had insisted she take.

Despite the heat, she felt boundless energy.

He's alive, Meres thought. *Ramose is alive.*

She knew it was foolish to trust a foreigner. Meres knew nothing about Queen Angelique or her subjects. What if they'd lied to her?

But that didn't make sense. What could they gain from lying?

Meres considered everything she knew about foreigners. They were dangerous and evil, so it stood to reason that they might lie to Meres for the fun of raising her hopes, knowing she'd be devastated to arrive in Annu and find Ramose dead.

But that didn't make sense either. Someone who would stoop to such a wretched act probably would want to see Meres' reaction. In that case, Queen Angelique would have insisted that Meres wait so the queen could take Meres to Annu herself.

Confused, Meres shrugged it off. Maybe the people in the land of Punt were different from other foreigners.

But this morning's conversation with Queen Angelique haunted

Meres. She'd felt unnerved when asked if she loved her husband. Would she have to prove it somehow to get him back? Or would she have to follow him to dangerous places?

Meres felt troubled by the queen suggesting that Meres and Ramose no longer had a home in the White Walled City. Meres had been so focused on finding Ramose that she hadn't thought about their future, but the queen was right. None of them could ever go home again.

The White Walled City was the only home Meres had ever known. She'd never wanted to go outside its walls. She loved her mud-brick house and the temple of Our Lady of the Absolute and everything else about the city, now lost to her forever.

Don't think about it now, Meres told herself. *Find Ramose first. Then we can look for Pu and the girls.*

After making her way between the bases of two adjacent rock mountains, the trail widened. Vultures wheeled in the sky above.

The vulture was one of the Pharaoh's protectors—why were vultures here now? Could it be a sign of being followed or watched by the Pharaoh? That seemed unlikely. If anyone had followed her, she would have heard the sound of crunching footsteps on the gravel trail behind her.

On the other hand, maybe the vultures were a sign of protection from Queen Angelique. So far, she'd been true to her word, but Meres refused to trust the foreign queen until she saw proof that Ramose still lived.

Vultures are birds of prey, Meres thought. *Maybe this isn't a sign from the gods. Maybe they've just found something to eat.* Watching them circle above, she considered that vultures typically ate prey already dead or dying.

Ramose. What if they'd lied about taking Ramose to Annu? What if they'd cast him out into the desert and he'd collapsed before he could reach Annu? What if the vultures were circling above him?

Unable to see over the trees and bushes lining the trail, Meres pressed forward. As the trail widened even more, she could see someone lying on an open stretch of desert up ahead.

As Meres ran toward the huddled figure, she noticed a vulture on the ground next to it.

"Hey!" Meres waved her arms furiously. "Get away from him!"

The vulture hopped away and tilted its head hopefully.

Screaming, Meres raced toward the vulture, and it finally took flight. Out of breath, Meres braced herself for the worst. If Ramose had died, at least she'd found his body and would find a way to have him buried properly so that he could live forever in the Underworld.

The still, huddled figure looked human. But it wasn't Ramose.

"Goddess Isis," Meres said as she knelt next to the unconscious girl, pale but still breathing. If not for yesterday, Meres might not have recognized her so quickly. But now she remembered that moment when she'd seen Pu and her daughters in the crowd during the parade and realizing how very much they looked like their mother. The unconscious girl on the desert floor was Pu's teenage daughter, Zalika.

CHAPTER THIRTY-TWO

"Hey!" Meres yelled at the vultures, waving her arms harder. "Get out of here!"

The vultures ignored her, tipping lazily in the wind.

Meres considered the situation. Although just a girl, Zalika stood nearly as tall as Meres and probably weighed nearly as much. Meres had physical strength, but not enough to pick Zalika up and carry her to Annu.

The vultures' shadows circled around Zalika's body, gradually growing smaller. They were getting closer.

Meres looked around. Maybe if she could find some materials she could make some kind of stretcher, roll Zalika onto it, and drag her to Annu. But she saw nothing in the desert but sand and plants.

And a few rocks. Meres picked up a handful and threw one at a vulture right above her head. The rock flew short of the vulture and hit Meres on its way back down.

Wincing more with embarrassment than pain, Meres backed away so she could throw in an arc instead of straight up in the air. No matter how hard she threw, the rocks didn't come close to hitting the vultures, who didn't seem to notice Meres at all.

Meres believed she could run to Annu and bring back people who could help within the hour, but she didn't dare leave Zalika alone and unconscious. Meres glanced at the town in the distance as if it might have magically grown closer since the last time she looked.

As if sensing that Meres might try to make a run for it, the vultures landed on the desert floor. Spread out, the birds were far enough away to still be safe from getting stoned.

What do I do? Meres thought. *I can't leave her here, but we can't stay here indefinitely either.*

And if vultures were drawn to Zalika now, did it mean she was dying? Maybe Meres could keep them at bay, but what would happen at night? Wasn't that when the jackals came out?

"Get out!" Meres yelled and threw every rock she could find while staying close enough to Zalika to protect her in case one of the vultures tried to slip in behind Meres. "Get out, get out, get out!"

The vultures raised their wings as if surprised. One of them looked at Meres as if she'd hurt its feelings.

It dawned on her that maybe Zalika wasn't as close to death as she appeared. What if Zalika could wake up?

Meres knelt next to her, looking for any sign of injury and finding none. Maybe the girl had simply gone too long without food and water. Meres stroked her niece's hair. "Wake up, Honey. I need you to wake up."

Zalika remained motionless, except for the shallow rise and fall of her chest as she breathed.

Meres took the girl's hands, which felt cold and clammy. Meres kneaded them. "Zalika, you must wake up now. Please."

She stirred like a child having a nightmare.

Meres rubbed her hands harder and raised her voice. "Please!"

She looked up startled at the rustling sound of feathers. The vultures had crept up closer but were startled when Meres raised her voice. They looked at Meres with hope in their tiny eyes.

Letting go of Zalika, Meres scooped up handfuls of sand and rushed at the vultures, flinging it at them. The vultures took a few hesitant steps back as the wind picked up the sand and blew it back at Meres and Zalika.

Furious, Meres prepared to rush the birds when she heard Zalika cough.

Kneeling next to her, Meres said, "Zalika?"

Groggy, the teenager opened her eyes, squinting at the bright sunlight. "What happened?"

"I don't know," Meres said. She retrieved the water container given to her by Queen Angelique's servant, removed the cap, and raised it to the girl's lips. "Take little sips."

Zalika obeyed and stopped to cough again. Looking at Meres, Zalika's voice dropped and her voice cracked with fear. "Who are you?"

Meres smiled. "I'm your Aunt Meres. I'm married to your mother's brother."

Zalika locked her gaze on Meres. "I don't have any aunts or uncles. Who are you really?"

Goddess Isis, Meres thought. *Pu never told the girls about us.*

"I'm telling the truth. My husband—your Uncle Ramose—never wanted your mother to join the royal harem. When she did, he stopped speaking to her and refused to see her."

Zalika's voice cracked, this time with suspicious. "Then why haven't I seen you?"

"It's not allowed," Meres said. "When Ramose gave up his right to meet you and your sisters—the Pharaoh's children—I lost mine, too."

Zalika shrieked in pain.

One of the vultures was trying to eat her toes.

Meres pounced toward the bird and barely missed catching it. She chased it and its friends away, yelling, "Stay away from her!"

Rage rushed through her with the intensity of a mother protecting her young.

The teenager studied Meres' face as she slowly sat up. Finally, she started to cry.

Meres knelt by her again, wrapping her arms around the girl and holding her close. "I won't let them hurt you again—I promise."

Pressing her face against Meres' shoulder, Zalika said, "Are you really who you say you are?"

"Yes. We're family. And as long as you're with me, I'll protect you."

Zalika cried harder. "They're dead! I saw them get killed!"

Meres held onto the girl tightly, taking a breath to steady herself. "Who's dead? Who did you see get killed?"

"My family! Jabari murdered them!"

Automatically, Meres said, "Jabari? That's impossible."

"I saw it happen! He shot them. I saw them covered with blood. I was hiding. He couldn't find me."

"Are you sure it was Jabari? Maybe it was someone else."

"He drove us out of the city. We were alone in the desert with him. I saw him get a gun and shoot them."

Stunned, Meres took a deep breath. She wanted to rock Zalika in her arms, but there wasn't time. Murder was the most heinous crime imaginable. Zalika had to be delirious. But if Zalika truly had witnessed the murder of her mother and sisters, it stood to reason that her life was in danger.

CHAPTER THIRTY-THREE

Pu trudged through the desert on the road to Rosetjau. She'd had nothing to eat since leaving the White Walled City and little to drink. She'd risen with the sun and lapped dew from the sagebrush and any other vegetation she could find. She kept a flat, sharp rock in one pocket and ate the juicy fruit of any cactus in her path. Her one saving grace was the bottle of sunscreen she'd slipped into her other pocket. It had been intended for the girls when they'd watched the parade.

Her legs felt as heavy as boulders. It took all of Pu's remaining strength to drag one foot forward and then the other. The thought of seeing her daughters once more and apologizing for failing them inspired her to keep moving.

The Underworld wasn't anything like what Pu had always imagined it would be. She'd pictured it as a vast, flat desert of pale white sand, soft and fine. She'd thought each hour that Ra traveled would be marked by massive gates that rose high up into the sky. She thought the monsters living in the Underworld would be fearsome, magical, and easy to recognize.

But none of that was true. The rolling and uncertain desert of the Underworld had coarse and brown sand, sometimes covered with rocks. And she'd seen no monsters here. Even Wepwawet, the guardian of the gate to the Underworld, had looked like nothing more than an oddly-colored jackal. Maybe it was because she'd been shot. Maybe this is what it felt like to be dead. Maybe it was the weakness she felt from going for days without food. Maybe she struggled to think because she'd had so little water. Or maybe it was because she'd spent days walking in the hot sun. Whatever the reason, Pu began to question what had happened to her and her children.

What if Jabari was the monster? What if the man she'd secretly loved since childhood—since the day he'd killed the crocodile attacking her—had become a monster without her realizing it?

What else could explain the ease with which he'd killed her and her daughters? How could any Black Lander commit murder, especially of someone he had once loved?

Pu shook her head. Nothing made sense anymore.

She stopped walking when she noticed a shimmering thread in the distance. *Don't get excited,* she told herself. *It's probably just an illusion, just like all the others.*

Sometimes Pu had seen wavy lines on the horizon that looked like a lake in the distance. But she'd soon realized that no matter how far she walked, she could never get closer. Finally, she'd decided there had to be some kind of cruel magic that existed only in the Underworld to torture troubled souls like her. "Don't do it," Pu said. "Don't be tempted. You'll only feel hurt again."

But maybe that was the point, to accept pain as payment for the grief she'd caused by being a traitor to her nation and placing her children in such grave danger. With a heavy sigh, Pu dragged herself toward the new illusion. But it was different this time. Instead of wavering on the horizon, a thin diagonal slice of water in the distance slowly became larger and more clear. It didn't look like a lake. She saw a thin stream flanked by great, sloping banks.

It was real.

"Thank you, Isis," Pu said as she quickened her pace, flush with new energy. Even though she'd spent nearly all of her adult life in the royal palace, she'd never given much thought to religion. She considered the paradox: she belonged to the Pharaoh—a living god. But maybe Pu felt no connection to the gods because she'd learned to take her husband—the living god—for granted. Maybe it was because she felt neglected by him. As one of the members of his harem, she often wondered if he even remembered her name. Maybe she resented the gods because she resented the Pharaoh, and he was one of them.

"Thank you, Osiris!" Pu said as she reached the high banks. Even though the river flowed far below, she could almost taste its fresh water. Step by step, she dug her heels into the sandy dirt, taking a foothold on any rock she could find. Her journey downward proved to be long and tedious, but joy flooded her heart when she knelt by the thin stream of water. With her first swallow, Pu felt her body respond like a sagging plant to a welcome rain. She splashed water on her sun-tightened arms and face, feeling immediate relief.

But Pu paused as she sensed a low rumble. The ground itself trembled beneath her. The sound of rolling thunder pierced the air, but as Pu looked up, she saw nothing but clear blue sky. She saw the wall of water in the distance, contained within the high, sloping river banks. Like the banks, the wall of water stood as high as the Temple of Our

Lady of the Absolute. Pu froze, mesmerized by the strange sight, feeling as if she were in a dream.

She saw the wall of water crashing toward her.

Pu raced up the same bank she'd descended, trying to reach the top before the water came. Just a step away from climbing up onto the desert plateau, the river swept her away.

CHAPTER THIRTY-FOUR

With Zalika leaning against her, barely able to walk, Meres led them both into the city of Annu. Buildings flanked its paved main road while homes fanned out behind.

It wasn't until Meres dragged Zalika into one of the large buildings—a healing center—that she realized how pitiful they both must look. Before they reached the front desk, a large man wearing a simple white kilt approached them from the nearest hallway. He barked orders to the receptionist at the front desk. He scooped Zalika up into his arms as if she were a jackal's pup.

Big and beefy with pale skin and close-cropped brown hair, the man's arms looked like pure muscle and bone. His furrowed brow and strained concentration convinced Meres that they'd stumbled into a safe place. His name tag read "Dave."

Meres ran to keep up with him as he raced through a maze of hallways.

"What happened to this girl?" Dave said.

"I don't know. I found her in the desert."

"How long was she there?"

"I'm not sure. At the very most, she was there for—" Meres paused. How many days had passed since the day when Ramose had been cast out of the White Walled City in a sarcophagus and into the Nile? "A day or two."

"How do you know that?"

"The last time I saw her was two days ago. She was fine."

"So you know her?"

"Yes. She's my niece."

Like a heron searching for fish in a pond, the man's gaze darted into each room they passed. Finally, he carried Zalika into an empty room, laid her gingerly on an empty bed, and disappeared.

Meres held Zalika's limp hand. The girl had lost consciousness. Zalika's hand felt cool and clammy. Her own sweat plastered her hair to her face. Meres felt anxious for Dave to come back.

He'll come back, Meres told herself as she stroked the back of Zalika's hand. I gave her water. She'll be fine.

Dave barreled back into the room with an I.V. bag on a wheeled stand. He inserted and taped the I.V. needle into the back of Zalika's other hand. "It's easy to get dehydrated out there," he said. "We'll give her some rest, let her soak up some fluids, and keep an eye on her for now. If she doesn't perk up soon, there're plenty of tests we can run. My money's on dehydration." His gaze finally drifted lightly upon Meres and his tone turned casual. "What are you girls doing here?"

Meres felt something flinch inside as she realized the Pharaoh might be looking for Zalika. "Traveling."

"Where from?"

Meres remembered Neferita, the woman whose young son had peed on the sacred statue of the Pharaoh. "Elephantine," Meres said. "My niece was recently orphaned, and I agreed to help take care of her. I traveled to her city and we lost our way on the way back to Elephantine."

"Mmm," Dave said as he stared at Meres.

Suddenly, Meres remembered why she'd come to Annu. "I'm looking for my husband—when Zalika and I lost our way, we lost him, as well. Has anyone arrived within the last day or two?"

Dave shrugged. He took one last look at the sleeping Zalika. "Don't know. I can check, but there's healing places of all kinds here. He could be at any one of them." Gently, he smoothed the hair back from Zalika's face. "You can stay here with her. I'll check back in an hour."

"Please!" Meres said, frantic with worry. "I was told my husband came here. I need to know if he's alive!"

Dave nodded. "Let me see what I can find out."

"Thank you," Meres said as Dave left the room. She pulled up a chair next to Zalika's bed, allowing herself to feel real hope at last. Zalika was safe and in good hands.

And Ramose had to be here, somewhere in Annu.

But an hour later, Dave returned with the news that although Ramose had indeed come to Annu, he had died before Meres and Zalika arrived.

CHAPTER THIRTY-FIVE

Meres drifted into the hospital room where Zalika rested in bed. Motionless, Zalika stared at the ceiling, her face still blank with grief.

Meres registered Zalika's presence but didn't acknowledge it. Meres clung to the necklace the girl had been wearing as if it were a lifeline. The world didn't feel real any more. Her vision seemed hazy, as if she were trying to see through thin linen cloth. Sounds were distant and unrecognizable. Although Meres steadied herself against the wall, she couldn't feel its texture. She couldn't even feel her feet against the floor. She seemed to be floating—not walking—into Zalika's room.

Is this what it's like when you die and your spirit separates from your physical body, Meres wondered. *When you die, is it normal to feel numb all over?*

Was this how Ramose had felt when he died yesterday?

Meres sank into a chair next to Zalika's bed, remembering the day this nightmare began. When Pu had confided her pregnancy and that news had stirred up all the deep longings that Meres tried to keep hidden. Meres ached to have children of her own, and she felt like the only woman in the White Walled City who couldn't conceive. She was a failure. A joke. A waste of time.

Meres didn't feel like a woman. She didn't feel human at all.

Becoming a mother was the only path to becoming a real woman. And until she had a child of her own, Meres felt doomed to living a useless life. Except it wasn't really living. It was simply existing.

Because Zalika looked like her mother, she also looked like Ramose.

In the most distant and secret chamber of her heart, Meres thought of Ramose as a man who could give her what she wanted. It was why she had married him—she needed a good, strong man to show their children how to become good, strong people. And she needed him to impregnate her. During the past year or so, in that secret heart chamber, Meres had wondered if she'd made a mistake by marrying him. Of course, that meant assuming that he was the reason they had no children.

What if Meres was the problem? What if she left him and married another man and still had no children? Wouldn't that prove she was barren? And if Meres had that proof, what possible reason could she find to go on living in a land that placed family and children above all else?

The truth was that the reason she'd stayed with Ramose wasn't because she loved him. She'd stayed because of her fear of what could happen if she left.

Tears streamed down her face. Her heart rumbled with a rushing sound like the distant churning of the Nile just before it flooded the farm lands every year to fertilize them with the rich, black silt that had been collecting at the bottom of the river all year long. Memories flooded Meres' mind like healing waters. Memories of Ramose. How he'd comforted her when they failed to conceive. How he'd encouraged her to work as a scribe at the temple of Our Lady of the Absolute, and how being in the presence of the home of the goddess Isis had brought solace into Meres' life. And simple memories: the way he looked at her, cooked for her, made love to her—

"Ramose," Meres whispered, realizing for the first time that she *did* love him—not as a potential father but as the friend and lover who stood by her side, day in and day out. The floodgates inside her broke open, and the secrets rushed out of her heart, leaving it clean and empty.

Comfort yourself, she remembered Ramose saying every time she lost hope of having children. What can you do to comfort yourself right now?

He's with the priests now, Meres reminded herself. It's what Dave had told her. Ramose's body was already being prepared for his journey to the Underworld. *Ramose is safe in their hands. He'll be with Osiris soon.*

It was why she had run after Ramose when he'd been put in the sarcophagus, carried out of the White Walled City, and thrown into the Nile.

It was why Meres had flung herself into the Nile, determined to follow him.

It was why she had come here to Annu after learning from Queen Angelique that her men brought Ramose to Annu for healing.

All along, Meres kept hoping Ramose still lived. But if he didn't, she would find his body and make sure he'd receive a proper burial. Without that, Ramose's spirit would be destined to wander between worlds, lost and alone. But properly mummified by priests, Ramose would journey to the Underworld until he reached the Field of Reeds and the House of Osiris. If Ramose's heart weighed light, he'd be welcomed into the land ruled by Osiris, where he could live happily forever. And there was no reason for Ramose's heart to weigh heavy. After all, he was the best man

Meres had ever known.

Meres gazed at Zalika and considered using her as a bargaining chip with the goddess Isis. If Isis appeared to Meres right now and offered to restore Ramose back to life in exchange for Zalika's death, Meres wouldn't hesitate.

I'd choose Ramose, Meres thought.

Zalika coughed.

Meres jumped to her feet and took Zalika's hand in hers, placing her other hand on the girl's forehead, feeling for a fever. Suddenly worried the goddess might have heard her thoughts, Meres said, "Are you all right?"

Zalika nodded and pointed at a pitcher of water on a bedside table.

Trembling, Meres poured a glass and helped Zalika drink.

Please, goddess Isis, Meres thought. *I have no right to offer that kind of trade. Zalika's life belongs to her and no one else.*

Flushed from coughing, Zalika looked as if she'd come to life at last.

"Where am I?" Zalika said.

"Annu. It's a place of healing."

"Are we still in the Black Land?"

Meres nodded.

"We can't go back," Zalika said. Panic broke her voice. "Jabari will kill me." She looked at Meres with the wide-eyed fear of someone who expected to be brushed aside like a silly, bauble-headed girl.

Meres still found it hard to believe Jabari had killed Pu and Zalika's sisters. But she couldn't think of any reason for Zalika to lie.

Assuming Zalika told the truth, it was no longer safe to stay in the Black Land.

CHAPTER THIRTY-SIX

"Good morning, sweetie," Mrs. Dempsey said, beaming as she pulled a tin of muffins from the oven.

Sekhmet had walked down the stairs and into the kitchen. For the past few days, she'd spent her time soaking in a cold bath to relieve the pain of her sunburn, lying down in a plump and soft bed, and sleeping. Miraculously, her red skin had faded to pale pink and was now turning brown. Mrs. Dempsey said that Black Landers were lucky. Even people as pale-skinned as Sekhmet rarely burned, and when they did, they rarely blistered or peeled.

The idea of her skin doing such a thing sickened Sekhmet. Fortunately, the turquoise dress given to her by the priests—as well as the black tattoos covering her nose and outlining her eyes—had protected much of her body. Mrs. Dempsey had seemed surprised by the tattoos, but she'd never asked Sekhmet about them.

"Come on then," Mrs. Dempsey said brightly. Her voice had a musical tone, almost as if she were singing instead of talking. "I've set a place for you at the table."

Until today, Mrs. Dempsey had brought offerings of food to Sekhmet on a portable altar that she'd rest on top of Sekhmet's bed or on the floor next to the bathtub. Here in the kitchen, two chairs flanked a large altar with legs. Sekhmet slid carefully onto one chair, grateful that her skin no longer stung.

"I figured today is a good day for blueberry muffins," Mrs. Dempsey said as she placed a basket full of them on the tabletop, along with a plateful of bacon.

Yesterday Sekhmet had eaten bacon for the first time in her life and discovered she loved it. Seeing another plateful today made her happy but even more confused. As a child, the priests in the White Walled City had used her in whatever way they liked. As an adult, they'd made her a god and treated her with respect. The victims they provided feared her.

Mrs. Dempsey was the first person Sekhmet could remember who treated her with kindness, which undermined Sekhmet's desire to kill the woman. After all, Mrs. Dempsey had fed Sekhmet well and healed the wounds inflicted upon her by Sekhmet's own father, the sun god Ra. Perhaps Mrs. Dempsey worshipped Sekhmet. She knew from the priests that everyone worshipped Ra, but he had many children who were also gods and goddesses. Any Black Lander had the freedom to choose which of Ra's children to worship in addition to the sun god.

"And we need some juice," Mrs. Dempsey said as she opened the refrigerator door.

Sekhmet seized a handful of bacon and dropped it on her plate. She chose a muffin and bit into it. The world stopped for a moment as Sekhmet discovered the taste of blueberries and muffin. She shivered in ecstasy. She'd been well fed inside her tomb, but the meals had been very basic, consisting mostly of hunks of meat. By contrast, Mrs. Dempsey gave her the kind of food that ought to be the food of the gods: spicy green beans and moussaka and red curry and lasagna and chocolate cake and pecan pie. Every day brought a new adventure in discovering how wonderful food could be.

Sometimes Sekhmet thought she could stay here forever and convince herself to forget why the priests had sent her out into the day.

"Here we go," Mrs. Dempsey said. "Some nice chilled tomato juice."

Sekhmet froze, staring at the drinking glass before her that Mrs. Dempsey had filled. "Tomato juice?" Sekhmet said.

"That's right. Don't tell me you've never tasted tomato juice either?"

Why did Mrs. Dempsey call it juice? Sekhmet knew the truth. Blood filled the glass.

The killing lust murmured in the pit of Sekhmet's belly. She looked up slowly until she met Mrs. Dempsey's gaze. "No," Sekhmet said softly. "I know its taste."

Mrs. Dempsey wolfed down a muffin as if she hadn't seen food for days. She drank from her own glass.

Sekhmet leaned back, stunned. Mrs. Dempsey drank blood! Sekhmet had never seen a mere mortal drink blood, which was her own sacred right.

Maybe it wasn't blood, after all. Maybe it just looked like blood.

Sekhmet drank, immediately recognizing the tangy taste of human blood as it danced across her tongue and down her throat. Quickly, she drained the glass, hungry for more.

Cheerfully, Mrs. Dempsey poured a new glass of blood for Sekhmet. "Thirsty this morning, aren't we?"

What kind of creature was this woman? Had she been sent by the priests to check up on Sekhmet?

Or—and Sekhmet believed this was more likely in light of the fact that Mrs. Dempsey drank blood as easily as Sekhmet herself—could she be some kind of goddess? Had Sekhmet's father sent Mrs. Dempsey to find out if Sekhmet was indeed a goddess herself and worthy of his attention?

Either way, Sekhmet realized with a certain sense of relief, it would no longer make sense to kill Mrs. Dempsey.

Instead, it was time to focus on the reason why Sekhmet had come out into the day: her mission to track down the mortal Meres and bring her back to the White Walled City for punishment.

And with any luck, the priests would allow an audience of mortals to watch, and Sekhmet would take her greatest pleasure in hearing their cries of terror.

But, taking another muffin from the basket, Sekhmet had to admit she'd miss the taste of blueberries.

CHAPTER THIRTY-SEVEN

Swept away by the towering wall of water rushing through the deep riverbed, Pu tumbled near the surface. At first, she'd been stunned. Now, she fought panic by reminding herself that she had already died and nothing else could hurt her. Still, seemingly without volition of her own, she instinctively fought to push through the surface so she could breathe.

No matter how hard she kicked or pulled with her arms, Pu proved no match for the power of the flooding river. She might as well have been a leaf carried off by the wind in a storm. As the water continued pressing against her chest, Pu exhaled the last of her air, giving in to the instinct telling her to get rid of the old air and inhale.

But the river hit a rocky outcrop, resulting in a wave that pushed Pu up into the air. She cried out, her wet hair blocking her vision. She reached out but found nothing to hold onto. She skidded across the desert floor. Gasping for air, she pushed the hair out of her face.

Winded and choking, Pu found herself several feet from the river's edge. Here, the land dipped low enough that the water crashed up and over its banks. As a result, Pu landed in the midst of a small and shallow pool, caused by other waves washing over the side of the obstruction. Pebbles, twigs, and other debris littered the bottom of the pool.

Pu placed a hand on her flat belly. She first thought of her unborn child. Little more than a week had passed since she'd suspected her pregnancy. She'd missed her monthly cycle, a tried-and-true sign. The ram-headed god Khnum had swept up a bit of fertile soil from the Black Land and placed it on his potter's wheel, shaping the body of her new child. Then Khnum placed a new spirit inside it. Her missed cycle meant that Khnum had already placed that tiny body and spirit inside Pu, even though it would still be months before her condition would be obvious to others.

Because Pu had already died, did that spell the death of this child, too—or had the child's spirit already been set free? Would she meet it when she saw her children in the House of Osiris?

With a heavy sigh, Pu rose from the shallow pool of water. Although drenched and muddy, the warmth from the sun god would dry her skin and clothes quickly.

These flooding waters must be the yearly Inundation heading to the White Walled City. There, the river would flood all the farmland surrounding the city, fertilizing it before the season of planting. And if the Nile had carried her back toward the White Walled City, that meant Pu had traveled even farther away from the House of Osiris. It could take all day just for her to return to where she'd resumed her journey through the Underworld this morning. "Osiris, help me," she said. If her body had been prepared for a proper death, plenty of amulets would have been tucked into the linen wrapped around her. "Why can't I have just one amulet to bring me luck?"

Something glinted in the water that barely covered her feet. Pu retrieved the object. It was an amulet: a djed, the symbol of the tree that had consumed Osiris's body, later cut down and carved into a column for a king's palace.

Tears of gratitude welled in Pu's eyes. Amulets were given to the dead to protect them during their journey through the Underworld. And this amulet had magically appeared at her feet. It had to be a gift from the gods. A sign of hope. A recognition that her wish to see her children one last time was worthy of granting.

Pu broke into a grin. Closing her fist around the amulet, she continued forward along the banks of the Nile, looking for the road to Rosetjau, which had to be nearby.

❧❧

Pu came upon a place where the Nile ran close to the base of a red rock mountain. Like many of the mountains in the Black Land, the mountain stood slightly higher than Pharaoh's palace, and it looked like the castles that children made when they dribbled sandy mud into high, tower-like piles: soft and rounded. A narrow path meandered between the mountain and the sharp drop into the raging waters below. The narrow path looked easy to walk.

She forged ahead with the rocky wall to her left and the Nile to her right. Water pooled in depressions around the mountain's base. Suddenly, a crocodile lunged out of a shallow pool toward her.

Screaming, Pu ran a few steps back without looking and stumbled on the path's edge, nearly falling into the river.

The crocodile hesitated, thrashing its tail back and forth while eyeballing her, as if wondering how to catch her without losing her to the Nile.

Pu's heart pounded so loudly she thought she could hear it. Since childhood, nothing had terrified her more than crocodiles.

But you're already dead, Pu told herself. *There's nothing to be afraid of.*

She knew the Underworld was a dangerous place. There were scorpions and poisonous snakes at every turn. And, apparently, there were also crocodiles. But in the Underworld, these were simply creatures to outwit and defeat. They posed no real danger to her. Not anymore.

Pu reached out and touched the mountain as she stepped back slowly, taking care to feel for the path. At the same time, she slipped the djed amulet between her teeth and the inside of her cheek, knowing she might need both hands.

The crocodile lunged again, but this time Pu scrambled up onto a round perch on the mountain, just high enough to get out of the creature's reach. She clung to natural holds with each hand, struggling to keep her balance.

As the crocodile rose on its hind legs and leaned its body against the mountain rock, just inches away, Pu stepped onto a slightly higher ledge. As she searched for a new handhold, a rock twice the size of her fist came loose in her hand.

The crocodile edged closer, snapping near her feet.

Pu froze as another wave of fear rushed through her.

You're not a little girl cornered in the garden, Pu told herself. *You don't need anyone to come and save you.*

With a sweeping motion, Pu ducked down and shoved her hand into the open mouth of the crocodile, jamming the rock to prop its mouth open.

Startled, the crocodile lost interest in Pu and shook its head, unable to dislodge the rock in its mouth.

Pu let her momentum carry her off the wall and on the other side of the frustrated crocodile. She realized its teeth had scraped her hand and arm, which were now covered with thin streams of blood. She hurried ahead to escape the crocodile, its mouth still locked open.

On the other side of the mountain base, the path opened up into the desert again. Pu froze at the sight of someone running toward her.

According to the Book of the Dead, she shouldn't encounter anyone during this part of her journey. Dangerous creatures, yes. Gods and goddesses, no.

As he came closer, she recognized him with a shock.

"Pu!" Ramose shouted as he ran toward his sister. He stopped short when he saw the blood on her arm. "By the gods," he said. "What have they done to you?"

She stared at him, drinking in every detail of how he looked. He'd lost the nemes he'd worn in the parade, but otherwise he was still dressed like Osiris, including the broadcollar similar to the one she still wore. It had been sixteen years since she'd seen him last. She realized how much she had missed him.

Overwhelmed, Pu sank to her knees and sobbed.

Pu looked up when she felt his hand on her head. He knelt beside her.

"What's wrong?" Ramose said.

Pu gazed at him, longing to embrace him and pretend they hadn't spent the past sixteen years not speaking to each other. But that was a luxury Pu had not earned.

She wrapped her arms around herself and rocked back and forth, trying to control her tears. *I'm so sorry,* she thought, unable to bear saying the words out loud. *I didn't know they killed you, too.*

CHAPTER THIRTY-EIGHT

"Tell me," Ramose said. "Why is your arm bleeding? Who hurt you?"

Calm down, Pu told herself. *I'll be destroyed by the monster-god Ammit in the House of Osiris, but Ramose will live forever in the Underworld. Along with our parents, he can take care of my daughters.*

That thought brought her solace and eased the guilt she'd felt because her children had never met him. Now, they could spend eternity with their uncle.

Wiping the tears from her face, Pu said, "It was a crocodile." When she spoke, the amulet fell onto her tongue, and she removed it.

Ramose's face flushed and he looked away in embarrassment.

He still feels bad that he did nothing when I was attacked all those years ago, Pu realized. At the same time, she knew she still faulted him for it.

"I had walked down the banks of the Nile so I could follow the river," Pu continued. "Then the flood came—the Inundation. There wasn't time for me to climb out. The river took me with it and threw me up on shore. I was coming back when a crocodile came out of nowhere."

Ramose looked at her again, brightened with curiosity. "What did you do?"

As Pu told her story, Ramose grinned. He yelped with delight when she described how she shoved the rock into the crocodile's mouth, propping it open.

Laughing, Ramose said, "I bet he lost interest in you real quick." He clapped her back enthusiastically.

Pu broke into a smile. "I can't believe I did it! One moment, I was trying to run away. This rock came loose in my hand, and all of a sudden I was tired of being scared. That rock made me feel like I could do something, instead of waiting for something to happen to me."

Ramose raised his palms toward the sky and looked up, speaking directly to the sun god above. "Thank you!" Clasping his hands together in triumph, Ramose said to Pu, "That's what I've talked about since we were kids. Taking charge of your life! When did this happen?"

"Just now. The crocodile's back there—"

Ramose threw his arms around her, holding Pu close and mussing her hair as he let go. "You're wonderful! But let's take care of that arm." Jumping to his feet, Ramose offered both hands to his sister.

It was strange for Pu. She'd spent so many years being angry and frustrated with Ramose, all the while resenting him for not protecting her. All those feelings still swirled around her, and she wasn't sure she wanted to let them go. Not just yet.

Still, Pu reminded herself, *there's not much time left. Once I reach the House of Osiris and say good-bye to my girls, I'll be destroyed.*

Taking his hands, she allowed him to help her stand.

"What's this?" Ramose took the amulet from her hand. "I think this is mine. Must have lost it." Handing it back, he said, "Keep it."

Ramose led her a few steps down the steep bank. He held onto her tightly as she dipped her arm in the Nile, letting the rushing water clean her wounds. As she let the warmth from the sun god dry her skin, Ramose tore a strip from the bottom of his linen kilt. He wrapped it around her arm, splitting one end of the strip down the middle and tying it at her wrist.

Maybe he hadn't had the courage to protect her when they were children, but he took care of her now.

Pu cleared her throat. This could be her only chance to swallow her pride and make things right with Ramose. "You were right about Pharaoh. I never should have joined his harem."

Ramose took one last look at his handiwork, patting her arm gently to make sure the bandage was firmly in place. "Why do you say that?"

"That day in the White Walled City," Pu said. This time, she glanced away from his gaze in embarrassment. That day, she'd been the one who had stood by and let him get hurt. "The day Priest Hennet had you put in the sarcophagus and thrown into the Nile, Meres was helping me. I needed to take my daughters out of the City." Pu gathered her courage, looking her brother directly in the eye. "I'm pregnant by a foreigner. I've committed treason."

"I know. Meres told me."

Pu felt as if she'd been slapped. "Meres betrayed me?"

"You know Meres—she always keeps her word. But sometimes keeping your word can spell disaster. Meres needed help. And she knew I'd want to help you."

"You?"

Ramose smiled and shrugged. "You're my sister. You're the only blood family I've got left."

Pu remembered that day in the city. There had been a moment before Ramose had been forced into the sarcophagus, a moment when it seemed as if he'd looked through the festival crowd and smiled at Pu. She'd assumed it had just been her imagination.

He'd helped her. He'd sacrificed his own life to protect her.

And it had all been for nothing.

"And it worked," Ramose said. "But where are your daughters? And what are you doing out here in the desert?"

"That's what I'm saying—you were right about Pharaoh all along. We escaped from the city, but Pharaoh had us all killed."

Ramose stared at her for a moment and then started laughing.

Horrified, Pu shouted above his laughter, "We were murdered! Just like you!"

Ramose paused, but the corners of his mouth still turned up in a smile. "No one's been murdered."

Pu crossed her arms. "Then what are we doing in the Underworld? And why are we dead?"

"We're not in the Underworld—we're still in the Black Land." Ramose mussed up her hair again. "And we're not dead."

CHAPTER THIRTY-NINE

Ramose and Pu agreed to head North and follow the Nile down-stream, away from the White Walled City. Pu insisted the Nile would lead them back to the Road to Rosetjau, which in turn would lead them to the Field of Rushes and the House of Osiris.

Ramose simply wanted to put as much distance as possible between himself and the royal city. Ever since the day he'd been locked inside a sarcophagus and thrown into the Nile, he couldn't get rid of the memory of Meres simply standing by and watching. How could he have been so stupid to believe she'd choose him over her loyalty to Isis and the other gods, which by default included the Pharaoh? Once Ramose and Meres had discovered they couldn't have children, she'd turned all the love she'd wanted to give as a mother to the gods. He'd witnessed her descent into a depth of sadness that threatened to drown her. Ramose had always believed becoming a scribe in the Temple of Our Lady of the Absolute had saved his wife's life.

In childhood, standing by and doing nothing when a crocodile attacked his sister had become the greatest shame of Ramose's life. But finding a way to reach into the depths of his wife's sadness and pull her out of it had become his greatest success. He may have failed Pu in childhood, but that failure gave him the courage and determination to save Meres. But now that Meres had chosen the gods instead of him, Ramose felt grateful that Pu had come back into his life.

They trudged along the banks of the Nile, shouting to make them-selves heard above the constant roar of the racing waters.

"But I saw Jabari shoot my daughters!" Pu said. "And I felt bullets hit my chest when he shot me. How can you possibly believe we're not dead?"

"Show me where you were shot."

"Why?"

"Just show me."

They stopped and Pu opened her dress to expose her ribs.

"Ah ha!" Excited because he knew he was right, Ramose pointed at her skin. "Look at those bruises!" He touched the small, round bruises gently. At the same time, Pu strained to see her own chest. "You've always bruised easily," Ramose said. "Something hit you all right, but you weren't shot with bullets. These are bruises, not scars."

"Impossible," Pu said. She covered herself up again. "What about the blood? It was everywhere—all over me, all over the children. Look at the blood stains on my dress!"

Ramose pointed at the red splotches on the front of her dress. "You mean that's not the way it's supposed to look?"

"No! It's blood! This is what I've been telling you all along—this is where I was shot!"

Ramose laughed again. "No, it's not."

"Of course, it is. I remember being shot!"

"But—"

"Shut up!"

Without thinking, Ramose let himself go back to the way he'd fought with his sister when they were young. "You shut up!"

"No—*you* shut up!"

His sister's frustration made him laugh again. But when her face flushed and she stared angrily ahead, Ramose vowed to reach her, the same way he'd reached Meres when she'd thrashed in sadness all those years ago.

"I'm sorry," Ramose said as he kept pace by her side. "But there aren't any holes."

Pu frowned, but she kept looking straight ahead.

"In your dress. There aren't any bullet holes."

Pu stopped abruptly, touching the red splatters on her dress. She looked up at Ramose, pale and confused.

"If you had been shot with a gun, the bullets would have gone through your dress. Bullets leave holes, and there aren't any holes or rips or tears in your dress. But the bruises on your skin match the red pattern on your dress. That means something hit you, but you weren't shot. You're bruised, but you're not dead."

Pu stared at him for a long moment.

"You're a smart girl," Ramose said. "You always have been. But your fatal flaw has always been not using that perfectly good brain inside your head when you need it most."

"But it's red," Pu said. "It's blood."

Ramose shook his head. Pointing at her dress, he said, "That's bright red. Haven't you ever seen blood after it's dried? It should be brown or rust colored. What's on your dress looks more like paint."

He leaned forward to touch and sniff her dress. "I think that's exactly what it is. Paint."

Pu examined the red spots. "You're saying I was shot with paint?"

Ramose shrugged. "Maybe. Whatever it was, that's what your daughters were shot with, too."

"You think they're alive?"

"I think we're all alive."

Pu's eyes darkened. "Or maybe you just can't accept the truth. Why would Jabari shoot us with paint? Why had he and my children vanished when I came awake in the Underworld?"

"Why would Jabari shoot you and your daughters at all?"

Pu answered with a crisp and matter-of-fact tone. "Because I'm a traitor. Why wouldn't Pharaoh's guard shoot a traitor and that traitor's offspring?"

"Because he loves you."

"That was long ago."

"Jabari still loves you—don't you know that?"

"Jabari is married and has children of his own." She dug into a pocket and pulled out the scroll, now soaked. When she opened it, she found the ink smeared and difficult to read. "Besides, everyone knows that when you die, the gods tell you that you're dead. Here's the message they gave me."

Ramose laughed and pulled a similar scroll from a pocket in his kilt. "I got one, too. Telling me my body is being mummified and giving me directions. But it's all nonsense." Taking a new tack, he said, "Wager me."

Pu pursed her lips, looking suspicious. "What?"

"We'll go to the Field of Reeds. We'll go into the House of Osiris. If you're right, you can do what you've been planning all along—say good-bye to your children. But if they aren't there, that means they're not dead, and I'm right."

"And then what?"

"I don't know yet. I guess it depends on what we find. Deal?" Ramose spit in the palm of his hand and extended it toward his sister.

Pu spit in her own palm and shook hands with Ramose. She grimaced as she wiped her hand off on her dress.

Ramose grinned. "Let's go find Osiris."

CHAPTER FORTY

After walking across the desert for two days with a teenager, Meres wondered why she had ever wanted to have children.

"I'm tired," Zalika whined. "Why can't we get some horses? I can't keep walking like this forever."

Zalika had complained constantly from the moment they'd left the city of Annu. Mostly, she said the same thing over and over again. It was as if she thought Meres hadn't heard her the first time and that repeating herself incessantly would make a difference. Or maybe it was her age—Meres had heard that teens were notoriously difficult to tolerate.

"Can we stop for awhile?"

Meres took a deep breath, reminding herself that she cared about her niece, the only family she had left in the world. "We stopped ten minutes ago."

"But it's too hot!"

It was only mid-morning, and they were already exhausted. "Drink some water."

Sighing with disgust, Zalika drained the last of her water. "I'm out. We have to go back to the Nile and get more."

Before leaving Annu, Meres had asked for directions back to the White Walled City. In case anyone came looking for Meres or Zalika, she wanted them to think they were returning to the city. In truth, Meres wasn't sure where they were. Queen Angelique had told Meres to go to that light, and Meres believed it represented her last and only hope. In the vast desert, Meres had chosen a trail that seemed to head toward the light.

The girl hadn't spoken the obvious: if Jabari had found her, he would have killed her, too. Instead, he'd carried the bodies of her sisters into the Jeep and driven away, leaving Pu's corpse behind. Once Jabari had disappeared, Zalika had panicked and run in the opposite direction, not knowing what else to do.

Now, she veered away from Meres.

"Zalika! Come back!"

Without turning to look back, Zalika waved a careless hand.

Meres had lost track of the number of times she'd recalled conversations she'd had with Pu in the past. Whenever Meres had voiced her longing to be a mother in order to feel complete, Pu had cautioned her. "It's easy to think having children is romantic. Don't get me wrong—it's rewarding. But mostly it's hard work and a lot of aggravation. Don't get lost in the romance, Meres. It's not worth it."

Finally, Meres understood what Pu had meant.

Meres dashed to catch up with Zalika, grabbing her arm and stopping the girl in her tracks. "I'm your aunt. Your job is to listen to me."

Smirking, Zalika pulled free of Meres' grasp. "I'm the Pharaoh's daughter. My father is a god. You want to get in trouble with him?"

This time, Meres dug her fingertips down to Zalika's arm bone. Zalika cried out in pain but couldn't wriggle out of Meres' grip.

"The man who killed your family is the Pharaoh's guard. Hasn't it dawned on you yet that your father is the one who ordered them to be murdered?"

Zalika blinked hard, processing this information. "I don't believe it. Why would he do that?"

Meres hesitated out of habit. She'd given her word to Pu to keep her secret. Meres had already broken her word once by telling Ramose. Was it wrong to break her word again, especially with Pu dead?

If it meant saving Zalika's life, then yes. Meres would break her word again and again to keep her niece safe. *Don't be afraid to tell the truth,* Meres told herself.

"Because your mother committed treason against him. It wasn't her intent. She fell in love with a visiting foreigner. She was carrying his baby when Jabari killed her."

"I know. She told me. Right before he shot her." Zalika's eyes brimmed with fear.

I've been too hard on her, Meres thought, surprised to hear that Pu had confided in her daughter. "Let's stop at that outcrop over there and take it easy for the rest of today."

Zalika lit up, smiling for the first time since she and Meres had met. "Really?"

"Really. We'll eat and sleep all day. We'll walk tonight, when it's cooler."

Zalika glanced up at the sky nervously. "Will it be safe? Without Ra to guide us?"

"We'll have the moon and the stars," Meres said. "And we'll have each other."

And besides, Meres thought, *that's when the beam of light connecting the great pyramid to the heavens above shines brightest.*

Even if it does lead us to evil.

CHAPTER FORTY-ONE

Sekhmet felt tired of waiting for Mrs. Dempsey and eager to get back to the desert to hunt down her prey. Sekhmet had planned to slip out in the early morning hours, but she'd overslept. Mrs. Dempsey had insisted on making a hearty late breakfast. Afterwards, she commanded Sekhmet to take one more cool bath to soothe her slightly pink skin.

After toweling off, Sekhmet dutifully smeared her skin with Aloe lotion. She had to admit she loved the way her tight skin drank in the lotion and softened.

Following Mrs. Dempsey's instructions, Sekhmet sipped tea at the kitchen table while the old woman rifled through all of her own belongings throughout the house. Sekhmet drummed her fingers on the table, wanting nothing more than to leave as she gazed out the window at the tumbleweeds rolling down the main street of the empty town.

Sekhmet nearly jumped out of her chair when the cuckoo clock on the wall opened its tiny doors and the wooden bird emerged to chirp the hour. She'd heard it every hour on the hour, day and night, and it scared her every time. She'd even learned how to wind the clock, when Mrs. Dempsey had suggested that becoming more familiar with it might help.

It felt strange, being here. About the only thing Sekhmet could remember since childhood was her tomb buried in the depths below the White Walled City, the priests, and the prey they brought from time to time for her hunting pleasure. It had been a shock to come out into the day, and especially to see her father, the sun god Ra, for the first time in her life. Days alone in the desert with nothing to eat and little to drink had left her weak. Discovering her father had burned her skin had been painful.

But as Sekhmet took another sip of tea, she realized she'd gladly do it all again if it meant spending time with Mrs. Dempsey, the only resident remaining in this lost and forgotten town. From the moment they'd met, Mrs. Dempsey had shown nothing but kindness and concern for Sekhmet.

The old woman breezed into the kitchen, her hair disheveled and her face slightly pink from exertion. She gazed at Sekhmet. "You know you're welcome to stay as long as you like. I'm the only one who lives in this abandoned town, and I wouldn't mind the company. At least, not yours." Mrs. Dempsey paused. Her face tightened as she looked out the window behind Sekhmet. "Those people threw me out like trash all those years ago, and somehow I found this old town. It's a crazy world out there, but this place is a sanctuary. I grow good food, the well never runs dry, and there's nothing as wonderful as the silence of the desert."

A lump rose in Sekhmet's throat, and she couldn't find the voice to speak.

Mrs. Dempsey looked back at Sekhmet, and the tautness that crossed her face softened. "I know. You have to be on your way. It was just a thought." As quickly as she'd come into the kitchen, Mrs. Dempsey exited to another room.

No one had ever treated Sekhmet like this before. When Sekhmet thought about her childhood and how the priests had used her, she felt ashamed of being given such care. She didn't deserve it. She was nothing. She meant nothing.

But at the same time, Sekhmet was a mighty and powerful god, daughter of the Almighty Ra, the one and true god of all the Black Land. When she thought about how she'd become a god and how the same priests who had used her now bowed down before her, being cared for by Mrs. Dempsey felt like finding fresh, cool water in the desert. Sekhmet drank in every moment she could remember of her days here. Everything Mrs. Dempsey had done for her made Sekhmet stronger.

The lump ached in Sekhmet's throat as she realized how much she'd miss Mrs. Dempsey. She calmed herself by remembering what had happened just yesterday. Mrs. Dempsey had not only served up a glass of blood to Sekhmet but had downed her own glass filled with blood! Because no human would do such a thing, Mrs. Dempsey had to be a goddess herself.

But which one?

It was a puzzling question. Mrs. Dempsey certainly wasn't Isis, because Sekhmet lived under the White Walled City, the royal city of the Pharaoh ruled by Isis. Surely, Isis wouldn't leave the city that worshipped and needed her. Besides, Isis had wings—Mrs. Dempsey didn't.

The most obvious goddess was Hathor, the goddess with the ears of a cow, the mother goddess of nurturing. Mrs. Dempsey did have unusually large ears, but it didn't make any sense that Hathor would drink blood.

Maybe, just maybe, Mrs. Dempsey could be Maat, the goddess of justice. Sekhmet knew that Maat weighed the hearts of the dead as they entered the House of Osiris to determine the worthiness of each to live in the Underworld. Those who weren't deemed worthy were destroyed forever.

Yes, Sekhmet thought. *This would explain everything. Evil has been done against the Pharaoh, and I am the arm of justice. Of course, Maat would journey from the Underworld to help me!*

"Here we are!" Mrs. Dempsey said happily as she entered the kitchen with full arms. She plopped everything she carried on top of the kitchen table and explained every item. "First, here's an old pack. It's seen better days, I'm afraid. I wish I had something nicer to give you, but at least it's functional."

Sekhmet held her cup of tea close to her chest as she watched the old woman.

Mrs. Dempsey held up two bottles: one pale green and the other white. "This is sunscreen. Put it on first thing in the morning and keep putting it on throughout the day. This is the Aloe lotion we've been using on your sunburn. Slather it all over your skin at night."

She put the bottles in the pack and held up a cap. "Always wear a hat with a brim to protect your face."

She's telling me that I must protect myself from the power of my own father, Sekhmet thought as she took a sober sip of tea. *She's telling me he'll hurt me again if I give him the chance.*

"Do you still have your sunglasses? Good. Don't forget to wear those, too."

Funny. Sekhmet wondered for a moment why Priest Hennet had given her sunglasses and nothing else to protect her. Did he think the sunglasses would make her keep her distance from her father? That they would make her fear the sun god?

Mrs. Dempsey handed a pair of white socks to Sekhmet and put several more in the pack. "Put these on your feet. And these. We should wear the same size, as far as I can tell." She gave Sekhmet a pair of white shoes.

Sekhmet quickly grasped the concept of socks, snuggling her feet into them, filled with awe at the softness—but the shoes were a challenge. Mrs. Dempsey helped her wedge her feet inside and taught Sekhmet how to tie and untie the shoelaces.

After a few moments puttering around the kitchen, Mrs. Dempsey added food and a small jug of water to the pack, followed by a folded pair of shorts and a couple of long-sleeved T-shirts. Finally, she showed Sekhmet how to use the zipper to open and close the pack and its compartments.

Mrs. Dempsey gazed at Sekhmet wistfully. "That's it, my dear."

Sekhmet nodded, drank the last of her tea, and stood.

Mrs. Dempsey smiled and opened her arms.

At a loss, Sekhmet stared at her. Was Mrs. Dempsey really Isis, after all, ready to sprout wings and reveal her true identity? Or was she simply stretching?

Mrs. Dempsey walked to Sekhmet and threw her arms around her. "It's been a pleasure having you here. Come back any time."

At first, Sekhmet felt startled by the embrace. Her first impulse was to push the old woman away. Sekhmet had never seen people embrace each other before, much less been held herself.

Mrs. Dempsey held Sekhmet close. "I'll miss you," the old woman said.

Instead of pushing her away, Sekhmet remembered how safe she had felt in this house. Gradually, Sekhmet raised her own arms and put them around the woman/goddess who had taken care of her.

CHAPTER FORTY-TWO

Pu and Ramose followed the trail deep into the Underworld. Pu was the first to spot the settlement in the distance. "Look! It's a town—maybe even a city!"

An enormous valley opened up before them. The high gray mountains marking the boundaries of foreign lands stood beyond the valley to the North and East, while the familiar rock mountains of the Black Land rose to the South and West of the valley. Unlike the red sand and gravel desert floor, dotted with cactus and other desert plants, a thin ribbon of pine trees stretched into the lush valley from the mountains. Rows of whitewashed houses and large sandstone buildings emerged from behind the strip of pine forest and throughout the entire valley.

"Thank Isis and Osiris," Ramose said. "I'm so hungry I was ready to go back and eat that crocodile you killed."

"I didn't kill it. I just shoved a rock in its mouth."

"Wedging its jaw open. It can't eat, so it's probably dead by now. We could've feasted on a royal delicacy—" Ramose paused, and the enthusiasm drained out of his voice. "But I forget. You're part of the royal family. You probably have crocodile for dinner every week."

"It's nothing special. It tastes like chicken." Pu stared at the settlement in the distance. She was still convinced they were both spirits roaming through the Underworld, despite Ramose's argument that they were still alive. Pu didn't feel alive. Watching her children murdered had shattered her heart, but she believed she knew where the pieces lay. She still believed her daughters must be safe in the Field of Reeds, watched over by Osiris himself.

If the settlement turned out to be just a town or city in the Underworld, they could ask for directions to the House of Osiris and find out how much longer their journey would take. However, that settlement might be the Field of Reeds itself. In that case, Pu's time grew short.

"There's something I need to say to you," she said, stopping in her tracks and holding onto Ramose's arm to make him stop, too. "I'm sorry about all the bad blood between us. I don't know how we came to this."

Ramose shifted from one foot to another and looked away. "It's because we're both pig-headed. It's just part of who we are, Pu."

I have to make this right, she thought. *This may be my last chance before I'm destroyed.* "I'm glad I joined Pharaoh's harem because he gave me four daughters and I love them dearly. But if I had to do it over again, I'd listen to you. You were right. Living in the royal palace was fun, but it didn't make me happy. Neither did the jewels or the dresses or being desired by every man because I belonged to Pharaoh. I would have been better off if I'd married Jabari instead."

Ramose looked at her sternly. "Look—I still say nobody's dead, but Jabari did something that makes you think he shot you. Now you're saying you'd be better off with a man who you claim shot you and your daughters. That's trading one evil for another."

"I can't believe Jabari is evil. He's one of Pharaoh's guards. He was probably just following orders."

Anger crept into Ramose's voice. "And that's not evil?"

"He was just doing what he was told."

"Would you murder someone if the Pharaoh told you to?"

"Of course not. But I'm just one of his wives."

"What difference does that make?"

"Jabari was doing his job."

"So his job is to do whatever he's told, no matter what? If Jabari kills you or your kids or anyone else, it's Jabari's fault. He's the one who pulled the trigger. He could have said no." Ramose's stomach growled loudly. Glancing ahead, he said, "Let's go."

Pu kept pace by his side as they forged ahead.

Ramose is right, she realized. *I saw no one other than Jabari, the girls, and me. He could have let us go. He could have gone with us.* Out loud, she said, "But if Jabari had disobeyed Pharaoh, we could have all been killed. Pharaoh could have sent other guards after us."

"So what? At least you would have had a chance. And Jabari would have done the right thing instead of caving in like a coward." Ramose laughed bitterly. "How heavy do you think Jabari's heart will weigh on Maat's scale of justice when *he* dies?"

Pu frowned at the puzzling question. "Jabari was doing Pharaoh's will. Pharaoh is the god who lives among us, so Jabari was doing the gods' will."

"Since when do the gods say that murder is ok?"

"I betrayed Pharaoh. If I betray Pharaoh, I betray all the gods."

"By getting pregnant?"

"By a foreigner! All foreigners are evil."

"So your baby is evil? Is that what you're saying?"

Pu placed her hand on her belly. How could a baby be evil?

"And what about the foreigner? Did he force you?"

"No," Pu said softly.

"Is he evil?"

"He's a good man. A kind man."

Gazing at his sister, Ramose softened. "You love him."

Pu nodded.

"So why would the gods sanction the murder of a woman who loved a good man?"

"I don't know."

Ramose slipped his arm around Pu's shoulders and hugged her briefly. "You're smart. Always have been. I just want you to think for yourself instead of buying into whatever nonsense they feed you in the palace."

Pu stopped, throwing her arms around his waist and holding him close. She wished she could hold onto Ramose forever and make up for all the years they'd lost by not speaking to each other. But moments later, she let go, knowing she couldn't put off the inevitable. "Hold my hand the rest of the way," Pu said. "Please."

"You're not dead. I promise."

But he held her hand anyway as they walked toward their destiny.

CHAPTER FORTY-THREE

They stopped at the edge of a wide field of papyrus plants that encircled the city like an enormous green moat. A narrow stone path cut through that moat from the desert to the city. A green wooden sign stood by the entrance like a silent sentinel. Words had been carved into the sign and painted gold. It read, "Welcome to the Field of Reeds."

"Told you so," Pu said.

"Very interesting." Ramose gazed long and hard at the sign. "Let's see what happens when we get inside."

And so they walked the stone path through the Field of Reeds. Now that Pu neared her destruction, anger flared inside her. "At least I'm glad you'll finally meet my daughters."

Ramose's jaw tightened. "Now we get to the heart of why we haven't spoken for the past sixteen years."

"My oldest wasn't even born when you wrote me out of your life."

"I'm not talking about your kids. I'm talking about the way you act. Poor Pu. Poor little girl. I wrote you out of my life because every time I try to help you, you make me out to be some kind of bully."

Pu felt as if someone had wrapped their hands around her throat, making it hard for her to talk as tears welled in her eyes. Feeling attacked, she wished she had a corner she could back into. "That's what you are. It's what you've always been."

Ramose snorted in disgust. "I have the guts to say what's true, and you find it convenient to criticize me so you'll have somewhere to hide." Ramose shook his head in frustration. "And I was so proud of you these last few days. You stood up and defended yourself against a crocodile. You told the truth about the mistakes you've made. And now you're doing what you always do. I feel sorry for your kids—between you and the Pharaoh, they have no one to look up to."

"You're horrible!" Pu sobbed. She wished she'd never seen Ramose again. She wished she could have traveled here alone.

"It's called honesty," Ramose said evenly. "Sometimes the truth hurts, but lying and pretending are a lot worse. I wish you could understand that."

They walked the rest of the stone path in silence. All the while, Pu wished for Ramose's heart to weigh heavy on Maat's scale of justice. She wanted nothing more than to see him devoured by Ammit, the horrific monster of destruction that waited hungrily by Maat's side as hearts were weighed.

The stone path continued where the Field of Reeds wound through another wide circle of farmland and finally into the city itself. The royal city of the Underworld resembled the White Walled City in many ways. The streets were laid out in a similar pattern, and they were lined with white-washed mud brick homes. City residents—the spirits of the dead—went about their business: grinding grain, washing clothes in buckets, and bustling toward the market. Young, naked children played in a shallow reflecting pool in the garden outside a nearby home.

"To the House of Osiris," Ramose said.

"What?"

He pointed to another sign with an arrow toward the street in front of them. A palace rose in the distance.

Now Pu's anger at her brother grew, along with the terror of facing her own destruction and the satisfaction of realizing her dream of seeing her children once more.

Without saying a word, they walked side by side toward the House of Osiris.

❧❧

"Name?" The receptionist looked old enough to be their mother. She wore a heavy necklace made up of several rows of vertical beads and gold scarabs, several turquoise-and-silver bracelets on her upper arms and around her wrists, and far too much makeup.

"Ramose and Pu," Ramose said.

Pu added, "My full name is Senetenpu."

The receptionist raised an eyebrow.

"It means, 'She is our sister,'" Pu said.

"I know what it means," the receptionist said coolly. "What is the family name?"

The lobby of the House of Osiris was a large room of polished white marble. Sunlight streamed in from the narrow, horizontal windows cut into the walls near the high ceiling, like a row of squinting eyes. Towering potted plants surrounded the space behind the curved wooden reception desk.

"Patrick," Ramose said.

The receptionist raised her other eyebrow.

"Ramose Patrick and Pu Patrick—we're brother and sister."

"I see." The receptionist typed at her keyboard for a few minutes and studied the monitor. Without looking up at them, she said, "You can have a seat. Someone will be with you shortly."

Dozens of plush chairs and sofas dotted the enormous waiting room. Alone in the room, Ramose plopped on a loveseat.

Someone will be with you shortly.

Pu's time was running out. She didn't want to be alone. Not now.

She eased herself on the other half of the loveseat, even though Ramose looked away as she sat down next to him. She rested her elbows on her thighs and her face in her hands. She didn't want him to see her cry any more than she wanted to see the disappointment on his face.

CHAPTER FORTY-FOUR

The wisest strategy was to follow the Nile, Mrs. Dempsey had told Sekhmet. The quickest route to death—especially in the desert—was thirst, not hunger. And following the Nile had two advantages: it was a constant supply of drinking water and a sure path to civilization, because all towns and cities depended on the Nile for their water.

Sekhmet never told Mrs. Dempsey of her mission to track down Meres and take her back to the White Walled City. Instead Sekhmet said she had lost her way while traveling.

It wasn't long before Sekhmet arrived at the Nile as it cut its way through a lone stretch of desert. It wasn't until that moment that she realized she didn't know which way to go. For a moment, panic washed through her like the churning waters of the Nile below her.

Remember who you are, Sekhmet told herself. *You're the goddess of death and destruction. You are the powerful child of the Almighty God himself. You have successfully hunted and killed every victim ever brought to your tomb.*

Gradually, her heart stopped racing and slowed to its normal beat.

All this time, Sekhmet had kept the photograph of Meres in her pocket. She pulled out the photograph and stared at it. Who was this woman? And why did Priest Hennet want to punish her?

Sekhmet stood by the river bank and sniffed the desert wind for clues. After several minutes, she gave up, smelling no trace of anything mortal.

She considered her options. If she followed the Nile to her right, it would lead her deeper into the Underworld and unknown danger. If she followed the Nile to her left, it would lead her back to the White Walled City. Sekhmet shrugged. Maybe she should give up and return to the royal city.

Sekhmet turned left.

Many hours later, she recognized the outskirts of the White Walled City. Sekhmet picked up the scent she'd detected when she'd first come out into the day from the underground catacombs.

The scent of Meres.

Sekhmet perked up. She'd wandered through the desert for many days, in addition to her time at Mrs. Dempsey's house in the deserted town.

Hunting Meres would be even more pleasurable than hunting in the stone column forest of her tomb. Sekhmet could be inventive about making her dangerous presence known without revealing herself.

It could be great fun.

Sekhmet smiled and crept far enough from the Nile so she wouldn't be seen by the city guards until she deemed it safe to walk in the open again.

A short time later, Sekhmet stumbled upon them. Still following the Nile, the scent she followed suddenly became pronounced. Pausing, she'd scanned the landscape until she saw two figures lying in the shade of a cluster of tall cactus plants nearby. Sekhmet approached slowly and quietly, circling to hide behind the plants.

It was the woman, Meres! And a younger one with her.

Sekhmet's heart sank. They were dead already.

The young one turned.

No. They were merely sleeping. They were probably hungry and had succumbed to the heat of the day. The thing to do would be to let them get a good night's sleep and then play with them in the morning when they rose.

Satisfied with her plan, Sekhmet walked ahead to where she believed the women would walk past her in the morning. A small hill rose above the Nile, and Sekhmet climbed it, finding her own shade below its highest point. Settling in as the sun began to set, she opened her pack and cried softly in delight when she discovered a plastic bag containing a few blueberry muffins.

Sinking her teeth into her new favorite food brought back memories of Mrs. Dempsey and the way she'd taken care of Sekhmet after her own father had burned her skin.

The Almighty God Ra still ignored her and kept his distance. Sekhmet still struggled between giving up on him and wanting to prove herself and gain his recognition. Why should she fight so hard to please him when he'd done nothing but hurt her—just like the priests?

For now, Sekhmet realized, all she wanted was to enjoy the taste of a blueberry muffin.

CHAPTER FORTY-FIVE

Pu had tears in her eyes as she studied the paintings on the walls of the waiting room. They were typical paintings that would decorate the walls of a tomb where a mummy would be laid to rest. There were scenes of men hunting birds among the reeds and farmers using cattle and plows to prepare their land for planting seeds. There were paintings of a feast laid out for the dead: beef and chicken, figs and grapes, nuts and honey cakes. And, of course, a series of paintings along one wall illustrated what would happen next: meeting Osiris and the Weighing of the Heart. But Pu and Ramose had been waiting so long that instead of feeling anxious, she became bored.

Ramose nudged Pu to get her attention. He pointed at a clock that hung on the wall between larger-than-life images of Isis and Osiris. "We got here at noon," Ramose said. "And it's 5:30. Let's go see if we can get some food."

Pu crossed her arms. "It's our duty to wait until the gods are ready to see us."

"It's been almost six hours, and we're the only ones waiting to see them! I'm starving—it won't hurt them to wait on us for awhile."

Pu stared at him long and hard. "Keeping them waiting could be enough to make your heart weigh heavy with sin. Do you want to be destroyed forever, too?"

Ramose snorted as he rose to his feet. "I've had enough of this—"

The receptionist's voice emerged from a loudspeaker, even though she sat behind her desk at the opposite end of the waiting room. "The gods will see you now. Please follow the green stripe into the House of Osiris."

Ramose said, "Let's go see what the gods have to say for themselves."

Pu whispered, "Blasphemer!"

Glancing around the waiting room, Ramose said, "Where's the green stripe?"

One of the painted walls slid open, revealing a narrow hallway with a pale wooden floor with a wide green stripe painted down the middle.

They followed the stripe down a long hallway. When the hallway turned sharply to the left, the pale wooden floor gave way to black carpeting. The walls and ceiling were painted black, and the only illumination came from tiny, dim lights set into the seams where the floor and walls met, stretching onward like a runway of stars into eternity. As they walked, the hallway narrowed, and the hair on Pu's arms rose. She reached for her brother's hand in the dark. When he took her hand in his, she thought she felt him tremble.

The hallway kept twisting and turning like a maze, and the darkness grew deeper with every step they took. Finally, a golden glow beckoned in the distance, and when they turned the next corner they saw a bright light at the end of the hallway.

Ramose squeezed Pu's hand.

Their eyes adjusted as they walked slowly toward the bright light. When they reached the doorway, Pu realized they had arrived at the threshold of the throne room of Osiris.

A pale golden light bathed the entire room, like late afternoon sunlight on sand. The floor and walls were painted pale yellow, and the light seemed to emanate from every surface. On the ceiling, neat rows of painted yellow stars crowded close together against an indigo background, simulating the night sky.

Two rows of three enormous columns with lotus capitals, painted the same pale yellow as the rest of the room, formed a pathway into it. The columns were covered with larger-than-life figures of the gods. Between the columns, Pu caught glimpses of paintings of fish and fowl on the floor, as well as tomb paintings on the walls, like the ones in the waiting room. It made Pu feel on the brink of rising from the floor of everyday life into the arms of the gods.

At the end of the pathway formed by the columns, the king of the Underworld sat on his throne, on a raised platform. Just as legend said, his skin was the pale green color of new growth in spring, symbolizing his return to life after death. He wore the white elongated hat that served as his crown and held his royal scepter in one hand and his flail in the other. The images of bound and gagged foreigners decorated his footrest so that when he rested his feet, he symbolically would crush those who opposed the Black Land.

His wife Isis stood behind him, dressed in a simple white sheath. The long feathers of her wings hung down from each arm.

Pu felt Ramose's grip tighten on her hand, making her feel less frightened. This was the time to stand up and face the gods with honesty and candor.

A dark figure stepped out from the shadows behind Ramose and

Pu. He had the head of a jackal and the body of a man.

Startled, Pu jumped and let out a tiny shriek of surprise. Ramose's grip tightened even more.

"Welcome to the Underworld," the jackal god Anubis said, even though his lips didn't move and his voice seemed a bit muffled. "Follow me."

Anubis walked toward the gods Isis and Osiris, dutifully followed by Pu and Ramose. As they passed the last columns that blocked their view of most of the room, they saw what flanked the raised platform.

A large but simple set of scales stood to the right of the platform. Maat, the goddess of justice, knelt next to the scales. Like Isis, she wore a simple sheath and had winged arms. But unlike Isis—who wore a crown shaped like the letter "L" to symbolize the royal throne—Maat wore a simple headband sporting a single white feather.

The monster Ammit stood on the other side of the platform. He had the head of a lion, the torso of a hippopotamus and the lower body of a crocodile. Like Anubis's strange jackal head, Ammit's entire body seemed stiff and unreal, as if he were made out of wood.

Facing Ramose, Anubis raised one hand with outstretched fingers, saying, "Ramose Patrick, long have you journeyed through the Underworld to arrive at the House of Osiris in the Field of Reeds. And now I take your heart."

With his other hand, Anubis reached into Ramose's chest. Anubis withdrew his hand and opened his fingers to reveal a heart amulet in his palm, shaped like a vessel and carved from red jasper.

Taking slow, dramatic strides, Anubis delivered the heart amulet to Maat. She placed it on one pan of the scales and took the feather from her headband and placed it on the other pan. The scales see-sawed: the feather raised higher one moment and the heart amulet higher the next. Finally, the scales came to a rest.

Ramose's heart rested in the higher pan. The feather weighed heavier than the sins he had committed over his lifetime and that were stored in his heart.

Anubis turned and held out one hand toward Ramose. "Congratulations, brother Ramose! Come and meet your new king, Osiris."

Ramose shook his head, still holding Pu's hand. "Not until you weigh my sister's heart. We'll meet Osiris together."

For a moment, Pu felt angry at Ramose's disobedience. He'd shown the same kind of disrespect toward Pharaoh when she'd first decided to join the royal harem.

"As you wish," Anubis said. This time, he walked swiftly toward Pu and thrust his hand into her chest without warning.

Pu's jaw dropped in surprise. As a child, she'd once fallen to the ground while playing on top of a tall pile of rocks, and the impact had been hard enough to knock the wind out of her. That's what Anubis's touch felt like. Even after he withdrew his hand, she still struggled to breathe.

"Pu Patrick, here lies your heart," Anubis said. It looked just like Ramose's heart.

"Wait!" Pu said, remembering why she'd decided to come here. "I wish to see my children first."

Anubis gave her a blank stare.

"They probably came here days ago. Four girls: a teenager, twins, and a toddler. They would have arrived together."

Anubis turned to face Osiris, whose face was equally blank. The jackal-headed god faced Pu again and said, "We've seen no girls like that lately."

Frantic, Pu blurted, "But I have to see them before I—"

"Never mind," Ramose said loudly, drowning her out. To Anubis, he said, "Carry on."

"No!" Pu called out. Panic-stricken, she began to run toward the gods, but Ramose caught hold of her and held on tight. Pu struggled to get free against his strong grip. "Let me go!"

Anubis handed the heart amulet to Maat, who weighed Pu's heart against the feather.

Defeated, Pu gave up her fight and collapsed in her brother's arms. *This is it,* she thought, suddenly wishing she'd done more with her life. Suddenly wishing she could go back in time and listen to her brother's advice. Suddenly wishing she had never set foot inside the royal palace in the White Walled City, even if it meant her daughters had never been born.

But they had been born, and they meant everything to her.

She whispered to Ramose, "Please find my girls and take care of them."

She closed her eyes, waiting to be devoured and destroyed forever by the monster Ammit.

A hand took hers. The hand of the monster.

Hand? Pu thought. *The monster Ammit should have paws or claws or hooves.*

"Welcome to the Underworld."

Opening her eyes, Pu discovered she held the hand of the great god Osiris himself, who had left his throne and now stood before them. Speechless, she could do nothing but gaze into his eyes.

"Your heart is lighter than a feather," Osiris said. "Welcome to eternity."

CHAPTER FORTY-SIX

After being escorted through a door at the back of the throne room, Ramose and Pu walked through another dark, maze-like hallway. They saw a heavy door labeled with a sign reading "Exit" in red lights. Ramose pushed the door open, and they both squinted as they walked outside the House of Osiris.

The door closed with a thud behind them. It had no doorknob or handle, making it impossible to get back inside. In fact, the door blended so seamlessly with the building's exterior that it nearly hid the door.

As their eyes adjusted to the bright sunshine, they took stock of their surroundings, here in the royal city of the Underworld, flanked by the Field of Reeds. They stood alone in an alley between the House of Osiris and another large building. At each end of the alley, they caught glimpses of the city, which in some ways resembled the White Walled City.

"If I didn't already know we were dead," Ramose said dryly, "I'd swear we were back home."

"Very funny." Pu stared at the red piece of paper in her hand. Anubis had given it to her as they were leaving the throne room. That paper bore an address: 3517 Luxor Lane. The jackal-headed god had told them this would be their new home in the Underworld. "I don't understand what's happening."

"First, we died," Ramose said with a tad too much enthusiasm. "Then like good little spirits, we each hiked through the world of the dead until our paths crossed. We found Osiris, got our hearts weighed to prove we lived good lives, and now we'll spend eternity in our own little bungalow on Karnak Court."

"Luxor Lane," Pu said, correcting him. "But this makes no sense. We're not dead."

Ramose succeeded in keeping a straight face. "Really?"

Pu realized she had new admiration for her brother. "You've known all along. How?"

He gave her the same smile that he'd given the moment before he'd been placed inside the sarcophagus during the parade in the White Walled City. They'd been separated by a crowd: Ramose had been in the parade and Pu had seen him moments before escaping the city with her children. He must have seen her and flashed that hint of a smile at her.

"The sarcophagus had plenty of good padding inside. There was even an oxygen mask. I got banged up and bruised, and water leaked inside so I got cold. I kept thinking that it couldn't be real. That any moment somebody would fish me out and it would turn out to be a big joke." Ramose shook his head slightly. "It was no joke."

Pu's voice cracked. "How long were you inside?"

"Most of the day, I think. Finally, I came to a slow part of the river and some fishermen guided the sarcophagus to the banks. They heard me yelling and broke it open."

"So you knew all along? That you were still alive?"

Ramose shook his head again. "It's the first question I asked when the fishermen pulled me out. But nobody would give me an answer."

"Why not?"

Ramose shrugged. "Never could find out. But they told me I'd crossed the boundary and had landed in the country of Punt. It's when they took me to their queen that I knew I was still alive."

Pu felt baffled. Leave it to Ramose to make a story more confusing by explaining it. "How?"

"Do you remember the week after Jabari saved you from the crocodile? When the Pharaoh's mother came to our house to meet you?"

"Vaguely." Pu frowned as if frowning could somehow help her sharpen her memory. "I remember Mom and Dad talking about it incessantly for years after. But mostly I remember what she wore: her silver dress and lots of jewelry and her crown. It was a hat that looked like a gold vulture with its wings flapped down to cover her ears."

Ramose laughed. "That's not what I remember. She was the prettiest woman I'd ever seen. I never forgot her face. That's why it was so easy to recognize her when I saw her again in Punt."

Pu shivered as the fine hair on her forearms stood up. "That's impossible. Queen Angelique died when we were children."

"Then how could she end up being the Queen of Punt?"

Pu rubbed her arms to chase away the willies. "It's not her. It's just someone who looks like her."

"Do you remember what happened the day she came to visit? What she gave you?"

Pu reached automatically for her earlobe. Angelique had removed diamond studs from her own ears and given them to little Pu more than thirty years ago. Pu had removed her own little girl earrings—special turquoise ankh earrings that her mother had made herself—and given them to the queen in appreciation. Pu had put the diamond studs in her ears and never removed them.

Like always, she wore them now.

"She was still wearing your earrings, Pu. The turquoise ankhs."

"No. That's impossible. I remember going to her funeral parade."

"You asked me how I knew I'm not dead. It's because I saw her. She's not the same—she's older. I called her by name. I got down on my knees. She sent all the servants away, like she didn't want anyone to know I remembered her. And I asked her: Is this the Underworld? Am I dead?"

A cool breeze swept through the shadows in the alley. Pu shivered. "What did she say?"

Ramose laughed. "She said, What do you think? She said I should see a doctor and offered to send me to Annu. I stayed in a hospital for a few days. They told me I was dead and drove me out into the desert. They said it was time for me to make my way through the Underworld, but I knew they were lying."

Pu pinched herself. She still felt alive.

"Think about it, Pu. The Pharaoh was a teenager when his father died. By law, he should have taken over the Black Land, even though he was a boy. But Angelique took the law into her own hands and made herself Pharaoh. The priests said she died in her sleep, but nobody ever saw her body. All we saw was the sarcophagus they said she was in when they carried it in the funeral parade."

"What are you saying?"

Suddenly, Ramose's eyes glazed over and he looked over Pu's shoulder.

"Ramose? What's wrong?"

His eyes darkened. "I know that woman."

Pu turned and saw a petite woman kneeling at one end of the alley, gathering something she had dropped and oblivious to the world around her.

"By Isis and Osiris," Ramose said. "That's Neferita."

Chapter Forty-Seven

Pu stared at the petite woman kneeling at the end of the alley. "If she's a friend of yours?"

"She's no friend," Ramose said under his breath. "She came from Elephantine. Meres caught her little boy peeing on a statute of the Pharaoh, and Priest Hennet decided it would do the woman good to stay with us and put her son in the orphanage for a few days." Ramose shook his head in disgust. "In hindsight, I think they used her to spy on us, and through us, to spy on you."

Pu's heart sank. She should have known that asking Meres for help would put her and Ramose at risk, too. "What is she doing here?"

"That's a very good question."

When Neferita finished gathering everything she'd dropped, she stood and walked away.

Ramose ran quietly down the alley with Pu on his heels. Where the alley met the street, they peered around the corner and wove themselves among the dozens of other pedestrians and followed Neferita. She walked another block and turned right.

Ramose and Pu kept a casual pace and took the same right turn into a narrow alley filled with lines of fresh laundry: men's kilts and women's sheath dresses—ranging from white to turquoise to coral—hung from horizontal ropes strung between two stone buildings. The alley was empty of people, and the rows of laundry facing them swelled in the wind like ocean waves.

They ducked under lines and between the clothes until they saw Neferita sitting alone with her back to them in a small courtyard where the alley ended. She muttered, swearing under her breath, as she hunched over her work.

Ramose and Pu stepped through the curtain formed by the last row of laundry. "Hello, Neferita," Ramose said.

Startled, she jumped to her feet and spun to face them. A man's kilt fell onto the ground from her lap. Neferita's eyes widened in surprise as she recognized Ramose.

He smiled. "Fancy meeting you in the Underworld."

❧❧

"Yes," Neferita stuttered. "I'm sorry to see you've died." She paused, as if calculating her next move. "And I'm happy to see you've arrived safely from your journey."

"The last time I saw you, you were with my wife. Before the parade. What happened? How did you die?"

"Crocodile," Neferita said very quickly. "I was attacked by a crocodile when I left the White Walled City to go back home to Elephantine."

Ramose stepped forward slowly and picked up the kilt that Neferita had dropped. He examined it for a few moments, raising it so Pu could see what he had discovered.

Green. She saw a pale green smudge on the white kilt.

Pu frowned. "That's the same shade of green as Osiris's skin."

Ramose handed the kilt to his sister. "The pale green of new spring growth."

Pu took the cloth in hand and studied the smudge. Suddenly, she felt light-headed with disbelief. She looked up at Ramose. "It's makeup. Green makeup."

He nodded, not surprised. To Neferita, he said, "Why don't you try telling the truth this time?"

Neferita glanced nervously around the courtyard. They were surrounded by high walls. The only route of escape was the alley beyond Ramose.

"There's nothing to be afraid of," Ramose said. "We're all dead. Our hearts have been weighed. And we'll be living happily here in the Underworld for the rest of eternity." He paused for a beat. "We might as well be friends."

Neferita eyed Pu nervously. "Who's she?"

"My sister."

Neferita stared blankly at them for a moment. All the color drained from her face.

"That's right," Ramose said smoothly. "She's Pu, member of the royal harem. Accused of treason." Ramose gave Neferita a hard smile. "But that's all over now. Like I said, we're all dead here. None of us can do any more harm than we've already done. So why not make a fresh start?" He took one step closer to Neferita.

Her legs buckled in fear and she sank onto a nearby bench. She spoke fast, as if she were reasoning out loud. "My son—the priests promised to take care of him. He'll be a priest himself one day. It's the best thing that ever could have happened for him."

Pu stifled her anger. This woman's son lived when Pu still wondered if all of her daughters had been murdered. But Pu knew how to talk to a fellow mother. Gently, she said, "Your son's with the priests in the White Walled City?"

Neferita nodded, now hugging herself as she rocked back and forth.

"There's nothing we can do to change that," Pu continued. "He's in the world of the living, and we're in the world of the dead. We have no say in his world."

"Sekhmet," Neferita said. "She's the one who killed me."

Ramose's eyes crinkled in puzzlement. "Sekhmet?"

Pu laid her hand on Ramose's arm. "She's real. I've never seen her, but Jabari has."

A distant look replaced the puzzlement in Ramose's eyes. "I know. He told me."

Pu saw the same look in Neferita's eyes as she kept rocking back and forth on the bench. "Priest Hennet took me under the city and into an underground temple. It was full of stone columns, hundreds of them. And she stalked me for hours and hours until she finally gave mercy and killed me. When I woke up, I was covered in blood." Neferita looked up at Ramose. "And Priest Hennet told me I was dead."

Ramose and Neferita were each told they were dead by someone in authority, Pu realized. Someone you wouldn't think to question.

"Did you walk through the desert?" Ramose said.

"No," Neferita said. "One of the priests drove me here."

"They drove you?" Pu said, outraged. "I had to watch my children die and woke up alone and walked for days by myself in the desert... and you got a ride?"

She felt Ramose slip a firm arm around her shoulders. "We're all here now—that's all that matters."

Neferita stopped rocking. She stared at Pu. "You saw your children die?"

Pu pushed her anger down deep in her belly. It would keep. For now, there were more important things to do than just be angry.

Pu held up the kilt with the pale green makeup stain. "What do you know about this?"

But now Neferita gazed at Pu with compassion. "It must have been hard. To watch your children die."

For a moment, Pu saw her as just another mother. Only another mother could really understand. "Yes," Pu said softly. "It was horrible."

Neferita nodded and answered Pu's question. "Priest Hennet said he'd give me a very special job here, as a reward."

A reward for spying on Ramose and Meres, Pu thought. *A reward for identifying me as a traitor to Pharaoh and all the Black Land.*

Neferita continued, oblivious. "I work for the gods. I help to keep everything they need clean and in order. Even the wings."

"Wings?" Ramose said.

Neferita nodded and smiled with pride. "The wings that the goddesses wear. I take care of them when they don't need them."

"Where are they?" Ramose paused and softened his tone. "We'd be honored to see the vestments of the gods."

Since when? Pu wondered, turning her gaze to him in curiosity.

Neferita recoiled, shaking her head like a little girl. "My duty is to keep them safe."

Ramose gave her his most charming smile. "Then you must be very important."

Sly dog! Pu thought. *What are you up to?*

Neferita relaxed and took the bait. "I'm not so important. Mostly, I just do laundry."

"Which makes you a servant of the most important gods," Ramose said. "You might as well be handmaiden to Osiris! But my sister and me—we've just met him and will probably never see him again for the rest of eternity."

"But I believe there are festivals here in the Underworld," Neferita said. "Surely the gods will come out of the House of Osiris on those days."

Ramose shrugged. "So we'll see them from a distance. Here's our one chance to see their vestments up close one more time, and you're denying us? Despite being a guest in my home and betraying me and my wife?"

Neferita's lower lip trembled. "You betrayed the Pharaoh."

"No," Ramose said softly. "I protected my sister from him. Isn't that like what you did? Sacrificing yourself so your son can live and have a good life?"

"That's what they told me I was doing." Neferita stared into empty space, the wheels in her head clearly turning again. "But why? All my little boy did was pee on a statue."

"A statue of the Pharaoh," Ramose said. "That's a crime as serious as treason."

"But he didn't mean any harm!"

"Neither did I," Pu said.

Neferita stared at them long and hard. Finally, she said, "Follow me."

As Neferita began to lead them out of the alley, Ramose reached out to Pu, grabbed her necklace, and jerked it off. He took his own

ging her feet through the sand, Zalika said, "Are we there yet?"

"I don't think so." Meres led the way on the trail as it wound around the base of a rock mountain and up a sharp hill. As she reached the top, the sight of a road startled her.

Zalika trudged up the hill to catch up. Once Zalika reached Meres' side, she jumped in surprise. "What's that?"

"I think we've just crossed the border. We're not in the Black Land anymore."

"We're in a foreign country? Just like that?"

"I think so."

"Which one?"

"I'm not sure." A few foreign countries surrounded the Black Land.

Zalika paced nervously. "Why should it matter? All foreigners are evil. We're going to die."

Meres took a deep breath. The same thoughts had been running through her mind, and she'd been trying to calm herself.

"I want to go home." Zalika turned and headed down the hill.

Meres caught Zalika by the arm. "Your home is with me now."

Zalika yanked herself free.

"I'm sorry about everything that's happened to you," Meres said. "But you're not going back to the Black Land. I won't let Jabari kill you, too."

Zalika's body shook as she sobbed, and Meres held her close. Sometime later, Meres took her by the hand and turned to lead the way into foreign territory.

Suddenly, two beams of horizontal light cut through the fading night and swept across them.

"Who is that?" Zalika whispered.

"I don't know," Meres said. "I think it's a foreigner."

They watched as the car parked in front of them. A man in a blue uniform emerged and walked toward them. "I can take you to the light."

Terrified, Meres stood in front of Zalika to protect her.

The man smiled. "I thought you people believed that everyone's family. Men and women are brothers and sisters."

"But you—"

"I'm an evil foreigner?" The man laughed. "I'm not as foreign as you think. There's family waiting for you at the light." Walking back to the car, he opened the door to the back seat. "Trust me. The walk's a lot longer than it looks. I can get you there faster."

The man's eyes looked true and gentle. Meres decided to trust him and led Zalika into the car.

As they drove away, the man picked up a cell phone, dialed, and spoke into it. "Tell Bruce she made it. We'll be there in about half an hour."

Chapter Forty-Nine

Sekhmet woke up with the dawn. Even though it had been many days since she'd ventured forth into the day from the White Walled City, she felt disoriented and alarmed every morning. She felt strange, as if she were coming alive inside a dream. The light inside her tomb was always dim and never changed. The air was always cool and comfortable. She was used to feeling cradled by the slim interior of her sarcophagus where she slept. She was used to a world of stone.

Just like every morning she'd come awake in the desert, Sekhmet regained her consciousness with a start, as if she were the one being stalked. Before becoming fully alert, she jumped onto her hands and knees, lips snarled, ready for a fight. The dry heat that chapped her lips felt alien. It always took a few minutes for Sekhmet to realize where she was and what she was doing there. She'd sit on the desert floor and think about food.

It had been different when she'd stayed at Mrs. Dempsey's house. The first two nights, Sekhmet had drifted asleep in the white bathtub in a few inches of cool water to ease her burning skin. It felt like being back inside her own sarcophagus. After that, Sekhmet had slept between crisp, clean sheets on a soft bed. It had been a strange sensation at first—sleeping on a soft surface—but Sekhmet had felt so drained that the bed offered a welcome sanctuary.

But now she slept out in the open again, and that made her feel alone in the world.

Sekhmet shook her mane of blonde dreadlocks, stretched, and yawned herself awake. Her father had not risen above the horizon yet, but early morning light announced his approaching arrival.

Her stomach growled, and Sekhmet covered it with her arms, remembering her mission. She'd found her prey at last, now ready to stalk and kill the woman.

Slipping on her pack, Sekhmet crawled behind the underbrush toward where the women slept.

They were gone.

Sekhmet stepped out into the open.

They'd been here last night—Sekhmet was sure of it.

She found evidence of their presence: scuff marks in the hard sand where they'd slept and walked.

In one breath, Sekhmet berated herself for letting them get away. In the next breath, she saw this as an opportunity to prove her herself as a keen and fierce huntress and worthy of being recognized as the Almighty Ra's goddess daughter.

Studying the landscape and direction in which the scuff marks led, she couldn't tell how long it would take to catch up with them. Taking off her pack, Sekhmet sank to the ground. It would be wise to fill up her stomach before beginning today's trek. She still had plenty of food, but when she pulled out the last blueberry muffin, Sekhmet felt caught off guard when tears welled in her eyes.

"By the great god Osiris," she said harshly to herself. "It's only a muffin."

And yet she had to eat slowly because of the lump that kept rising in her throat.

⁊⁊

In the back seat of the car, Meres and Zalika held hands. For the first half of the journey, they were surrounded by the desert landscape they'd always known. Eventually, they came to a foreign civilization, where hundreds of homes surrounded by walls lined the road, although none of the walls rose as high as those around the White Walled City.

Meres stared in wonder as they passed block after block of neat houses, none of them made of white-washed mud bricks like the houses in the White Walled City. Instead, they were as beautiful as the homes of priests and administrators. Instead of dirt roads, every street was paved. Instead of traveling by foot, the streets were full of the kind of vehicles used by high officials.

Surely, this must be the royal city of whatever foreign country they had stumbled into.

But why were these foreigners so willing to escort Meres and Zalika to the light they were seeking?

"Who are you?" Meres asked.

He met her gaze by glancing in the rear-view mirror. "Officer Carl Rodriguez, Ma'am."

"I don't understand what's happening. You seem to know—" Meres stopped talking when Zalika tugged her hand. Her face pale with fear, Zalika shook her head, silently begging Meres to say no more.

"Like I said, Ma'am, we're all brothers and sisters here. I'm taking you to folks who can explain it better than me. It's best for you to just sit back and wait to meet them. They'll take real good care of you. I promise."

Zalika shuddered.

Meres gave Zalika's hand a reassuring squeeze. "Officer Carl Rodriguez?"

"Ma'am?"

"Don't be afraid to tell the truth. It will make you free."

This time, his eyes crinkled when he glanced in the rear-view mirror, as if he were grinning. "I have to agree with you there, Ma'am. But like I said, there's other people who are better at doing it than me."

All the while, the fading vertical beam of light grew closer.

Meres sat up sharply as they turned south onto a great roadway with many lanes of vehicles. After several minutes they turned east onto another great roadway lined with tall buildings. But within the next few minutes Meres and Zalika encountered a world that shocked them both.

Brightly lit palaces loomed ahead in a city made for the gods themselves.

Zalika closed her eyes and clung to Meres.

Officer Rodriguez entered a small road parallel to the avenue of great palaces, through the opening at the base of a great Sphinx, and stopped his car at the front entrance of a great black pyramid, towering high toward the sky.

A powerful beam of light shot up from the pyramid's cap into the sky above, while bits of white light crawled up and down its corners.

Officer Rodriguez parked, opened the back door, and helped Meres and Zalika step out. Men wearing black shorts and bright yellow jackets stood on each side of the driveway. Up ahead, one of the men used a long-handled roller to apply fresh amber paint to a long, narrow bump that bisected the driveway. In front of the pyramid, a few people waited with large bags by a section marked off with black rope. A long white vehicle waited nearby.

Holding Zalika by the hand, Meres took a few cautious steps out from underneath the Sphinx. It rose, high above the dozens of hundred-foot high palm trees that flanked it, and the great black pyramid rose far higher above the Sphinx. With its back to the great pyramid, the Sphinx faced the Almighty sun god Ra as his golden glow peeked above the horizon, greeting the god and the giant obelisk between them.

A cool breeze blew in the quiet morning, and a passing vehicle in the air above broke the silence with a chopping sound. Small gardens of flowering pink and red flowers, shrubs, and benches lined the pyramid's base. Like the giant black snake Apophis, a strange long vehicle slid silently on tracks high above the ground in the distance, disappearing into a palace called Mandalay Bay. Meres gasped when she saw it: a fantastic, great palace that shimmered like gold in Ra's light. Beyond that palace lay a vast, empty space of concrete and desert and far-away mountains.

"Thank you, Carl."

Meres turned to see a woman dressed in a simple white sheath standing on the sidewalk behind them. Feathered wings hung from the woman's arms.

He smiled. "We'll keep patrolling, just in case there's more coming."

The winged woman smiled at him.

Weeping in terror, Zalika dropped to her knees.

But Meres kept standing. Meres had seen Isis's face on statues and paintings every day in the temple. She knew every detail of the goddess's face. "Stand up, Zalika," Meres said. "This isn't Isis. Or Maat. Or any kind of goddess."

"You're safe now," the winged woman said. "No one can hurt you here."

"I don't understand," Meres said as she helped her trembling niece to her feet. She looked up and realized that when the sun god came forth to begin a new day, the light connecting the great pyramid to the sky vanished. "Where are we?"

The woman who wasn't Isis smiled. "Welcome to Las Vegas."

Chapter Fifty

"What?" Meres said.

"Las Vegas," the winged woman said. "It's in Nevada."

Zalika piped in. "Nevada is an evil country full of sinners. Everybody knows that."

"That's not true," the winged woman said. "It's just what you've been taught to believe."

Still standing in front of the great pyramid, more foreigners circled around them, most dressed in shorts and T-shirts. But neither the men nor women wore kohl lines on their faces to elongate their eyebrows or underline eyes. Foreign men wore no makeup at all, while the women wore colors on their eyelids and cheeks and lips, as well as thick black eyelashes.

Ever since they'd arrived, foreigners had been staring at Meres and Zalika. Their uninvited gazes made Meres uneasy. To the winged woman, she said, "Can we go somewhere else?"

A man shouted as he emerged from the great pyramid and ran toward them. "You're here!" His face lit with joy, but when he reached the women, that joy evaporated. "Where's Pu?"

"She's dead!" Zalika yelled, launching herself forward and pummeling the man with her fists. "They murdered her and my sisters!"

"No," the man said. "How can Pu be dead?"

"Because of you!" Zalika cried, hitting him harder.

He's the one, Meres realized. She studied his face. His eyes were narrow, his hair black and straight, and his skin had a yellow cast.

Many races lived in the Black Land: black and brown and white. But Meres had never seen anyone like this man before. He had to be the father of Pu's unborn child. Pu had insisted that the father's difference from all other Black Landers would show up in her child. Everyone would see by looking at the child that the Pharaoh could not be the father—and that Pu had committed treason.

The winged woman tried to intercede, but Meres stepped between her and Zalika. "Let them be," Meres told the winged woman. "He deserves it."

The winged woman looked from Meres to the man and back again.

The man caught Zalika's fists in his hands. "You're the oldest—you're Zalika. Let me help you. I'll keep you safe. No one will ever hurt you—"

Wrenching one hand free, Zalika slapped him hard across the face.

Someone in the growing crowd around them gasped.

The winged woman said, "Let's go inside," and herded them all into the great pyramid. They walked through one of many doors at the opening of its base, where the air became cold. Meres gawked at the interior of the pyramid as it rose high above them. The interior seemed to be one great, vast space. To their right, a winding line of people waited to approach an impossibly long counter. Endless rows of hundreds and thousands of machines of lights and music filled the pyramid's interior.

Meres held Zalika close as they walked. She looked up sharply when the man spoke to her.

"I'm Bruce Wong. I've been expecting Pu—and her daughters, of course—since last week." He hesitated. "I'm sorry. I don't know who you are."

Meres ignored him, holding on tightly to Zalika as they walked through the strange building. Palm trees grew inside the pyramid. A few people were scattered among the machines and sitting in front of them. Another handful of people sat around one of many tables jammed next to each other in a small space. Others simply walked past, dragging bags rolling on tiny wheels.

And then Meres saw her up ahead, walking across the room.

She wore black pants and a blue shirt, like a man, but she walked on high heels. In her forties, she looked fit and trim with brown skin and long black hair tied at the nape of her neck. She walked quickly, as if she really wanted to run but it wasn't allowed.

But Meres wasn't afraid of rules against running. Taking Zalika by the hand, Meres sprinted toward the woman ahead. When they reached her, Meres knelt, pulling Zalika down to the floor with her. "Isis, help us!"

Startled, the woman took a step back. She turned and walked away, deeper into the rows of machines of lights and music.

Meres didn't understand why the goddess would behave like this, but she didn't care. Again, pulling Zalika along, Meres rose and chased after the goddess until she caught up with her. "I know you," Meres said.

The woman stared straight ahead as she kept walking.

Meres and Zalika kept pace. "And you know me. I'm the scribe at your temple in the White Walled City. I see your face every day. I'd recognize you anywhere."

The winged woman caught up. "Please," she said to Meres. "Come with me."

Meres shook her head. "Not until my goddess tells me what she's doing here in this gods-forsaken foreign land."

Finally, the woman stopped and acknowledged them. "I'm not a goddess. I'm—"

"Look!" Zalika pointed at something pinned on the woman's chest. "She's wearing her name!"

It was a black name tag that read "Isis."

Meres dropped to her knees again. "Isis, help us. I pray to you."

Isis rolled her eyes and shot an accusing look at the winged woman. "I've got to get to my table before my shift starts." Again, Isis walked away.

This time, they all followed: Meres, Zalika, the winged woman, and Bruce.

"Please," the winged woman said. "There's been an incident."

"It's your job to handle the fallout from that freak show, not mine," Isis said, still walking. "I've worked too hard to become a dealer."

"Don't worry about coverage," Bruce said. "I'll find someone to work your shift. I'll make it worth your while if you take today off and help us."

Isis snorted and kept walking. "Asking me to put my job at risk..."

"Wait," Bruce said, pulling cash out of his wallet and holding it up for Isis to see. "Here's a thousand dollars. I'll talk to Jack. I've got seniority over the pit bosses. Your job is safe."

Isis stopped short and snatched the bills from his hand, giving them a once-over before stuffing them in her pants pocket. "All right, but let me do it my way. You and the fake goddess stay out of it."

Crestfallen, the winged woman said, "The Hathor Room is set up. I'll alert everyone in the back of the house."

"We're not going back of house. Not yet." Isis removed her nametag and shoved it in her pocket, next to the cash. "That's where you people always go wrong. They're not ready, unless you want to traumatize them even more than they already have been."

Bruce answered his ringing cell phone, covering his other ear with his hand as he turned away.

The winged woman said, "But there could be someone they know."

"What?" Meres said. "How could someone we know be here?"

"Sometimes death is just a coverup," the winged woman said. "Just because you've been told someone is dead doesn't mean they are."

Zalika clung to Meres. "Mama," Zalika whispered.

Isis crossed her arms. "I'm telling you they're not ready."

"My husband was put in a sarcophagus and thrown into the Nile," Meres said, wrapping her arm around Zalika's shoulders. Meres didn't want the girl to be hurt any more than she already had been. But people often thought they were being kind when they were actually too afraid to say the truth. Zalika needed to know the truth as much as Meres. "Zalika saw her mother and sisters murdered. They can't still be alive. It's impossible."

"See?" the winged woman said to Isis. "They've got to find out—" She stopped abruptly and said to Meres, "Nobody gets murdered in the Black Land. They're too crafty to let that happen."

"But I saw it with my own eyes," Zalika said. "I saw them shot and killed."

Pocketing his cell phone, Bruce leaned in toward Isis and said, "Something's come up. Keep me posted."

As he hurried away, Isis glared at the winged woman. "If you want my help, you've got it. But if you want to do this yourself, then let me go."

The winged woman argued, "Of course we need your help. I'm just saying—"

"That's the problem," Isis said. "Either take care of this yourself or get out of my way."

Taking Zalika by the hand, Meres walked to the nearest craps table and climbed on top of it. Zalika scrambled up next to Meres' side, and Meres wrapped both arms around the girl. At the top of her voice, Meres yelled, "I want to talk to my goddess!"

For a few moments, everyone standing nearby stared up at Meres and Zalika.

"See what you've done!" Isis said to the winged woman.

The winged woman, like everyone else, simply stared at Meres and Zalika.

Angry, Isis turned her back on the winged woman and headed toward the craps table. Looking up at Meres, she said, "Let's go to the Hathor Room, and we can talk as much as you want."

"No." Meres held on tight to Zalika, not budging from where they stood on the tabletop. "I want to see that place she talked about. Where she said there might be people we know."

Isis gazed long and hard at Meres. "He won't be there—your husband. Just like her mother and sisters won't be there. You're the first new people we've seen in a long time."

Meres' heart suddenly felt like a hard lump weighing heavy in her chest. The goddess's eyes were clear and full of truth. "We need to see for ourselves," Meres said.

Isis sighed. Finally, she offered a helping hand up toward Meres. "All right. But don't say I didn't warn you."

CHAPTER FIFTY-ONE

Isis led them to a wall and a set of doors reading "Authorized Personnel Only." Once through the doors, Meres and Zalika followed Isis down a hallway and a short flight of stairs. "This level is for employees," Isis said. "There are four thousand of us at this hotel alone."

Meres and Zalika held hands as they walked through a maze of hallways, but Meres couldn't tell which of them was more scared. Meres fought the constant temptation to cling to Isis as if she were their mother.

The underground level of the pyramid bustled with life. Men and women walked in and out of rooms. Many of them noticed Meres and Zalika, stopping abruptly to stare at them.

"Hey, Isis!" A man's voice called out.

Meres felt her heart skip a beat, hoping to see Ramose.

It had been in Annu that the same doctor who'd treated Zalika had checked nearby hospitals for Ramose. Zalika's doctor had learned Ramose had died the day before and his body had been sent to the priests who prepared it for burial. But what if the doctor had been wrong? What if he'd learned about another man named Ramose? What if someone else had died, not her husband? What if Ramose was still alive?

A short, squat man walked toward them. "Who are they?" he asked, eyes sparkling with excitement.

"Not now," Isis said. "We're not ready to announce them yet. They've just come out of the desert—they don't know anything yet."

Oblivious to her words, the man's eyes widened. "That's Tarahk's girl. She has to be." Making an abrupt about-face, he hurried away.

"That's not my Mama's name," Zalika said to Meres, as if they were the only people in the room.

Meres understood. For all they knew, this was an elaborate trick set up by evil foreigners determined to get information from them about the Pharaoh. They'd been warned all their lives to never trust foreigners.

But as Meres looked into the eyes of the faces surrounding them, she realized she felt safe. For the first time, she wondered why foreigners would want to question her. Even though Meres worked as the scribe of the most important temple in the Black Land, her breadth of information covered only the religious holidays and festivals they celebrated.

Zalika was a royal princess among dozens. Zalika may have lived in the royal palace, but she rarely saw her father. Pu had once admitted that Zalika had never spent any time alone with him. The Pharaoh treated all his children the same way he treated his harem: as possessions. Zalika probably had never seen or heard anything that could be of value to foreigners. And if Meres and Zalika—two of the most famous people in the Black Land—knew so little, wouldn't that mean that most people knew nothing of value?

So why had they all been warned since birth of the dangers of speaking to foreigners?

Meres wanted to talk to the people surrounding them but still felt bound by fear. To Isis, she whispered, "That man—he's wrong. Zalika's mother's name is Pu."

But Isis pressed forward, ignoring Meres. "You must be hungry. They feed us for free here. Come with me to the cafeteria, and we'll get something for you and the girl."

They followed Isis into a great room with many tables and chairs and then into a greater room with many food stations. Meres' stomach rumbled. To Zalika, she said, "Do you want anything?"

Zalika shook her head.

Taking Zalika by the hand, Meres led them slowly around the food arena, seeing no sign of Pu. Meres led them back out of the cafeteria and looked for another place to explore.

"Wait!" Isis called out, catching up with them. "You can't just wander around—"

"Show us," Meres said. "Show us everywhere that Pu could be."

Isis took them to the dry cleaning shop, where employees picked up and dropped off their uniforms each day. Next, they went into the women's dressing room. She took them to the bank of information stands, the monitors where employees accessed human resource details. Finally, she took them to the dealer's lounge, a room with a big-screen TV, walls of lockers, and tables and chairs where the dealers who stood on their feet forty minutes out of every hour could sit and relax. Right now, a handful of dealers in black pants and blue shirts played gin rummy at a small round table.

"This is all there is to see," Isis said. She pointed at a closed door down the hallway. "There's a meeting room down there. Let's go there, and I'll tell you everything you want to know."

Meres wondered if Isis was right, if she and Zalika should trust the goddess and do whatever she said.

But at the same time, something held Meres back. She felt a strange sensation, as if someone invisible held her hand and told her to stay just a moment longer.

Zalika turned slowly in place, studying every face in the room. She looked pale and drawn and hopeless. "Where is she?"

The short, squat man plowed his way into the room, followed by a man and woman in their fifties. "Great gods," the man said as the woman stood by his side, her mouth agape. "It's Meres!"

The man ran at her so fast that Meres didn't have time to react. Suddenly, she felt his arms holding her so close that she gasped for air, feeling as if he'd squeezed it all out of her lungs.

Whooping with joy, he lifted her off the ground and spun in circles. "I knew we'd see you again!" Stopping abruptly, he lifted Meres up above his head, as if she were a little girl. Her head nearly brushed the ceiling.

Dizzy and discombobulated, Meres stared down at the white-haired man holding her up toward the gods. Startled, she realized something about him looked familiar.

He lowered her slowly to the ground and embraced her again, more gently this time. "That's my good girl," he said. "I'm so proud of you."

"She doesn't remember you, Tarahk."

When Tarahk let go of Meres, she felt as if something knocked the air out of her lungs again. The woman who had entered the room with Tarahk now stood within arm's reach. And she looked so much like Meres that Meres might as well have been looking into a mirror showing how she'd look twenty years from now.

"I'm Dendera," the woman who looked like Meres said.

Tarahk clapped Meres hard on the back. To Dendera, he said, "Meres knows who you are!"

"I don't think so," Dendera said softly. "It's been too long since she's seen us." To Meres, she said, "You don't remember us, do you, Honey?"

Meres stared at the woman who looked like her but wasn't. The world turned inside out, and Meres felt like she had fallen from the Black Land and up into the sky, now tumbling among all the stars out in space, lost and alone. Still breathless, Meres shook her head.

Dendera smiled, but tears welled in her eyes. "We're your parents, Honey. We're your mom and dad."

CHAPTER FIFTY-TWO

In the Hathor Room, Meres insisted on sitting between Isis and Zalika. Tarahk and Dendera sat on the opposite side of the table. Zalika tackled a plate full of bacon and eggs. Isis filled her plate for the third time, inhaling food as if she'd never seen it before.

A single croissant lay centered, untouched, on Meres' plate. She studied Tarahk and Dendera carefully. "They told me you were dead."

"Bastards!" Tarahk said. He leaned back, crossing his arms. "Those pricks destroyed our lives. Every day we wanted to come back for you, but—" Tarahk's face tensed and he clenched his fists. "But we couldn't risk it."

His words made Meres feel hurt and angry. A question that had been nagging the back of her mind finally surfaced. Why had her own parents left her behind? What kind of people would abandon their own child and let her grow up in an orphanage? Meres spoke, her voice soft and distant. "Why?"

"Because they threatened mass murder," Tarahk said, his voice breaking in horror. "They said they'd poison the water supply and kill everyone in the Black Land if anyone ever came back."

Meres laughed. "That's ridiculous. Who told you that?"

"Priest Hennet," Dendera said.

Meres paused. None of this made any sense. No Black Lander would ever commit murder, especially not a priest.

As if reading her mind, Isis said, "It's true. Things like this have happened before."

Meres protested, "Not in the Black Land!"

"No," Isis said. "In places like Jonestown. But it could happen in the Black Land just as easily as it happens anywhere else."

"She's back," Dendera said. Since they'd entered the room, she hadn't stopped staring at Meres. "That's all that matters."

"You still haven't told me what happened," Meres said.

"It doesn't matter," Dendera said.

"Are you crazy?" Tarahk said. "She needs answers. It's the least we can do for her. Never be afraid to tell the truth. It will make you free."

"By the gods," Meres said. "That's what I always say!"

Tarahk grinned. "That's my girl!"

Dendera smiled, looking hopeful. "Go ahead. Tell her."

"I saw something I shouldn't have." Tarahk shrugged. "That's how it began. I was the scribe at the temple—"

"Our Lady of the Absolute? I'm the scribe there!"

Tarahk relaxed into a grin, gazing at Meres with pride. "Like father, like daughter, eh? Anyway, I stumbled across some papers, financial information, I think. I should have ignored it, but I made the dumb-ass mistake of asking a priest about it. And those bastards set us up. First they called you and your mom and your sister to the temple."

"Sister?" Meres gripped the edge of the table, feeling as if she were about to fall off the world again.

Dendera looked up sharply. "Ruka."

Meres shook her head. "In the orphanage, they told me I had no brothers or sisters."

"Goddess Isis!" Dendera cried.

Isis looked up briefly and kept eating.

Dendera moaned. "What happened to Ruka?"

Tarahk gave his wife a quick hug. "Chin up. Meres found us. Ruka can, too."

Dendera cried in little sobs that sounded like muffled hiccups. "What if they killed her?"

Tarahk kissed the top of her head. "Don't worry about that now. Meres is what's important." He winked at Meres.

Meres gazed at Tarahk's bright, open face. The only reality she'd ever known was being an orphan, barely able to remember anything about her dead parents. Being told they were alive—and sitting in front of her face—felt too overwhelming to believe just yet. But Tarahk's wink came like the first ray of sun on the morning horizon.

It gave her hope.

"When you all arrived at the temple, they managed to separate you girls from your mother. They interrogated us until they thought they understood what we knew." Tarahk laughed bitterly. "They made assumptions. They jumped to conclusions. We didn't know anything! All they had to do was tell me to forget what I saw or even make up some stupid excuse to explain it away, and we could still be living in the White Walled City, none the wiser."

"None the wiser," Dendera said, resting her elbows on the table and her chin on her hands. "You make it sound like a good thing."

"Damn straight! To be back home, surrounded by my children and grandchildren? What could be better than that?"

Dendera shook her head, baffled.

Tarahk reached across the table, extending one arm to shake hands. "Speaking of grandchildren, what's your name, Sweetheart?"

Her mouth full of scrambled eggs, Zalika stared at his hand and then at Meres, as if looking for an explanation.

"She's not mine—I can't have children."

Concerned, Tarahk withdrew his hand. "What's she doing with you?"

"Zalika is my niece—the daughter of my husband's sister."

Zalika swallowed her eggs and announced, "I'm a princess."

Tarahk and Dendera exchanged worried glances.

Zalika noticed. "It's not like that. I'm not one of them. They shot my mother dead. My sisters, too."

Simultaneously, Tarahk and Dendera burst out laughing, and now Zalika recoiled. Recovering quickly, Dendera said, "That's impossible."

Zalika's cheeks flushed with anger. "I saw it!"

Still chuckling, Tarahk said, "I don't doubt it. But you got to remember you're dealing with a bunch of manipulators. They'll do anything to make you believe what they want you to. And they're damn good at it."

Dendera said, "What did you see?"

"They shot them."

"With guns?"

Zalika nodded, too upset to speak.

"Did you see blood right away?"

Zalika nodded again.

"What color was the blood?"

Zalika pointed at a plate of strawberries.

Tarahk sighed. "They got you and got you good, like they did us."

Zalika pushed her plate away. "Why should I believe you?"

Becoming more serious, Tarahk said, "What if I show you how they did it?"

"How?"

"Come with me and Dendera, and we'll show you right now."

Zalika turned to Meres.

Meres nodded. "Let's go."

"Why don't you stay here with me?" Isis said through a mouthful of cantaloupe. "You haven't been debriefed yet."

She's my responsibility, Meres thought, looking at Zalika. *We've just met these people—can we trust them?*

And Meres felt a touch on her arm that came as light as the landing of a dragonfly and as startling as a hand reaching into her chest and wrapping its fingers around her heart.

It was Isis.

Of course, Meres realized. What else would the touch of a goddess feel like?

"It's fine," Isis said. "She's safe with them."

Trusting the goddess, Meres gave her consent.

CHAPTER FIFTY-THREE

Isis opened another door, and Meres followed her into an adjoining room. Sunlight spilled through a glass wall overlooking several large outdoor swimming pools. Inside the room, photographs, maps, and framed newspaper clippings lined the walls. An enormous table dominated the center of the room. A model of the desert covered the entire table.

"What's this?"

Isis pointed at the edge closest to them. "We are here."

Of course! Meres saw a tiny sign reading "Welcome to Las Vegas" and a strip of buildings, including the black pyramid and the other palaces she'd seen, each one no taller than her thumb.

"And that," Isis said, pointing at the far end of the table, "is the Black Land."

Because the table took up most the room, Meres had to edge her way through the narrow space between the table and the walls. As she approached the model of the Black Land, she paused to get her bearings. It was easy to find the White Walled City, because she recognized the tiny versions of the royal palace and the Temple of Our Lady of the Absolute. But when Meres located the Nile, the model confused her. A blue strip of the Nile ran down a mountain South of the White Walled City and alongside the city gates and up North. But that same blue strip snaked West and South again, back to the same mountain with a large blue circle at the top. "The Nile..."

"The water comes from an aquifer." Isis pointed at a mountain sliced open to show its interior of layered rock and water. "Some of it goes to the White Walled City and other towns throughout the year, but most of it runs the course of the Nile and is pumped up to a reservoir. Once each year, that reservoir is opened and the water rushes down the mountain and flows over the river banks to flood the crops surrounding the city. That's what you know as the Inundation."

Meres shook her head. "No. The Nile is a river. The Inundation is a gift from the gods."

"The Nile is man-made, and the Inundation is controlled by machinery."

Meres grasped the table's edge to steady herself before the room could spin out of control. "Who would do such a thing?"

"This room tells the story," Isis said, gesturing at the walls surrounding them. "These are the people who created the Black Land."

Meres wandered slowly, dragging her fingertips across the wall as she stared at brown-and-white photos and articles, now yellow with age. Here was a photograph of Queen Angelique in the old days when she was Pharaoh Angelique. Next to it she saw a photo of a woman grinning as she stood by a sign reading "Ghost Town"—a label identified her as Rosemary Dempsey. Meres stopped suddenly, staring at a photograph she saw every day at work, framed and hanging on a temple wall.

It was a photograph of Isis.

Meres turned toward her.

Isis smiled. "That's not me. It's my great-great-grandmother, Fatima. She came here from Egypt in the late 1800s. She worked for an American woman who'd settled in Cairo. When her employer died unexpectedly, Fatima brought her body and belongings back to the woman's brother here in Nevada. His son fell in love with Fatima and married her—but he fell just as much in love with his aunt's paintings and journals of Egypt, so he called his new wife 'Isis.'"

Meres turned back to the wall and found an article about Dusty Newman that called him the king of the Silver Rush and described how he'd amassed a fortune of $100 million as a mine supervisor, owner, and investor. "Dusty Newman married Isis?"

"No. She married his son, James. Fatima worked for Dusty Newman's sister, who fancied herself an adventuress." Isis walked to the glass wall and pushed a button. The top half of the wall slid open, and dry, hot outdoor air flooded into the room. "Sobek! Come here!" Isis opened up one fist to reveal a handful of small fish.

Meres remembered seeing the fish on the breakfast table in the other room. But why had Isis called out the name of the crocodile god?

"After his own son died in World War I, James lost faith in this country. As the years went by, he thought his family wasn't safe, so he decided to buy all the land surrounding his home and create his own nation. He flew in dozens of women from Egypt for his harem and hired workers to build the White Walled City and the Nile. Eventually, the Black Land became a cult that recruited new members to serve the Pharaoh. James was the first Pharaoh, and the oldest son in each generation has been the next. It's been so long since James created the Black Land that only the Pharaoh and the priests know the truth."

Isis leaned over the lower half of the glass wall, dangling one small fish between her fingers. "Denwen! Sobek!"

Curious, Meres squeezed her way around the table to the glass wall and looked outside. Palm trees shaded a large sunken pit below, surrounded by water. One crocodile lunged out of the water and onto the rocky surface of the pit. Another stood on its hind legs with its front feet pressed against the outside wall, jaws hanging open just below Isis's hand. She dropped one fish at a time into its gaping mouth. "There are more in the other room."

"Fish? You want me to get them?"

"Sobek is fine, but Denwen looks hungry."

Meres still believed Isis might be a goddess and felt honored to serve her. Meres retrieved a platter full of fish.

Isis backed away, gesturing for Meres to take her place.

Terrified, Meres felt the color drain from her face. "But they're dangerous!"

Isis nodded. "There will always be predators in the world. Predators like the priests and your pharaoh. And you always have a choice: you can either let them control you or you can display your courage and take control of your own life."

Meres stood frozen in place for a few minutes. Finally, she stepped into the empty place that Isis had left by the glass wall. Peeking over the edge, Meres saw the crocodiles circling below.

You have a goddess on your side, Meres told herself. *Don't be afraid.*

She took a fish off the platter and dropped it toward the monsters beneath her.

Chapter Fifty-Four

After Meres fed all the fish to the crocodiles, she leaned over the edge of the glass wall and watched them bask in the sun. To Isis, she said, "Why did you claim you're not a goddess?"

"Because I'm as human as you."

"Why are you here? Why don't you live in the Black Land?"

Isis stepped next to Meres, looking down at the crocodiles, too. "When my mother was a teenager, she and her friends saw something they shouldn't have seen. The priests took them to the border, pointed them toward Las Vegas, and told them if they ever came back, they and their parents would be killed. The priests told everyone else that the teens had gone swimming in the Nile and were killed by crocodiles."

Meres nodded. It all began to make sense. "And the parents believed that story because crocodile attacks are so common."

"That's what everyone thinks. The priests have trained people to be afraid of crocodiles, but all the crocodiles in the Black Land are kept in the Pharaoh's personal zoo. Sometimes the priests let one out, just to keep everyone scared and in line. And sometimes one escapes. But the point is that it's all a lie. Many, many lies are told in the White Walled City."

Meres glanced at the vast area beyond the crocodile pit. One woman swam laps in one of the swimming pools, reminding Meres of Queen Angelique. The other pools were empty. "That makes no sense. Everyone has a good life in the Black Land. There's no reason to lie."

"It's about money," Isis said. "I believe most people have good hearts and good souls, but it's hard for some people to resist temptation of power and wealth when it's dangled in front of them. And the fortune that Dusty Newman made is still enormous."

"But the White Walled City isn't like that! We live simply, but everyone's happy. We live our belief that it's important to treat every man like a brother and every woman like a sister."

Isis smiled wryly. "Unless they're foreigners."

Without thinking, Meres said, "Foreigners mean harm to us.

They're evil."

Isis sighed. "You've been taught well." She pushed a button, and the glass wall slid back into place, putting the barrier between them and the crocodiles firmly back in place. Meres followed Isis back into the adjoining Hathor Room. "I believe it's important to treat every man on this planet like a brother—and every woman like a sister."

The thought startled Meres. "Even when foreigners attack?"

"If you genuinely treat a man like your brother, he has no reason to attack. Besides, siblings fight all the time. It doesn't mean they have to hurt each other."

Meres felt something shift inside, as if the cold fear inside her started melting. She'd lived her entire life in the White Walled City, working for the priests, obeying the Pharaoh's laws, and worshipping the Almighty sun god Ra as well as the goddess Isis, wife of Osiris and mother of Horus. Isis, the gentle goddess, had traveled throughout the Black Land to retrieve the corpse of her husband after he been killed, dismembered, and scattered all over the country. She'd convinced the gods to bring him back to life for a day so she could conceive his son, who in time would avenge his father's death.

Osiris once had been a man born to a time of chaos, who led humanity into peace and true civilization. After his murder, Isis did what had to be done to regain peace and prevent the world from falling into chaos again. Every night, when the Almighty sun god Ra sailed his boat along the horizon and into the Underworld, Isis saved his life every night when monsters attacked. If not for her, the sun would never rise again.

Meres stared long and hard at Isis, convinced more than ever that no mere mortal stood with her.

"For awhile, nothing will feel real to you," Isis said. "You'll feel scared when you wake up each morning, because you won't know where you are. When you're awake enough to remember, it'll feel like a bad dream. That's how everyone feels at first."

"Everyone?"

"You're not the first. Many of the people you saw downstairs came here like you did. Both your parents did. There're hundreds of people who used to be Black Landers. They've formed their own little community here at the hotel. They're the dealers in the casino and the cooks and waitresses in the restaurants. They work as maids and behind the front desk."

Meres felt the same way she did when she walked into the temple of Our Lady of the Absolute every day: blessed and honored to be granted permission to set foot in the house of a goddess. This hotel—this pyramid that sent a beam of light into the heavens every evening—must be the true home of Isis. It was here that she watched over her people, the ones who had found their way to her.

Suddenly, Meres' life felt magical. She'd found her way to Isis, too. "Tell me what to do. I'll do whatever you want."

Isis sighed in frustration. "A lot of people say the root of all evil is money, but that's a lie, too. Real evil begins whenever one person tries to control somebody else. And that's what's happened in the Black Land: the priests and the Pharaoh manipulate everyone else because they want to be in control. And if I tell you what to do, what to say, what to believe—how am I any better than them?"

Meres held onto the edge of the table, because it seemed as if the world truly spun out of control. Everything inside her, every thought in her head seemed to turn inside out and upside down.

And yet, the words of the goddess shot straight like an arrow into Meres' heart. Her head throbbed, and everything burst into stars across a void for a moment as her vision readjusted. As the room came back into focus, Meres felt as if she were stepping from a dark place out into the sunlight and feeling its warmth on her skin for the first time in her life.

The door to the Hathor Room burst open. Zalika stood in the doorway, her cheeks flushed and jaw set in determination.

"We have to go back," Zalika said to Meres. "And find my mother."

CHAPTER FIFTY-FIVE

Zalika burst into the Hathor Room, brimming with new strength and the passion of purpose. For the first time, Meres saw the girl animated and focused.

For the first time, Meres saw Pu reflected in her daughter Zalika.

"Tarahk and Dendera—they took me to this place," Zalika said, pacing the room and gesturing with her hands as if painting a picture of what had just happened. "People go there and pay money and put on helmets and vests so they don't get hurt. It's this huge room, like inside the palace at home, but it's dark and there are things you can hide behind. And people shoot each other!" Zalika demonstrated, pretending she had a rifle.

Horrified, Meres said, "Are you all right?"

Zalika nodded. Of course, she was all right. "The first time I saw somebody get hit, I thought I'd pass out. This guy—his blood spattered all over his chest. His vest, I mean. I thought he was dead, but he acted like nothing happened."

Meres looked to Isis for guidance, but Isis simply sat back, listening to Zalika.

Excited, Zalika spoke so fast that Meres had to concentrate to understand her. "He had blood all over him, but all he did was hold his gun over his head and walk away." Zalika showed them with her invisible rifle. "And I saw other people with blood on their clothes, but it wasn't just red—it was purple and yellow and blue!"

"That's impossible," Meres said.

Zalika paused and smiled for a few moments, looking pleased with herself.

Meres thought back to what Isis had said about the root of all evil being the desire to control other people and realized that Zalika smiled because she had power. Right now, Zalika understood a certain truth and that knowledge gave her power. The thought chilled Meres for a moment, until she realized that this was probably the only time in Zalika's life that she'd owned any real power and needed to enjoy her moment.

"It's not impossible," Zalika said, still smiling, "if it's paint."

Meres shook her head, even more baffled.

"It's a game," Isis said. "As long as you wear protective gear, you don't get hurt. You get to fight without getting hurt. At the end of the day, everybody walks away, safe and sound."

"But why Pu?" Meres said. "And the girls?"

"He was going to shoot me, too. Mama and Jabari got us all out of the White Walled City, and we stopped in the desert. Jabari was off doing something, and I told Mama I had to pee. There wasn't any place private, so I went off and found one. When I heard the shots, I peeked out. I saw Mama and the girls with blood on them, and Jabari was holding a gun and looking around. He was looking for me—I know it. But he didn't know where I was, and there's no way he could have found me. He called out, but I never answered. After awhile, he gave up and drove away."

Zalika paused, seeming to re-live that moment. Suddenly, her confidence washed away. She crossed her arms and her voice cracked when she spoke. "I thought Mama was dead, but I should have stayed to help her."

"No," Meres said. "You had every reason to believe she was dead. You had to protect yourself. You did the right thing."

"I wish I'd known she was still alive."

"But we know now," Meres said. "And we can do something about it."

"Technically," Isis said, "you shouldn't go back. The Black Land is private property, and the Pharaoh's rule is that once you leave, you're not a Black Lander anymore—you're a foreigner, like the rest of us." Isis turned to Meres and said, "Tarahk and Dendera have dreamed of this day for decades. Now that you're here, they're not going to want to let you go."

Meres nodded. She understood, even though she still struggled to believe she actually had living parents and had never been an orphan. But if Pu still lived, Meres felt driven to help Zalika find her and stay by the girl's side, ready to protect her.

And besides, Meres thought, *if Pu and the girls are still alive, maybe Ramose is still alive, too.*

To Isis, Meres said, "Will you help us go back to the Black Land?"

Isis shrugged. "I've got the day off and a thousand dollars in my pocket. Why not?"

Meres took a deep breath to calm her rising nerves. "Tell my parents I'll come back."

Isis easily convinced Meres and Zalika to sleep for the rest of the day in one of the pyramid's empty guest rooms. After all, they'd been up for eighteen hours and had walked all night through the desert. True to her word, Isis spoke with Tarahk and Dendera, convincing them that Meres wouldn't be happy until she'd tied up her own loose ends. She'd spent hours in the employee city below the pyramid answering questions from other former Black Landers who clung to shreds of hope that maybe they could glean information about those they loved who believed they were dead.

Finally, at the end of the afternoon, Isis grabbed some lunch in the employee cafeteria and sat down at a table in a quiet corner.

Funny. The morning had started like any other. But once she saw Pam from Employee Child Care in that ridiculous goddess getup that they kept in Dry Cleaning, Isis knew she'd end up getting involved, whether she wanted to or not. Pam had good intentions, but she never knew what to do with Black Landers.

Isis closed her eyes, relishing her tortilla soup. Ralph, the new cook, was a godsend.

She'd grown up in Vegas, and all her family still lived here. She'd always known about the Black Landers—everybody did. But after being teased all her life about it, Isis had been anxious to leave Nevada and go someplace where no one knew of her relation to those loony tunes. She'd gone to school in Boston and stayed there, becoming a teacher in its public school system. She never called her job a piece of cake, but Isis always found a way to connect with her students each year and that made it all worthwhile. But in time, the state told her how and what to teach, all based on standardized tests.

Nobody told Isis what to do. Despite all her complaints and protests, somewhere deep inside, Isis thought she had just a bit of goddess in her.

Teaching made no sense anymore—not if it achieved nothing more than to create little human robots. Ever since the pyramid hotel had been built in Vegas, she'd become more irritated than usual with the snow and slush that packed Boston's streets for months on end. She missed the mountains and the desert and the heat. For the first time since she'd left home, she went back to Vegas to visit family and consider her options. Everything had changed. Vegas had exploded, and the Strip resembled nothing she remembered. It wasn't all about gambling anymore. It was about celebrity chefs and Broadway shows and shopping. It was about conventions and events. And a little gambling on the side.

She'd walked down the Strip one day, just to get a feel for it. Most of the hotels that had dominated the Strip from her childhood had been replaced by elegant showcases like the Bellagio and the Venetian.

Sure, the walkways were crowded with tourists in shorts and T-shirts, but there were also women in kimonos who shaded themselves with paper umbrellas as they walked with downcast gazes. And Paris Hilton wannabees in designer clothes who called in their reservations for VIP tables at the hottest night spots on the Strip. The crowds were skewing younger, and no one failed to notice the number of high-end visitors from China. When Isis learned that the dealers in the top casino earned six-figure incomes, she thought about it long and hard.

The first time she saw the pyramid hotel and its bright beam of light reaching up into the night sky, she felt as if she'd come home for the first time in her life. Maybe racial memory could explain it. After all, she was part Egyptian.

Isis never returned East. Instead, she stayed in Vegas and went to dealer school. At her first job, she worked the midnight shift at the Sahara. The joint jumped until 4:30 a.m., but things would slow down for a few hours. Most of the time she didn't mind the customers, except for when they were drunk and on a losing streak. When they were angry and swearing, she struggled to look composed. She'd lost that composure exactly once when a jerk lost his last dollar, whipped his thing out, and urinated on the table.

Thank God that was the worst she'd ever seen. She worked her way up through the years and tapped into her built-in inner circle at the pyramid hotel to get a better job there. Like most of her fellow dealers, she had no desire to gamble after having seen so many casino guests lose over the years. Instead, she'd bought her dream home and spent her vacation time in Hawaii to get away from the stress of her job. She hated watching people throw their money away, especially when they looked like they needed to hang onto it. She often told herself what a pit boss had once advised: many of the guests were people from little towns who'd saved up for years to come here. For them, Vegas meant the vacation of a lifetime. A dream come true. A Disneyland for adults.

That helped.

Isis suspected that the truth to her stress translated to the very fantasy of her job—that people came to her table with dreams of winning big. That people would rather believe in fantasy than live in reality.

That explained why she'd left Nevada as well as why she'd come back. She'd grown up hating her connection to the Black Land because it was nothing but a big lie. Every Black Lander lived a lie. But as time had gone by, Isis realized the rest of the country wasn't much different than the Black Land. She believed the vast majority of people are good, but there are always predators looking to seize control and benefit from it. And that most people are so overwhelmed by everyday life that they often don't have the wherewithal to question those who have taken over.

She'd promised herself she'd never get involved with any Black Landers again. She'd just put in her hours at the pyramid hotel and leave it at that.

Isis leaned back in her chair, sipping the last of her coffee. *Irony*, she thought, *is a funny thing.*

Despite her complaints and protests, Isis loved and admired most of the Black Landers she'd met, especially when they arrived for the first time in Vegas. When they learned the truth, they all reacted differently. Some cried, some went into shock, and others were mostly grateful to know the truth. But what she loved most about them was their willingness to stare reality in the face instead of turning away in denial.

Whenever Isis felt tired or blue or frustrated, she thought about the Black Landers, and that always gave her hope and perspective. It cheered her to know they were her lost family.

She glanced at her watch. Time to wake up Meres and Zalika and get this freak show back on the road.

On days like today, it was good to be a goddess.

CHAPTER FIFTY-SIX

Sekhmet had tracked them all day and sensed this hunt would soon be over. She could smell it in the traces of stale sweat that still hovered in the air.

The day-long trek had given her much to think about. She'd eaten all the food that Mrs. Dempsey had given to her, but Sekhmet still carried the empty pack because it reminded her of the woman.

It was a comfort she didn't deserve. Coming out into the light of day—under her father's watchful eye but forever distant from his arms—had forced Sekhmet to a horrible realization. The priests hadn't simply made her a goddess. They had also turned her into a monster. And when people like Mrs. Dempsey found out who and what Sekhmet really was, they'd run away and she'd be left alone.

Sekhmet growled, her voice rumbling deep from the bottom of her throat. She blamed Meres. If not for her, the priests never would have cast Sekhmet out into the light of day. She would never have met her father and had to suffer the pain of his constant rejection. She would never have met Mrs. Dempsey and learned what was possible in the world outside a tomb that lies deep beneath the temple of Our Lady of the Absolute.

She paused to study the sand. Yes. They had come this way.

As Sekhmet, tired and hungry and thirsty, pushed herself to keep moving, she drew strength from remembering what the priests had done to her, first as a girl and then after they'd made her a goddess and taught her how to love the hunt and the kill and the taste of blood. She re-lived every kill she had made, remembering how she'd been the one with the power for once, and the brief moment of relief that had brought, almost like a moment of hope that her life could have been different. Each kill felt like a dream where she could have been happy.

Sekhmet licked her lips, remembering her last kill, which had been the woman Neferita. When she concentrated, she could still taste her blood.

All morning, Sekhmet had been thinking of a plan. She craved taking vengeance on everyone and everything that had made her. And the first step in her plan was to kill the evil woman Meres and drain every drop of blood from her body.

CHAPTER FIFTY-SEVEN

That afternoon, while all the former Black Landers thought they were still sleeping, Isis drove Meres and Zalika out of Las Vegas and into the desert. Meres sat next to Isis in the front but kept an eye on Zalika in the back seat. The girl fidgeted, staring straight ahead and chewing her fingernails. And yet, she didn't seem angry. Instead, fire burned in her eyes and nothing distracted her.

As they drove in silence, Meres wished she had Zalika's focus. Meres trembled at the thought of going back to the White Walled City. Maybe she *was* a traitor. But she'd done it to protect Pu, not to hurt anyone.

She kept thinking of the day she and Ramose had marched as Isis and Osiris in the festival parade. The cool, hard expression on Priest Hennet's face haunted her. She'd been a scribe at the temple for the past ten years and proven her loyalty to the priests over and over again. She couldn't bear them thinking she'd betrayed them.

On the other hand, if she believed Isis, the priests and the Pharaoh had betrayed Meres and everyone else who lived in the Black Land. Meres may have told some small lies for a few days because she thought it necessary to save Pu's life. But the priests and the Pharaoh lived their lies day in and day out, all for the sake of being in control and reaping the benefits that came with it.

One moment, she raged with fury because that's why they had put Ramose in danger—to hold onto their control and their lies. The next moment, she wondered if maybe Ramose could have survived, after all. And if he'd survived, she could find him.

Isis pulled the car over and stopped the engine, just as the sun began to dip below the western horizon. As Meres and Zalika stepped out of the car, Isis popped the trunk open and pulled out two small boxes with shoulder straps. "Here. You've got a long walk ahead of you. The cooks at the hotel put something together for you."

Zalika reached out and took one.

Isis caught her by the hand. "Bruce doesn't know your mother's pregnant. He told her he'd take care of all of you if she could bring you here. He knew it was a big decision she had to make on her own. He never wanted anyone to get hurt."

Zalika gazed at Isis for a moment before pulling free and walking away toward the desert.

Isis closed the trunk and slipped back into the driver's seat, closing the door behind her.

Panic-stricken, Meres ran in front of the car, putting her hands on the hood. "Wait!"

Isis rolled down her window.

"Aren't you coming with us?"

Isis stepped out of the car, sitting down on the hood and gazing at the mountains. "I don't like what the Black Land has become, but good still exists there. People live happy lives. I think part of that is because they embrace the idea that every man is your brother and every woman is your sister."

Meres shrugged, sitting next to Isis. "Some more than others."

Isis laughed. "That's always going to be true." She cocked her head, looking at Meres. "But that's what they believed in ancient Egypt, too."

Ancient Egypt. How strange and confusing to learn her way of life was based on a civilization that vanished thousands of years ago. And even more strange and confusing to be sitting on the hood of a car next to the flesh-and-blood goddess she'd devoted herself to, even if that goddess claimed to be only human. "They felt that way about everyone? Even foreigners?"

"No," Isis said softly. "Sometimes they traded peacefully with foreigners, but sometimes they went to war with them."

"But you believe every man is our brother—every woman is our sister—even if they're foreigners."

Isis nodded. "Nothing else makes sense to me."

In that moment, Meres didn't care whether Isis was a goddess or simply human. It suddenly made sense that she'd spent her life worshipping her. Meres smiled. It seemed as if all the bright stars in the sky had rained down on Las Vegas, the new temple of Isis. It seemed as if time stopped, and Meres wished it never had to start again.

"I hate religion," Isis said. "I know it's good for some people, but there are too many predators in the world who use religion to manipulate others. That's why it's so important to question everything and everyone. Never take anything at face value."

Meres didn't know whether to feel shocked or puzzled. "Don't you believe in the gods?"

"I have my beliefs. I just don't want anyone telling me what they should be."

"That happens?"

"Think of it this way: when I die, I want to be cremated."

"But you'll be lost in chaos forever!"

"We don't know that. Every religion has a different belief in what happens when we die, but none of us will find out the truth until it happens. Some people tell me what to believe because they care about what happens to me or because they're afraid they won't see me again. But most people tell me what to believe because they're too afraid to admit there's no proof."

"Can I still believe in you?"

Isis shrugged, sliding off the hood of the car. "You can believe whatever you want. Just get off my car because I'm going back to town."

Obediently, Meres stood up. "But why won't you come with us?"

Isis opened the driver's door again. "Because I'm not your mother. And the sun isn't your father. Be careful what you believe, Meres. If you think any god is your parent, then you're deciding to be a child. The problem is that children aren't held accountable for their actions and decisions—adults are. I expect you to be a woman—you're responsible for everything you do. If you're not happy because of something you do or say, it's your fault and nobody else's. And it's up to you to make things right."

Meres gasped, feeling as if she'd been punched in the gut. Part of the pain included feeling the truth of Isis's words. Meres saw her entire life flash before her eyes, all the while expecting the gods to take care of everything instead of claiming her life as her own.

Stunned, Meres watched Isis drive away.

It hit her—the words Isis had said to Zalika, telling her that Bruce knew nothing of her mother's pregnancy.

Neither Meres nor Zalika had told anyone in Las Vegas about Pu's pregnancy, much less about Bruce being the father. It was impossible for Isis to know. Unless she really was a goddess.

Smiling and full of new hope, Meres picked up the lunch box she'd left on the ground and put her head through the strap. Maybe the Pharaoh and the priests were frauds, but the gods were real. Meres still felt a mix of shame and shock from what Isis had said, but taking control of her own life felt right.

And then she heard Zalika scream in the distance.

CHAPTER FIFTY-EIGHT

Sekhmet paused, watching her father—the sun god Ra—dip to the horizon, preparing for his night journey through the Underworld. Like always, he committed to his duty of traveling through this world and the next. After all, it was ultimately up to him to keep chaos at bay and maintain order.

Apparently, that meant he had no time to meet his daughter, much less get to know her. Since coming out into the day, Sekhmet had learned she might as well be an orphan. Her own father had rejected her by keeping his distance and ignoring her existence. The priests who had once used her for their own pleasure had made her a goddess so they could use her to kill others without getting blood on their own hands. But once she'd found the woman Meres—the catalyst who had destroyed Sekhmet's hopes and dreams of meeting a father who would love her—she'd go back to the White Walled City and destroy them all.

But for now, Sekhmet struggled to keep up the rage that had always fueled her in the past. She'd walked through the blazing desert. Her skin felt dry and tight, no matter how much sunscreen she slathered on it. Her mouth and throat were so dry and parched that she had nothing to swallow. Certain she'd lost weight since leaving the city, her legs felt like heavy weights that she had to drag forward, one slow step at a time.

She heard voices in the distance. They echoed against the mountain walls.

Looking across the desert ahead, Sekhmet noticed a sharp rise—an overlook. The voices seemed to drift from there.

Adrenaline kicked in, flooding Sekhmet with memories of the joy of the hunt in her tomb's stone forest. With the stealth she'd developed over the course of many years, Sekhmet crept ahead until she reached a rocky ridge. From here, the sight of a new world took her aback.

Far away, a city glittered with brilliant, endless lights. A column of light poured from the sky above down into that city. Sekhmet realized that column must be the source of the city's many lights and power.

That's his home, Sekhmet realized with a start. That's where my father lives—he must stop there every time he leaves the Underworld and before he begins a new day in our world.

Sekhmet wanted to run and keep running until she came to her father's glorious city of lights, but she had to meet him and convince him to take her there. Hours from now his journey would begin. If she waited until then, she could finally meet him. She could see her father face to face.

But the same hardness that enveloped her whenever she embraced the hunt locked into place.

No one invited you to his city, Sekhmet told herself harshly. *You're not welcome there.*

Then Sekhmet smelled her.

Sekhmet took several shallow breaths, flaring her nose to catch each nuance of the scent. It was the same scent she'd picked up many days ago, only to lose it.

The scent of the woman Meres.

But she was with someone. Sekhmet had never hunted more than one person at a time. Perhaps the best thing to do was, corner and kill one at a time.

Yes, that's it, Sekhmet thought. *One at a time.*

Thoroughly parched, she thirsted for the taste of blood, ready to drink her fill.

The setting sun cast long shadows, and Sekhmet slipped between them as she crept along the trail below the overlook toward the voices.

Suddenly, the prey rounded a corner on the trail ahead, striding purposefully, looking down at her feet.

Sekhmet raced from out of the shadows and pounced on her prey, pinning her to the ground.

The prey looked up at Sekhmet and screamed.

It wasn't Meres.

This girl was the scent Sekhmet been following all along. How could she have been so wrong?

"Sekhmet!"

She looked up and recognized the woman immediately from the photograph that Priest Hennet had given to her.

The true prey stood still, staring at them with wonder and horror.

CHAPTER FIFTY-NINE

The woman Meres looked frozen, and only her gaze moved from Sekhmet to the girl she'd pinned to the ground.

Good, Sekhmet thought. *I can use that.*

What a shame they weren't in her tomb. Sekhmet loved nothing more than a cat-and-mouse game in the forest of its stone columns.

But there was more than one way to catch a mouse.

Sekhmet kept the wriggling girl pinned and waited to see what the woman Meres would do next.

"You're real," Meres said, her voice shallow and stunned.

Sekhmet smiled. She perceived it as a good sign.

"Aunt Meres!" The girl cried out.

Sekhmet slapped the girl hard across the face and shushed her.

"Please! No!" Meres shouted as she stepped forward.

Sekhmet showed the woman Meres the palm of her hand to make her stop. Keeping her voice cool and even, Sekhmet said, "Don't you know who I am?"

"Yes! We're Black Landers—we worship you!"

Sekhmet didn't know which one she preferred to kill first. She needed to play with them awhile longer before she could decide. Maybe it would be fun to make the most fearful watch the other one die first. But that meant she needed to test them to figure out which carried the deepest fear in her heart.

"Tell me," Sekhmet said, "what you know about me."

The woman Meres stared at her blankly, as if everything she'd ever known had suddenly evaporated into thin air.

The girl beneath Sekhmet sobbed.

The woman Meres spoke. "The sun god Ra took human form and came to the royal city to learn more about the people he'd created from the tears of his loneliness."

Sekhmet tensed at the mention of her father's name. At the same time, it surprised her to hear that he had ever been lonely. If he understood loneliness, then why didn't he understand Sekhmet's pain?

"He stayed for a long time—until his human body grew very old. His memory faded, and he soon forgot to bring about the Inundation of the Nile every year. And without the Nile flooding the crops, those crops failed and people began to starve to death. They hated him and turned against him."

Sekhmet listened intently. No one had ever told her this part of her own history before. Was it simply a ruse on the part of the woman Meres? Had she decided to play along with the cat-and-mouse game?

"The sun god Ra—still in his frail human form—was enraged. We're all his children. If not for him, none of us would exist. Furious, he plucked out his own eye and cast a spell on it. That spell transformed his eye into a new goddess, and he named her Sekhmet. Ra sent her out into the desert on a mission: to kill everyone who crossed her path to teach humanity that they must never turn on him again. To make sure she carried out his order, he gave to her all his own rage."

Meres' words rang true. Sekhmet knew her own rage. It's what helped her kill. At the same time, she realized that her father, not unlike the priests, had used her.

"You let out a horrible roar and shouted to all people that they should hide in the desert and in the mountains and feel terror in their hearts. You told them that you are the goddess of vengeance and bloody death. And you slaughtered everyone you met, ripping them apart and drinking their blood. Men tried fighting against you, but you killed them all. Killing is what gave you pleasure.

"But you killed so many that people almost became extinct. Osiris pleaded with Ra to make you stop. When he saw you next, Ra admitted that he'd created you when he found himself full of rage and pain, and that now the killing had to stop. But he didn't understand that all you understood was fury, making it impossible for you to stop."

Startled by Meres' words, Sekhmet eased back on her haunches, letting go of the girl, who scrambled away. Everything Meres said made sense.

"You rebelled against your father's command and returned to the desert, looking for more people to slaughter. The gods brought all surviving people to the city of Annu for safety. Isis led many women to brew thousands of barrels of beer that the gods colored red to look like blood and placed those barrels at the entrance to the city. The scent brought you to them. You drank them all and fell asleep."

This was the part of the hunt when Sekhmet became frenzied and ripped her prey apart, devouring its blood. This was the part that Sekhmet could never remember, because the priests told her she always got lost in her own rage. Sekhmet was used to—no, that wasn't right. First, the prey would offer a ritual cup of its own blood. When she woke up later, the priests told her about the carnage she'd caused.

Shuddering, Sekhmet remembered the moment Mrs. Dempsey had offered an entire glass of blood to her, calling it tomato juice. After drinking it, Sekhmet should have gone into her blood frenzy and destroyed Mrs. Dempsey. How could Sekhmet have failed that day? Why hadn't she killed Mrs. Dempsey?

Something was clearly wrong.

There was no ritual cup this time. And Sekhmet felt mesmerized by the truth in Meres' words.

"When you were sleeping, Ra pulled the fury out of you. Today you are the protector goddess of the Black Land. No more do you kill Black Landers, but when anyone threatens us, you are like a fierce mother protecting her young."

Sekhmet looked at Meres sharply. The woman lied—Ra had never taken the rage away. It ran like veins through her body, intertwined with her very being.

Sekhmet bared her teeth.

Startled, Meres dropped to her knees. "Mistress, you came to me in my dreams, just weeks ago. Everything you warned me of is true—I know that now."

On her hands and knees, Sekhmet stalked slowly toward Meres. Lies made her angry and thirsty.

"You told me that the Pharaoh isn't a god. I didn't understand then, but we've been to the great pyramid. We met Isis. She told us the truth about the Pharaoh and the priests."

Sekhmet hesitated as fear crept onto her skin. Isis was her sister goddess, and Sekhmet suspected Isis knew all, including what the priests had done to her. For a moment, Sekhmet felt sick with shame. When she'd been little, she'd pushed thoughts deep into the back of her head, hoping to forget them forever. Sometimes, she'd slapped herself in the head, trying to knock those thoughts out only to push them down, and now they were rising up again. She feared that what the priests had done to her was her fault. If she'd been smarter or braver or prettier or nicer, her parents never would have left her with them. And if she'd been more obedient or helpful, the priests would have left her alone.

Everything that had happened in Sekhmet's life was her fault and her fault alone. And now, the woman Meres knew. Sekhmet had to stop her—kill her—before Meres could get back to the White Walled City and tell anyone else. Sekhmet would have to kill the girl, too.

"You warned me that nothing is black and white, that I had to understand shades of gray. You were right. Isis said that the root of all evil is the desire to control others." Meres' voice softened. "Understanding that changes everything."

Again, Sekhmet hesitated. The desert seemed to shake beneath her, but maybe Sekhmet was the only one trembling.

The desire to control others. That's what the priests had done to her. First, they'd locked her in a tomb underneath the White Walled City. For years, they'd used her at their whim for their pleasure. And finally, they'd turned her into a bloodthirsty goddess full of rage.

For a moment, the world seemed to turn inside out. Sekhmet steadied herself as light reversed itself: for several seconds, day turned into night and black turned into white. Sekhmet felt dizzy, and she could no longer hear what Meres said.

The priests. They were the evil ones, not Sekhmet.

But no, that wasn't entirely true. Sekhmet had long lost count of the number of innocent lives she'd taken and the pleasure she'd taken from killing. Although it wasn't exactly pleasure—it was more like a brief moment of relief that made her feel like she escaped her life and could imagine a different one.

The world came back into focus, and Sekhmet found Meres staring at her. The woman's eyes were soft with concern.

Suddenly, Sekhmet recognized the look in Meres' eyes as the same as the look in Mrs. Dempsey's eyes.

"Are you all right?" Meres said. "How long have you been in the desert?"

Sekhmet answered automatically, now on the verge of feeling faint. "Days. Many days."

Meres lifted a strap over her head and unzipped a box she carried.

Sekhmet's mouth watered at the sudden aroma of rich, wonderful scents.

Meres took out a water bottle from the box and opened it. "Take some little sips of water first—"

All this time, Sekhmet realized, her heart had been aching. She'd never known anyone like Mrs. Dempsey, and she'd assumed she'd never meet anyone like her again.

Sekhmet sat on the desert floor, covered her face with her hands, and began to cry all the tears she'd been keeping inside since the first day she'd been entombed under the White Walled City.

≈≈

Her heart still racing, Meres stared in disbelief at the weeping goddess. From the moment she'd seen Sekhmet pinning Zalika to the ground, Meres knew she needed to draw the goddess toward her, giving Zalika time to run away and save herself.

Instead, Meres' words had a shocking effect; gradually, the goddess had crumbled before her, and she now seemed more like a terrified little girl than a woman.

Behind Sekhmet's huddled figure, Zalika raised a large rock over her head and crept toward Sekhmet, aiming the rock at her head.

Meres held out her hands to signal her niece to stop, but Zalika didn't see her.

Scrambling, Meres hurried to Sekhmet's side and put her arms around the goddess to protect her.

Zalika stopped short, frowning and puzzled. She dropped the rock.

Something seemed to break apart inside Sekhmet when Meres touched her, and she cried out as if in pain with each sob.

Instinctively, Meres held her closer.

In that moment, Meres saw the sense in her own life.

All this time, Meres had longed to have children, feeling like an outcast and that she had failed herself and her husband. If she'd had children as she'd wished, she would probably still be living her everyday life in the White Walled City. She doubted she would have taken the risk of helping Pu escape, and she would never have told Ramose anything. He would still be alive, but Pu might have found her own escape, maybe succeeding, maybe not.

But even if Meres lived with Ramose and the children they never had, they'd all be living inside a lie.

All of Meres' life, she'd valued the truth above all else. Now that she'd learned she'd been living a lie, she could never live that way again.

And Sekhmet—as grief came pouring out of her, Meres held on tight, imagining herself to be an anchor that wouldn't allow Sekhmet to be washed out into the sea of her own tears.

All these years, Meres had wanted to be able to comfort her own children, and now a goddess had landed in her arms instead. Meres felt as if she held the entire universe and all of time in her arms.

Sekhmet, the fierce and bloodthirsty goddess of war and protection, had made herself vulnerable to Meres, giving her complete trust to a mortal.

This, Meres realized, *is the most magical thing that will ever happen to me.*

And it never would have happened if my life had turned out the way I wanted.

CHAPTER SIXTY

Priest Hennet waddled through the dimly lit hallways of the temple of Our Lady of the Absolute and into the private courtyard of the sacred lake. The priests bathed three times each day in this enormous reflecting pool.

Well, that was the idea. In theory, that meant stripping and thoroughly cleansing oneself morning, noon, and night. In practice, Priest Hennet and his colleagues did little more than grab a handful of water and sprinkle it across their bodies as a symbolic gesture.

In light of an especially hot morning, a quick dip sounded refreshing.

Back in his office, Priest Hennet had already shaved his head. In his youth, when his hair had been full and thick, he'd hated cutting it off. Because natural baldness had set in, he ran a quick electric razor across his head every day.

Being High Priest meant being the most powerful man in the Black Land, other than the Pharaoh. And considering that the current Pharaoh—unlike his mother before they joined forces to kick her out decades ago—cared for little more than his own daily pleasures, Priest Hennet had the most power in practice, free to run the royal city and the country however he pleased, with rare interference from the Pharaoh. And even when the Pharaoh raised a stink, it was usually a small one that could be manipulated into something to benefit Priest Hennet.

Dropping his white robes on a white plastic lounge chair, Priest Hennet walked down the shallow steps into the cool water.

Most priests observed the guidelines for bathing early each morning, but Priest Hennet liked coming later so he could have the pool to himself and do as he wished. It gave him the peace and quiet he needed to plan his strategy. And the gods knew he'd needed plenty of that during the past few weeks.

It had started when Meres had come to temple on her day off and startled him in the hallway. He'd been carrying spreadsheets that detailed the finances of the Black Land, and he'd accidentally dropped them. Meres had seen them when she helped him pick them up. The question was, did Meres understand what she had seen or might she forget it? If she revealed herself as too trusting to recognize that the Pharaoh's worth was far more than any Black Lander realized, then Priest Hennet saw no need to take action. Otherwise, Meres could become a problem requiring immediate attention.

However, she'd unwittingly brought him a solution. Meres had come to the temple that day to report a minor crime committed by a young boy from Elephantine; he had committed disrespect to the Pharaoh by peeing on a statue of him. Priest Hennet still smiled when he remembered the genius of making the boy's mother Neferita live with Meres and her husband in order to spy on them. And by the grace of the gods, Neferita stumbled upon a plot devised by Meres, Ramose, and his sister Pu, a member of the royal harem and mother to four of the Pharaoh's many children.

Or was it six? It was hard to keep track.

Priest Hennet broke the surface of the water, and leaned back to float in it, gazing up at the bright blue sky.

Of course, he'd immediately called in Jabari, who claimed he knew nothing of the plot or even of Pu's pregnancy. Priest Hennet had been more amused than concerned about the silly little plot, confident the troublemakers would be handled quickly and efficiently. People left the White Walled City all the time. Sometimes they were smart and asked too many questions, but it was easy enough to send them packing to Las Vegas and report they'd been killed by crocodiles. Sometimes, like Meres, they stumbled upon information they had no business knowing or simply became too much of an annoyance. Those troublemakers ended up in the Underworld or some other enclave in the Black Land, like Elephantine.

And, over the years, it had been easy to establish a reputation among outsiders that if any unapproved person attempted to enter the Black Land, it would become another Jonestown or Heaven's Gate.

What had troubled Priest Hennet the most was his suspicion that Jabari knew more than he admitted. Everyone knew Jabari's history with Pu. When Jabari came in for questioning, he'd been convincing enough. But Priest Hennet didn't attain his position by believing convincing people.

He chuckled, still pleased with himself at the strategy he'd devised before meeting with Jabari. The expression on his face had been priceless when Priest Hennet had proposed a way for Jabari to prove his loyalty: set up Pu to believe Jabari killed her and her children. Giggling gleefully, Priest Hennet recalled how easy it had been to read Jabari's face as he'd processed the directive. It forced Jabari to choose between obedience to his masters and lingering love for the woman who'd rejected him because she wanted to be one of the Pharaoh's sluts.

Jabari had wavered for several long moments, and Priest Hennet had worried that it might be necessary to send him off to the outermost regions of the Black Land. But Jabari had come through, just as Priest Hennet had anticipated, choosing himself over his former love.

Dragging himself out of the water, Priest Hennet plucked the top towel from a neat stack on a poolside table, dried off, put his robes back on, and went back inside the temple.

So unfortunate it had all been for naught. How could anyone misplace a child that should have been shot with a paintball gun? Priest Hennet didn't believe Jabari's explanation for a moment. Even if the girl had run away, anyone committed to the task would have found her. Jabari could have made an excuse, describing some type of game—isn't that what he'd done with the younger children after he'd brought them back to the city?

Or were they just too young to understand what had happened in the desert?

Either way, it was easy to explain that their mother didn't love them any more and would rather be with the gods.

Priest Hennet shrugged it off. These things happened. And once Jabari had revealed his true nature, he'd been sent elsewhere.

On his way to his office, Priest Hennet swung by the offering table outside in the front courtyard of the temple. By now, any citizen making an offering today would have done so. But the pickings proved to be slim: little more than figs and a few bananas. Wrinkling his nose in distaste, he turned his back on the offering table. Let the other priests have the figs and bananas.

Once settled at his desk, Priest Hennet checked the GPS locations of all the troublemakers, thanks to the devices planted in the jewelry he'd made sure each one had. Pu, Ramose, and Neferita were still in the Underworld. Good. Likewise, Jabari had been relocated far out West, and Meres and Zalika had managed to make their way to Las Vegas.

He removed the short dagger-like letter opener from its scabbard, opening today's mail. But Sekhmet's movement between the White Walled City and Las Vegas worried him. She'd nearly caught up with Meres, which had amazed and delighted him. He'd assumed Meres would either get lost in the desert or escape the Black Land. Either way, it would solve his problem of her having seen too much. He'd sent Sekhmet out as a matter of insurance, figuring her presence along the Nile would add one more layer of protection to the possibility of Meres coming back to the White Walled City. If Sekhmet actually succeeded in bringing Meres back, so much the better. He'd set up a session for Sekhmet to "kill" Meres, which would reward Sekhmet and put the fear of the gods into Meres before kicking her out of the country.

Tapping the point of the letter opener on his desk top, Priest Hennet made a phone call. "Send me a plate of honey cakes."

CHAPTER SIXTY-ONE

After walking all night through the desert, Meres and Zalika hid behind a cluster of sagebrush located a stone's throw from the east gate of the White Walled City. In the early morning hours, a small hint of light on the horizon promised the sun would be rising soon.

"Why are there so many guards?" Zalika whispered.

"I don't know." Meres spoke just as softly. "I've never seen more than one guard at any gate."

Something rustled in the desert, dark and foreboding behind them.

Zalika twisted to face the noise. In a raised whisper she called out, "Keep it down, Mistress of Stealth!"

"Don't," Meres said. "That's no way to speak to a goddess." Meres still marveled at the fact she'd held the weeping goddess in her arms hours ago. When Sekhmet's tears had dried, Meres explained that she and Zalika needed to return to the city unseen to help the girl's mother and sisters escape. Sekhmet had listened carefully as Meres had told her what they'd learned from Isis. She'd revealed that she knew how to lead them inside the city so that no one would know they'd ever been there.

Meres didn't discuss Isis's claim that the gods and goddesses didn't exist in human form. After all, any fool could recognize Sekhmet. Clearly, she *was* a goddess.

There was no other explanation.

Turning back toward Meres, Zalika complained. "She's been following us ever since she tried to kill me. And she's just as human as you and me."

"She wasn't going to kill you. And just because she looks human doesn't mean she is."

Zalika rolled her eyes. "You're just saying that because she likes you best. And she's not a goddess. There's no such thing. Isis said so."

I'm not so sure, Meres thought. *Just because someone says something is so doesn't make it so. Even if the "someone" is Isis.* Out loud, she said, "That's not what Isis said. She said the Pharaoh and priests lied to us and gave us an ancient religion to believe in. She said they want to control us by making everyone believe the Pharaoh is a living god and that we'll be punished if we don't do whatever he and the priests want. Isis said the gods and goddesses in every religion lead to the same higher power."

"'Isis said, Isis said,'" Zalika mimicked in a sing-song voice. "Who died and made Isis the Pharaoh?"

"She's not the Pharaoh," Meres said evenly. "She's a goddess."

Zalika rolled her eyes. "No, she's not! She's just a human being! She said so herself!" Heated, Zalika forgot to whisper.

A searchlight beam illuminated the desert twenty yards to their left.

Meres clapped her hand over Zalika's mouth. "Don't move," Meres said softly. She didn't know what would happen if the guards discovered them, but she didn't want to find out. They planned to sneak into the city and then into the palace, find Zalika's sisters, and slip away to make their way back to Las Vegas. If Pu was still alive and in the city, they hoped the girls would know where to find her.

Several guards walked from the gate and into the desert, flashlights sweeping the sand. Within minutes, they were bound to spot Meres and Zalika. It was already too late for them to run.

But the guards raced toward a commotion to their far left.

Meres jumped at the touch of a hand on her shoulder. Stifling a cry, she turned to see Sekhmet crouched behind them.

"Follow me," the goddess said.

As the guards searched elsewhere, the three women slipped away under the cover of darkness.

✿✿

It took an hour to circle the city wall while keeping a safe distance in the desert. Sekhmet led them to a secret nook, a place where a large thatch of papyrus plants hid an indentation in which a door blended in with the wall. Before walking into that nook, Sekhmet said, "Priests will be on the other side—I'll tell you how many. Most should be going to the sacred lake soon to wash. We will strike when there is only one priest left. I will lure him outside and kill him."

"Isn't there another way?" Meres said hastily. She wanted to show her respect and gratitude to the goddess, which meant not insulting her. "There's no need to kill, is there?"

"I kill," Sekhmet said matter-of-factly. "It's what I do."

"I know. But can't we do something else to disable the priest? Maybe knock him unconscious?"

Disappointed, Sekhmet sighed, examining a pile of loose rocks surrounding the papyrus plants. Choosing a sharp and heavy one, she gave it to Meres. "I'll draw him out. You hit him over the head." Sekhmet looked Meres up and down, sizing her up. "Hard."

Meres and Zalika sat down inside the nook, stationed behind where the door would be when it opened.

Sekhmet eased her ear to the door and listened. After a few minutes, she held up one hand, showing all five fingers.

Five guards.

Sometime later, Sekhmet frowned, quickly holding up four fingers, then three, then two, then one. She pounded both fists on the door, yelling, "Open!"

When the door cracked open, Sekhmet took several steps back, staring straight ahead. When the door opened wider, she lunged forward, and pulled a young priest out into the nook. Surprised, he simply stared at her.

Without hesitation, Meres ran forward and brought the rock down over his head. The priest collapsed at her feet. Meres stepped over him.

Zalika whimpered, sitting on the ground with her back to the city wall. Wide-eyed, she stared at the fallen priest.

Sekhmet darted through the doorway.

Meres extended her hand to the girl. "Do you want to see your mother and sisters again?"

Zalika gulped hard, and forced herself to stand and inch forward, as if walking on the ledge of the top floor of a skyscraper. Finally, she latched onto Meres.

Once the women were inside, they closed the door behind them, leaving the unconscious priest locked out of the city.

⁂

Sekhmet led them through the narrow underground passageways, pausing every so often to listen to the sounds echoing through. Once, she led them into a side tunnel, where they hid in the shadows as a few priests raced through the main passageway. When they were gone, Meres said, "I don't understand. What's happening?"

But Sekhmet didn't answer, choosing to focus on listening for trouble as they made their way deeper through the tunnels below the city. A lizard skittered up one wall, pausing to watch them. Finally, they came to a fork. Sekhmet pointed to the left. "This leads to the pylons that flank the gate to the temple. That's where you'll find her."

"What?" Meres said.

"I heard what the priests said. It's why they're running—they're scared. No one ever thought she'd come out of the temple."

Hope washed through Meres like the sun breaking through clouds as she reached for Zalika's hand and held on tight. "Who?"

Sekhmet blinked slowly, like a sleepy cat. "Isis. She's talking to the people—not the priests."

Surprised, Zalika turned to Meres. "She said she wasn't going to come."

Meres grinned. "She must have changed her mind. She'll help us!" Meres turned to say something to Sekhmet, but the goddess had vanished without a sound.

CHAPTER SIXTY-TWO

Alone, Sekhmet slipped through the maze of narrow passageways beneath the White Walled City. Once she had accomplished what she came here to do, she'd leave the city forever. Before that happened, she wanted one last look at the only home she could remember.

She'd paid close attention when the priests had taken her through this maze a few weeks ago, memorizing every twist and turn. Soon, she found it.

Sekhmet paused at the open door to her tomb. In the many years she'd lived there, the door always stayed closed, locked from the outside. Why did it stand open now?

She took a deep breath, inhaling the air drifting out into the passageway from the tomb's interior. Used to her own scent that normally filled the tomb, a strange and new scent startled her. It had a tangy sourness, as well as earthy spice.

It was a scent she'd never smelled before. Sekhmet listened closely but the tomb remained silent. Dropping to her hands and knees, she crept inside, heading straight for the stone forest of columns. Rising to stand again, she pressed her back against the cool, polished surface of one column, still listening.

Silence.

Sekhmet realized she was alone in the tomb. She walked through it slowly, trailing her fingertips along every stone surface, memorizing every detail so she could remember it for the rest of her life. But when she reached the stone sarcophagus, she paused again, and her nostrils flared.

It was stronger here—that sour, spicy scent.

Following her nose, Sekhmet held onto the edge of the open sarcophagus and leaned forward over it. The scent stayed strong.

Someone had been sleeping in her bed. Someone new.

Someone had replaced her.

A low growl stirred in the base of her throat. Sekhmet was a goddess, and this tomb was her sacred ground. No one had the right to trespass here.

And no one could replace her.

As her face hardened with anger, Sekhmet left the tomb. She had much to do today. It would take time to hunt down and kill each priest, one by one, and she didn't know where to go from here. But as Sekhmet traveled deeper and deeper into the heart of the underground maze, the path became clear to her.

The air weighed heavy with the scent of honey cakes, and it was a very easy scent to follow.

❧❧

Sekhmet discovered a narrow stone staircase that led her into a large hallway, dimly lit by shafts of light streaming through a window of vertical slots at the top of the outside wall, twenty feet high. The stone walls were carved and painted with images of the gods. Most of those images were of Isis, the woman with feathers attached to her arms, wife of the green-skinned Osiris.

So, Sekhmet thought, *this is the temple where Isis lives. This is where they worship her.*

Jealousy gnawed at her, but Sekhmet pushed it away. She had to stay focused.

Up ahead, two priests raced across the hallway for a moment, shouting. They didn't notice her. Once they were out of sight, Sekhmet walked up to the point where they'd suddenly appeared, an intersection of two hallways.

The scent of honey cakes was stronger here.

Sekhmet followed it carefully until she reached the door of his office. She eased it open. From the hallway, she saw Priest Hennet leaning back in his chair behind his desk, eyes closed, facing the wall to one side of his desk with his profile to her.

Sekhmet crept slowly into the room, watching Priest Hennet every moment.

Suddenly, he moaned.

Sekhmet froze, confused. Why were his eyes closed? Had someone else already injured him? Was he hurt?

A subtle motion caught her eye, barely visible from behind the side of the desk. Sekhmet took one soft step to her left. She froze again at the sight of the naked boy on his knees, facing the seated Priest Hennet.

For a moment, Sekhmet couldn't breathe.

She'd followed the scent of honey cakes, and she saw a plate full of them on the corner of Priest Hennet's desk, untouched. That scent reeked and masked another one—a scent she could now detect. A sour and spicy scent. The same scent she'd smelled in her tomb and in the sarcophagus. That scent came from the boy.

She took another quiet step to her left, moving very slowly so the boy wouldn't notice her, and checking to make sure Priest Hennet's eyes were still closed. That step let her see more, and the first thing she noticed was the pain on the boy's face.

Looking back at the honey cakes on the desk, she noticed something sharp and shiny. She'd found something like that once. Long ago, when she was little, someone must have dropped it and she'd found it inside her tomb. For several days, late at night, she'd held its sharp tip next to her beating heart, feeling for the soft place between her ribs. She'd told herself to push it in hard and fast into her heart, thinking it would probably hurt a lot so she'd have to be quick. She'd tried, again and again. But every time she felt the sharpness of the steel point on her skin, she'd been afraid. What if she didn't succeed? What would happen to her then?

Now, Sekhmet eased close to the desk and took Priest Hennet's letter opener in hand. Still, neither the boy nor the priest noticed her presence. Sekhmet took a moment to touch her own ribs, feeling for the space between them, making sure she knew the exact spot.

She wasn't afraid anymore.

This time, she made sure it happened quickly.

In a few quick steps, she rounded the desk, found the soft spot between Priest Hennet's ribs, and shoved the blade straight into his heart.

CHAPTER SIXTY-THREE

"Now what?" Zalika said to Meres as they stood alone in the underground passageway.

Meres had run back to the spot where the passageway had forked so she could look down every possible avenue.

Sekhmet had vanished.

What's going on? Meres thought. *Why did Sekhmet leave us, and why are the priests in an uproar? Has Isis come to her temple? Is she looking for us?*

"We do what Sekhmet told us," Meres said. Even if Pu still lived, until they found her, Zalika was Meres' responsibility. She had to keep the girl safe at any cost. "But we've got to stick together. We can't let the priests separate us."

Zalika's eyes moved back and forth quickly, as if she were trying to read Meres, and the girl's face slackened with fear. She took Meres' hand and held on tight.

They moved forward, staying in the main passageway when more narrow hallways branched off. Once, several bats flew past them, only to disappear into the cracks of the stone walls. They walked in silence for nearly an hour, until they reached a stone staircase that spiraled up, illuminated by shafts of daylight from above. Along with the light, a woman's voice drifted down.

"... have lied to you and all the people in the Black Land."

Isis!

Meres whispered to Zalika. "We'll go slow. Let's find out what's happening before letting anyone see us. If it's not safe, we can go back the way we came and escape."

Wide-eyed, Zalika nodded her consent.

As they crept up the staircase, Meres realized Isis spoke into a microphone—probably one from the temple used on festival days—and that her voice was being broadcast.

At the top of the staircase, Meres and Zalika found themselves inside one of the pylon gates at the entrance to the temple of Our Lady of the Absolute. The interior's walls sloped high and inward, and another staircase at the opposite end led several stories up to the rooftop of the pylon.

Meres trembled. Below the city, she'd thought only about following Sekhmet and protecting Zalika. It wasn't until this moment that she'd realized they were trespassing on holy ground. The pylons, like most of the temple, were reserved for priests only. Setting foot inside them insulted the gods.

But she remembered everything Isis had told her about the Pharaoh and the priests, and that made her angry. Holding on to Zalika's hand, Meres led them through the shadows and toward the open door leading outside to the temple's gate, which separated the city from the temple's courtyard.

A man's voice called out, but his words weren't clear enough to understand.

Looking outside, Meres first noticed the priests clustered outside the gate and around the Pharaoh himself. It was one of the few times Meres had seen him in her life, because he rarely came out of the royal palace. He wore the royal nemes, a turquoise-and-gold striped cloth draped over his head and shoulders, held in place with a gold headband with the head of a cobra. Like all other Black Landers, his eyes were lined with black kohl. He wore a gold necklace embedded with precious jewels and shaped like a vulture, so large it covered the expanse of his chest. Meres recognized the trappings of royalty, not the man. Without them, she wouldn't be able to recognize the Pharaoh.

Hundreds of Black Landers, many still dressed in their night clothes, crowded behind the cluster of priests. As the Pharaoh shouted, they all looked toward the courtyard.

Quickly, Meres led Zalika across the open doorway, but no one noticed.

In the courtyard, two figures stood on the base of the statue of Isis, flanked by her protective wings.

Meres' heart fluttered. This was the stuff of dreams. And magic.

Tears of joy spilled down her face as she beheld Isis and Osiris, dressed in all their regal splendor that Meres recognized from the walls of the temple. As Isis used her arms to gesture as she spoke, the red and blue and green feathers hanging from them rippled and waved. Osiris stood solidly by her side, his skin pale green, symbolizing his resurrection from the dead, like the growth of new grass in the spring.

"Tell me—how did you become Pharaoh?" Isis said.

Startled, Zalika let her hand fall free from Meres' hand. "Wait a minute."

This time, they could hear what the Pharaoh said. "I'm the first-born son of Pharaoh. I rule by right."

Shifting her view, Meres looked across to the other pylon. Something had moved inside.

Isis and Osiris stepped down from the statue and walked forward toward the Pharaoh. "Before you took control, your mother ruled as Pharaoh," Isis said. "You told your people that she died, leaving you to rule."

Zalika proclaimed, "That's not Isis—that's my mother!"

"That was a sad day for the White Walled City and all of the Black Land," the Pharaoh called out in response. "But I accepted my duty and took over her rule."

Isis and Osiris continued to approach the temple gate. "Then you will be happy to know we've brought her back to rule again," Isis said.

Meres gasped. She could hear it now—it *was* Pu's voice. The Isis they saw, walking next to Osiris, wasn't the Isis they'd met in Las Vegas. It was Pu dressed as Isis. From a distance, Pu looked like Isis simply because of the clothes, jewelry, and makeup she wore.

A cloaked figure stepped out from inside the other pylon and faced the crowd.

Meres gazed at the cloaked figure in awe. "I know her!"

"Citizens of the White Walled City," Pu-as-Isis said. "We, your gods, return your beloved ruler. We bring you Pharaoh Angelique."

As the statuesque woman dressed as a pharaoh faced the crowd, most of the priests shrieked in fear. Moments later, people in the crowd began shouting, "That's her! I recognize her!" Soon, the crowd cheered.

"That's not right," Zalika said, wavering between relief and anger. "She's lying! She's no better than the Pharaoh!"

Meres understood what Zalika meant. Turning toward the girl, she said, "No. She doesn't know what we know. We're the only ones here who met Isis. They all still believe everything we used to believe."

"We have to tell them!"

Meres looked outside, gauging the situation. The Pharaoh protested, looking like a young boy throwing a tantrum, surrounded by cowering priests and thousands of elated people. There stood Pharaoh Angelique, strong and calm before them.

His mother, Meres realized. Angelique—the Queen of Punt, the woman who had helped her look for Ramose—was the Pharaoh's mother. And now she claimed her right to rule in his place. But how had Pu met her?

A sudden hush fell over the crowd. Following their pointing fingers, Pharaoh Angelique turned around and let out a small cry.

Meres stepped outside the pylon for a better view.

From the temple, Sekhmet emerged from the temple, carrying a weeping boy in her arms. She hesitated, as if evaluating the possibilities. She stepped forward.

Gently, Sekhmet pried the boy's arms from around her neck and placed him in Pharaoh Angelique's arms. It was only then that anyone realized Sekhmet was covered in blood. The crowd rumbled, and Meres instinctively wrapped her arms around Zalika, holding her close.

As Sekhmet turned away, she paused and stared at Meres.

For a moment, Meres thought she remembered a moment from her childhood. These pylons—they seemed familiar. She thought she remembered being here before, when she was little, and watching herself disappearing into the darkness of one of them. But that was impossible.

Pharaoh Angelique studied the boy and held him out in her arms for the crowd to see. "He's fine. He's safe. We have been granted the protection of the great goddess Sekhmet."

The priests shrieked, running away, leaving the Pharaoh alone and confused. But the crowd cheered again.

Osiris noticed Meres and Zalika standing in the pylon doorway.

It wasn't until he took a step toward them that Meres recognized her husband. She was overwhelmed at first with joy and then with the fear that he didn't want her any more—not since she'd chosen the gods over him on the day Priest Hennet had put Ramose into a sarcophagus and cast into the Nile.

He reached back and pulled Pu-as-Isis forward, slipping his arm around her waist and pointing at Meres and Zalika. Crying out, Pu's face lit up and she raced toward them, scooping Zalika into her arms and spinning in circles.

Ramose, in all his green-skinned glory as Osiris, walked slowly toward Meres, staring into her eyes.

"I'm sorry," she said, choking back tears.

He held her head and kissed her.

It felt the same as the first time he kissed her. Light-headed, an unexpected passion rushed through Meres like the Inundation of the Nile, flooding all the land and making it new again. Breaking the kiss, Ramose held her close, kissing her forehead and her hair. When they finally released each other, he wiped away a tear, grinned, and flexed his green arms. "How do you like me now?"

Chagrined, Meres laughed. "I just want my husband back. I don't need to marry a god."

Pharaoh Angelique still held the boy in her arms.

Meres recognized him. "That's Neferita's son!"

Ramose nodded as he stood behind his wife and wrapped his arms around her shoulders. "So it is."

Pharaoh Angelique had now walked into the crowd, and everyone pressed around her, anxious to touch the new pharaoh to make sure she was real.

But once again, Sekhmet had vanished.

Chapter Sixty-Four

Three months later, Meres chewed on her thumbnail as Bruce drove them toward the White Walled City.

"What's wrong?" he said.

"Nothing." For the seventeenth time since they'd left Las Vegas this afternoon, Meres unfolded and re-folded the top of the white paper bag that rested on her lap. She reached down to touch the zippered box on the car floor next to her feet, making sure for the fifth time that she'd remembered to bring it.

"Don't worry," Bruce said. "Everything's going to be fine."

Meres nodded, sitting on her thumb so she wouldn't chew on it. Bruce didn't know that her own marriage might be over. He had his future with Pu to look forward to. What did Meres have left with Ramose? Bad memories. How she had failed him. Despite her joy at reuniting with her husband, Meres still worried. He'd asked her to make decisions she'd finally made today, and she wasn't sure how he'd respond.

The road led to the gate at the back of the royal palace. A guard smiled and waved them in. Moments later, Bruce and Meres entered the palace together. Bruce glanced at his watch. "We're staying for dinner?"

"Yes." They came here once every week, and how long they stayed depended on what they each wanted to achieve on any given day.

Bruce looked into her eyes for a long moment. "There's nothing to worry about. Trust me." Smiling, his voice brightened. "Well, then. I'm off to see our new Pharaoh and help her manage her millions. See you later." Whistling, he headed up the staircase toward Pharaoh Angelique's office.

"Aunt Meres!" Footsteps raced down the hallway, and as Meres turned to face them, Zalika threw her arms around Meres' neck, squeezing her close. Letting go, Zalika took Meres by the hand, leading her down the hallway. "Guess what?" Zalika said. "Bruce is drawing up papers today. Angelique's cutting Pharaoh out of the loop and making Mama next in line. She's telling Bruce to put it in writing—I'm next in line after Mama. Someday, I might be Pharaoh!"

For the first time today, Meres smiled. "That decision makes me very happy. Your mother will be a wonderful pharaoh, and you will, too." Meres hoped that the girl would continue to mature as she had since Meres had first met her in the desert outside of Annu. In the past few months, Zalika had displayed more awareness of others and interest in helping Black Landers adjust to their new world.

"I hope so," Zalika said. "I never want to become like Pharaoh."

Meres chuckled. "As long as you're mindful of that, you should be just fine."

Three months ago, the citizens of the White Walled City embraced the return of Pharaoh Angelique. Her son, the old Pharaoh, had given up. He soon moved into the pyramid hotel in Las Vegas. For the first month or so, Meres saw no evidence of him and assumed he sulked in his room. There were no secrets among the Black Landers who worked at the hotel, and she soon learned the Pharaoh ordered room service every day, along with the women who were sent to his room. But lately Meres had seen him often, usually in the casino or one of the hotel's restaurants. Once he'd emerged, he became popular among the wealthy and elite for the stories he told about ruling the most notorious religious cult in the United States. He never seemed to recognize or even notice Meres when she saw him. Usually, he'd drunk too much.

Now they entered Pu's office. Zalika's younger sisters chased each other around Pu's desk, shrieking with delight. Above the racket, Pu called out, "Zalika—can you take them out somewhere?" Pu's belly had a slight bulge. In another four months, her fifth child—Bruce's child—was due.

Zalika squeezed Meres' hand before letting go. "Duty calls," she said with a hint of annoyance. To her sisters, she shouted, "Who wants to see the baby lions at the zoo?" After repeating herself a few times, her little sisters finally flocked to her side and let themselves be led away.

Pu grinned, running forward to hug Meres. "Look at you!" Pu said, taking a couple of steps back and examining Meres from head to toe. "You've gone native."

Instead of the typical Black Lander linen sheath, Meres wore white linen pants and a chocolate brown tank top and jacket, each embellished with simple and small white embroidered designs. A ponytail stretched her hair back from her face, and she no longer wore black kohl lines around her eyes.

Meres shrugged. "I go back and forth. Some days I dress like this, and some days I dress the old way."

Pu touched the material, nodding her approval. "How do you get such clothes?"

"They have indoor markets. Come visit me in Las Vegas. I'll take you shopping."

Pu beamed. "I'd love that. I need a day off for myself. It's been so busy here—meeting with every family, bringing everyone from the Underworld and Elephantine and Annu and all the other towns. Pharaoh Angelique has been doing most of the work—I've just helped however I can, and I'm exhausted. I don't see how she does it."

The day that Pharaoh Angelique had returned, Meres and Zalika had talked with them all late into the night, sharing everything they'd learned from the real Isis in Las Vegas. Pharaoh Angelique felt as shocked as anyone else. In retrospect, she suspected her husband had known the truth and shared it only with their oldest son. And when her husband died young, Angelique named herself pharaoh because their oldest son was only fifteen at the time and she didn't deem him fit to rule. When the White Walled City prospered, he staged her death, had her transported to an area within the Black Land that he declared as a foreign country named Punt, and vowed to kill all her children and grandchildren if she ever showed her face in the White Walled City again. Everyone who lived in Punt served to enforce the Pharaoh's orders. It had been Ramose's idea to return her to power, and when he and Pu entered Punt dressed as Isis and Osiris, they met with no resistance. That happened again when they came to the White Walled City.

During the past few months, everyone in the Black Land had been called to the White Walled City so that people long believed dead could reunite with their families and friends. Every day, Pharaoh Angelique met with individual families to help them adjust and make decisions about whether they wanted to stay in the White Walled City or go out into the world.

It was a decision that Meres had yet to make. For now, she chose to live in the pyramid hotel in Las Vegas and spend time getting to know her parents.

Pu said, "Have you seen Ramose today?"

Meres shook her head.

"He still loves you. He was thrilled when he found out you'd gone out on your own trying to find him."

Meres looked away. All their married life, she'd focused on what she didn't have—children. But the day Ramose had been put in a sarcophagus and thrown into the Nile, she realized he was all she really wanted and needed. But she couldn't get rid of her guilt from trusting the priests when they put her husband in a sarcophagus and threw him into the Nile.

"Go see him at the construction site," Pu said. "They've finished and have been cleaning up all day."

Meres' heart raced. She'd brought the zippered box and white paper bag with her, and now she held onto them even tighter.

"Go ahead." Pu smiled. "I'll see you tonight at dinner."

≈

Meres walked across the city, welcoming the warmth she always felt just by being among the Black Landers. She paused in front of the temple of Our Lady of the Absolute.

She remembered a dream she'd had months ago, when she'd first learned of Pu's pregnancy. Meres had dreamed that Pu had turned into Sekhmet, and the great goddess had warned her that nothing in the world is black and nothing is white.

"Nothing is absolute," Meres said to herself quietly, gazing at the temple that represented the home of Isis. "It's all shades of gray."

Meres turned her back on the temple and walked through the nearby city gate into the desert.

Immediately, she met the dozens of workers heading back into the city, led by Ramose. Even though three months had gone by, her heart still got stuck in her throat every time she saw him.

"Hello, my beautiful wife," Ramose smiled warmly and kissed her forehead. He pointed toward the desert. "It's all yours now."

"Thank you."

"Thank Pharaoh Angelique. She's the one who paid for it."

As Meres took another few steps into the desert, Ramose walked by her side. She stopped and faced him. "I need to do this alone."

Ramose took her hands in his. "It's not safe—"

"I'm tired of arguing about it."

"You're not letting me protect you. How do you think that makes me feel?"

"Probably not very good. I'm sorry about that." Meres took a deep breath. "Thank you for understanding that I needed time to think about where we go from here. I've decided it doesn't matter where I live. I can live here or in Las Vegas or anywhere else that's close enough to come back and visit often. All I want is to live with you again. But about this one last thing—I need you to trust me."

Ramose pressed his lips together in frustration and said, "Don't you dare go and get yourself killed. Not after all we've been through."

Meres saw it on his face. Her husband was back. He'd probably never gone anywhere—he'd claimed he'd forgiven her about letting him be thrown in the Nile. As he'd told her all along, Meres finally realized that he'd been ready to embrace their marriage again. Meres had been the hesitant one. "I won't get hurt. I promise."

"I'm waiting for you right here. I'm not going back into the city without you."

Meres smiled and nodded. She turned and walked into the desert.

It stood a good stone's throw away. The statue of Sekhmet in front of her new temple took Meres' breath away. She knelt in front of the statue and prayed. Finally, she entered the temple.

Dusk had come, and it took several moments for her eyes to adjust to the dim light inside. But Meres already knew this temple inside and out, because she'd helped design it.

Neferita's son, now reunited with his mother, had gradually revealed what the priests had done to him and how they'd locked him inside the underground temple where he'd slept in an open sarcophagus and played in a forest of stone columns.

Meres had a hunch. Ever since the day that she and Zalika had come back to the White Walled City and discovered Pu dressed as Isis and Ramose dressed as Osiris at the temple gates, Meres couldn't shake the strange feeling that she remembered standing inside those gates long ago. That she'd watched herself disappear into the darkness that led to the secret passageways below.

Meres had no proof and had told no one of her suspicions, except for Pharaoh Angelique. Maybe Meres was right. Maybe she was wrong. All she knew was she felt compelled to follow her hunch.

The stone column forest stood to her right inside the temple with the sarcophagus in back. Meres approached the altar, kneeling in reverence first. She rose, opened the box, and laid out the food she'd collected from the hotel kitchen. The insulated box had kept the food warm. According to Meres' orders, the construction workers had already lined up several bottles of water. Finally, she opened the white paper bag and placed a variety of muffins on the altar.

Something seemed to stir within the stone forest. Out of the corner of her eye, Meres thought she noticed a shift in the light, as if someone had crossed from behind one column to another.

Meres knelt and stared directly at the altar. "I pray to you, Mistress Sekhmet. I bring you news from the White Walled City. There was a decision to report everything we've learned to the authorities outside of the Black Land, because we want to establish good relationships with them. They investigated the death of Priest Hennet, but they have no suspects. That investigation is over."

After thinking about what had happened when she first met her own parents and they'd asked what had happened to her sister, Ruka, Meres couldn't stop thinking about the temple gates.

"I believe what we have learned from Isis and Osiris: murder is wrong, and we must never do it," Meres said. "I believe that it is evil to try to control another person, and murder is a decision and an act that controls whether someone lives or dies. Therefore, murder is evil."

What if Meres' strange sensation of remembering herself turned out to be a memory of the last time she'd seen her sister? Her parents claimed they'd been called to the temple by the priests and thrown out of the city. What if Meres and Ruka had followed them there? Maybe Meres had hidden inside one gate and Ruka in the other. Maybe what Meres remembered was Ruka being pulled into the darkness.

Meres stopped at a sound deep in the stone forest, as if a small stone had been kicked accidentally. She took a deep breath and continued.

The more Meres thought about her hunch, the more she thought she remembered an expression on the girl's face the moment before she vanished into the dark. Sometimes Meres thought it was a look of fear, sometimes she thought she remembered it as a look of excitement.

More and more, Meres wondered if it had been a look of longing and resignation. The girl hadn't cried out.

What if Ruka had let herself be taken instead of Meres, thereby protecting her sister?

"But we know what Priest Hennet did. He was an evil man who did evil things to that boy. And maybe he did evil things to other children."

She heard a slight gasp from somewhere in the depths of the temple.

Meres didn't know much about Sekhmet yet. They'd only had that brief time together in the desert on the night they all returned to the White Walled City. But from what she'd learned from Neferita's boy and a woman who had recently come in from a ghost town—Mrs. Dempsey—Sekhmet had probably suffered greatly.

Gazing into the dark shadows of the temple her husband had built, Meres thought. *There but for the grace of Isis go I.*

"I know murder is wrong," Meres said. "But somehow, I have no problem with the murder of Priest Hennet. As far as I can tell, most people in the White Walled City feel the same."

Meres rose to her feet, searching the shadows for any sign of life and seeing none. "I believe in you."

She turned and walked toward the entrance to the temple. Unlike the temple below the city, this one locked from the inside, not the outside.

Suddenly, Meres heard a rustling sound behind her. Spinning, she saw nothing at first. But as she examined the array of food she'd left on the altar, she realized the blueberry muffins had vanished.

Meres nodded, making a mental note. If Sekhmet liked blueberry muffins, Meres would bring more next week. She tried using the name her parents used. "Ruka?"

The temple was silent.

Time, Meres told herself. *These things take time.*

She left the temple.

Unable to contain himself, Ramose ran across the desert to meet her in the temple courtyard. "Are you all right? Was she there?"

They both jumped at the sound of the heavy temple door closing and locking behind them.

"I don't understand you," Ramose said, shaken. He wrapped his arm around Meres and pulled her away from the temple. "Why would you risk being alone inside with that thing?"

"If you have to ask, then you've forgotten what it is to be a Black Lander," Meres said softly.

"What's that supposed to mean?"

It was something that Isis had reminded her of when they'd had lunch recently. They had lunch often. They were becoming friends. Isis told Meres that with all its faults, there were many wonderful things about the Black Land. To Ramose, Meres said, "We believe that every man is our brother and every woman is our sister."

"You can't mean—" Ramose shook his head. "That thing in there— she's a killer!"

It could take years before she lets me near her again, Meres thought, remembering the magical night when she'd held a weeping goddess in her arms. *But I've got all the time in the world.*

Meres smiled as they walked back into the White Walled City, the statue and temple of Isis greeting them. As she spoke, deep in her heart she hoped that one day her words would prove to be more than just symbolic.

"Sekhmet is a Black Lander," Meres said. "She is my sister."

ACKNOWLEDGMENTS

Thank you to everyone at Mundania Press for helping me make this novel the best it can be.

I'm grateful to Yvette Monet of MGM MIRAGE Public Affairs for her generosity and enthusiasm in showing and teaching me about what goes on behind the scenes. This information helped shape the story and characters in wonderfully unexpected ways.

Fellow writers Carla Johnson and Tom Sweeney worked their magic in critiquing and helping me pull together this novel. Along with Dr. Toni Moran, they also helped me iron out a significant kink.

Finally, my deepest gratitude to my friend Kris Engdahl, who held up a mirror that helped me see myself more clearly. For my money, this is one of the greatest and most kind acts a true friend can offer.

About the Author

Resa Nelson is the author of The Dragon-slayer's Sword, which was a Finalist for the EPPIE Award for Best Fantasy Novel and was Recommended for the Nebula Award. Nelson is a long-time member of SFWA (Science Fiction Writers of America). Her short fiction has been published in Marion Zimmer Bradley's Sword and Sorceress 23, Science Fiction Age, Fantasy, Tomorrow SF, Aboriginal SF, and many other magazines and anthologies. She has been the TV/Movie Columnist for Realms of Fantasy magazine since 1999. She also is a regular contributor to SCI FI magazine. As a journalist, Nelson has sold over 200 articles to magazines in the United States and the United Kingdom. She also has been a quarter-finalist for the Nichol Screenwriting Award and a semi-finalist for the Chesterfield Screenwriting Award. A lifelong fan of ancient Egypt, she has traveled throughout modern-day Egypt to visit ancient sites. Visit her website at http://www.resanelson.com.